In Front of God and Everybody:

Confessions of April Grace

In Front of God and Everybody:

Confessions of April Grace

by K.D. McCRITE

Tommy NELSON®

A Division of Thomas Nelson Publishers

NASHVILLE DALLAS MEXICO CITY RIO DE JANEIRO

Published in Nashville, Tennessee, by Tommy Nelson. Tommy Nelson is a registered trademark of Thomas Nelson, Inc.

Represented by Jeanie Pantelakis of Sullivan Maxx Literary Agency.

Cover design by JuiceBox Design.

Cover photo by Scott Thomas.

Tommy Nelson® titles may be purchased in bulk for educational, business, fund-raising, or sales promotional use. For information, please e-mail SpecialMarkets@ThomasNelson.com.

Library of Congress Cataloging-in-Publication Data

McCrite, K. D. (Kathaleen Deiser)
  In front of God and everybody / by K.D. McCrite.
    p. cm. — (Confessions of April Grace)
  Summary: In the summer of 1986, eleven-year-old April Grace, who lives on a rural Arkansas farm with her family, across a field from her grandmother, has her sense of Christian charity tested when a snooty couple from San Francisco moves into a dilapidated house down the road and her grandmother takes up with a loud, obnoxious, and suspicious-acting Texan.
  ISBN 978-1-4003-1722-6 (softcover)
  [1. Family life—Arkansas—Fiction. 2. Farm life—Arkansas—Fiction. 3. Christian life—Fiction. 4. Swindlers and swindling—Fiction. 5. Arkansas—History—20th century—Fiction.] I. Title.
  PZ7.M4784146In 2011
  [Fic]—dc22   2011005583

Printed in the United States of America

13 14 15 RRD 6 5

Dedicated to my husband, Brett,
who loves April Grace as much as I do!

ONE

Something New This Way Comes

♡

Summer 1986

I was sitting on our big front porch, reading a book and minding my own business, when a big black car gleaming like a new mirror pulled into the shady, narrow lane that leads to our farmhouse. I flipped my red braid over my shoulder and squinted hard. You just don't see shiny, new vehicles on Rough Creek Road, or even in Cedar Ridge—the town we live near here in Arkansas, right in the middle of the Ozarks. Folks here don't have money for fancy-schmancy automobiles, especially brand-new 1986 models, which I was sure that one was.

The minute I laid eyes on that car, something unpleasant shivered across my skin, the way the air feels before a bad storm. Worst of all, it dragged me back to a time three years ago when I was eight years old and saw something I hoped never to see again.

Here's what happened. I'd been invited to spend the weekend with Crystal Tomlinson, a new girl at school who'd moved to Arkansas from someplace up North. We became friends right off.

Her family lived in a brand-new, huge house with a swimming pool and a maid, and I had never seen such a thing in my life.

One weekend, a bunch of Crystal's relatives had come to visit, but they were all adults, and she didn't have anyone to play with. That Friday night, while the grown-ups gathered downstairs, Crystal and I sat in her pink-and-white bedroom, playing with about two dozen My Little Ponies. I was thinking I'd dream of multicolored plastic horses for three weeks when suddenly, Crystal grabbed my hand and tugged me to my feet.

"Let's get something to eat!" she hollered. Crystal was a bit chubby around the edges, so getting something to eat right then wasn't totally unexpected. In fact, we'd had supper in the kitchen with the maid only an hour or so earlier. But this was an adventure, so I merrily went along with her.

We ran down the back stairs to the kitchen, where we ate tuna sandwiches and potato chips and slugged down Pepsi-Cola until we belched like truck drivers.

"Now let's get some cake," Crystal squealed. I followed her into the dining room, where many people sat at a long table full of flowers and candles. They didn't see us as we went to the sideboard that held two kinds of cake.

While Crystal cut us big hunks of each cake, I looked at the adults. That was the first time I'd seen a table like that. It was covered with a bright white tablecloth, a bunch of sparkly goblets, and a zillion pieces of silverware next to each plate. And I had never in my life seen people all dressed up that way just to sit around and eat supper. The men wore dark suits, and the women's big hair was all stiff and poofy. Their jewelry glittered in the light from a big chandelier.

At our house, we wash our hands and comb our hair before we sit down to eat. If our clothes are dirty, we put on clean ones, but that's it. No high heels or ties or dangly earrings.

Everyone was laughing at something Crystal's dad had said, when her mother piped up in a nasally kind of voice.

"I'm not sure how much longer I can take living here,"

she said. "You cannot believe these people. They think Fifth Avenue is nothing more than a candy bar. And the last time any of them went to the theater, it was to the Grand Movie House in Cedar Ridge. They've no idea what real theater is. . . ."

About that time, she spied Crystal and me. "Oh, here's one of them now. Come here, little redhead. Tell us your name," she said.

Everyone stared at me, and I felt like I didn't have my clothes on, but I said, "April Grace Reilly."

She looked at the others, and all of them laughed.

"Isn't that name too much?" Crystal's mom laughed. "*April Grace*. And the way she says it, as if she's proud."

They laughed some more.

"Come here, dear," she said. "These people want to meet an actual little hillbilly."

I approached the table slowly, not liking the way those folks smiled.

"Say something," said a woman on the other side of the table. She had a long face with deep grooves running down both sides of her mouth.

I looked at her, then at Crystal's mother. Then I looked at Crystal, who shrugged.

"Say something, April Grace," Crystal said.

"I don't know what to say," I said.

"How about a poem?" asked a man near the end of the table. He pronounced it "pome." The man had a narrow, pointy head. In a voice that sounded like it came from his sinuses first, and which I suppose he thought sounded clever, he said, "Can *you-all* recite a poem?"

"Yes, sir," I said.

Every last one of them snickered.

"Go ahead," said the pointy-headed man.

I figured if I said the poem without a single mistake and without talking too fast, they'd quit looking at me that way. I cleared my throat and stood straight and tall, the way Miss Carmichael had taught us.

"I think that I shall never see a poem lovely as a tree," I began.

I was the only one in third grade who'd been able to remember that entire poem by Joyce Kilmer. I recited the whole thing right to the end, but the people at that table were all laughing their socks off.

"What's so funny?" I asked. "I did it right."

"It's the way you talk, April Grace," Crystal whispered right in my ear.

"See?" said Crystal's mother to her relatives. "That twang is just too much!"

She clapped her hands together, and I saw her long, red fingernails and a bunch of rings on her thin, white fingers.

"I actually overheard a woman the other day say she 'lived a right far piece from the Walmarts.' Oh, and that's another thing here. Life seems to revolve around trips to Walmart. Or church."

The pointy-headed man leaned away from the table and eyeballed my feet. "She's wearing shoes!" he said. "Her family must be rich."

Well, that got a big, fat laugh.

A youngish woman across the table had a long face *and*

a long, pointy head. She must have been the daughter of the other two. "Which one of your cousins will you marry when grow up?" she asked.

"Angela!" gasped Crystal's mother. "Shame on you." But I noticed she laughed as hard as anyone else.

"I don't have any cousins," I told her.

But that only made everyone laugh even harder.

"What's so funny about that?" I asked.

"One thing more, *Daisy Mae*," said the pointy-headed man, smirking as he said the name. "Is your house a single- or a double-wide?"

They all hooted like that was the funniest joke of the night. I didn't live in a trailer, but why would it matter if I did? I couldn't understand why they laughed and said all those dumb things, but something inside me got tight and burned like fire.

"What's so funny?" I demanded, but no one told me.

I looked at Crystal. She was grinning like a big goof. She probably didn't understand it any more than I did, but all of a sudden I couldn't stand the sight of her, or that big house, or those fancy, sniggering people.

"I want to go home," I said. Then I marched into the kitchen through a pair of swinging doors, found the telephone, and called for my daddy to come get me. I never went to Crystal's house again. A year or so later, her folks moved out of the Ozarks and back to whatever city up North they'd come from. Good riddance, I'd say.

So now, anytime I see some slick car or uppity, dressed-up people, my hackles rise in defense.

It was too bad about Crystal, because I had liked her well enough. In fact, maybe we still would have been friends. Maybe not. Sad thing is, my new best friend, Melissa, had gone away to summer camp at the end of our fifth grade year, and I didn't have a blessed thing to do that summer. As it turned out, though, things happened that made the summer of 1986 the most memorable time of my whole entire life. And it all started with that gleaming black car pulling up in front of my house.

TWO

Ian and Isabel Look for Their Roots

❀

On that warm July day, while I watched from the porch, that car just sat there, paused in our driveway. I could see two people inside talking to each other. They looked toward the house for a bit; then the car sort of oozed up the driveway and stopped near the porch.

Daisy, our big white dog who is older than dirt, slept in her favorite sunny patch by the porch steps. She woke up and looked up long enough to take note of the visitors. Then she thumped her tail once or twice, yawned, and lowered her head to her paws.

"Some watchdog you are," I told her.

I was wearing a baggy, raggedy pair of red terry cloth shorts and a yellow T-shirt with the arms cut out because I'd got into poison ivy chasing Grandma's spoiled white cat, Queenie, who is not supposed to get out of the house but does anyway. Just because of her, I'd spent the better part of that week begging God not to let me itch completely to death.

Mama and Daddy had gone over to Ava in Douglas County to pick up a part at the tractor place because in all of Zachary County, that particular part was not to be found. Although my grandmother lives just across the hayfield from us, my sister and I were home alone right then.

The blond-haired, pink-faced man in the car blasted his horn. It was as loud as a freight train and startled me so bad I jumped. Daisy lumbered up and woofed once.

The man motioned for me to come to his car door, but I

didn't do it for three good reasons. Number one: he might've been an ax murderer for all I knew. Though from the looks of that spiffy car and the diamond ring winking in the sunlight on his pinky finger as he beckoned me, he looked more like a banker than a crook. Number two: my poison ivy itched worse every time I moved. Number three: I was pretty put out that he just sat in our driveway and honked for me to come running like he was King of the World. Plus, Daddy and Mama have talked to me and my sister about being careful around strangers.

I looked at the scrawny boy in the seat beside him. Boy, that kid was some kind of ugly with a mug that was all ghostly white cheekbones and forehead. His black eyebrows dipped down toward a long, pointy nose. He wore his short, dark hair all slicked back so his face was just hanging there, and you just had to stare at it, kinda like a bad wreck on the highway.

The way that pair glared at each other, you could see they were both madder than a two-edged sword.

They began to argue, but I couldn't make out the words. Finally the man's window slid down, smooth as you please.

"You! Girlie! Is that creature vicious?"

I glanced around, expecting to see Grandma's cat, who has been known to bite the hand that feeds her, or anyone else's hand for that matter. Then I saw him eyeball Daisy, who had plopped back down in the sun and was lying there like melted ice cream. I laughed out loud. That dog would rather lick you than sic you, and that tight-faced man was the only person in the world who ever thought good ole Daisy might be vicious.

"No, sir, she ain't mean," I said when I finally quit laughing fit to be tied.

The man turned to the boy and said something. This time, with the car window down, that boy's answer came out loud and clear.

That's when I realized the homely kid was actually the most unpleasantest-looking woman I've ever seen in all my life, and that's putting it nicely. And let me tell you, she had a voice shrill enough to crack the Arctic ice cap.

"I am not getting out of this car, Ian! That child is covered with sores, and there's no telling what rural diseases she has."

Well, she didn't need to make it sound like I had the cooties. We Reillys take a bath every single night before bed. My sister, Myra Sue, who is fourteen years old and is in love with herself, bathes about five times a day even though she's too lazy to do a blessed thing to get herself dirty.

"I got poison ivy," I hollered at the woman, who continued to gawk at me as if I were something disgusting. "It's not catchy, like the measles or head lice."

There was just the tiniest silence, as if they were both surprised I could speak. After a moment, the man gave me a big plastic smile that stretched his lips halfway to both ears. He obviously didn't wear dentures because they would've popped out from all the grinning.

"Well, then," he said heartily, "can you tell us if this is Rough—"

"What's the matter with you, Ian?" screeched the woman. "She's a child. She doesn't know anything!"

Ian jerked his head around to look at her, and I got a real good view of his bald spot turning a peculiar shade of purple.

"Isabel! Be quiet! You haven't shut your yapping mouth since we left San Francisco."

Well, I hate to say it, but watching this business was almost better than reading. I put my book down so I could pay attention. What were those people, anyway? Crazy?

The woman shrieked as if she had been goosed.

"Don't you tell me what to do, Ian St. James," she said. "This whole move is your idiotic idea. I was perfectly content at home, in the middle of civilization!"

His next words came out like little soldiers in a row, all stiff and even.

"Kindly remember that our home is gone."

"And it's all your fault!" she screamed.

The little soldiers continued to march forth. "I told you that someday I wanted to get back to our roots," he said.

"Roots? Back to our roots? We were both born in Marin County. California, Ian. *California!*"

"But my grandfather came from West Memphis."

She looked so mad I thought her eyeballs would pop right out. She leaned into him.

"Have you ever looked at a map?" she asked. "West Memphis is at least two hundred miles from this odious place. We don't have hillbilly roots!"

They glared at each other for a spell and cussed each other out pretty good, then she slung herself back against the car seat, crossing her arms.

"Idiot!"

By then it seemed evident they weren't ax murderers or dangerous in any way except maybe to each other, but all that screeching and cursing made me itch and gave me a head-ache. I'd had an earful more than I could stomach. I got up and went into the house, letting the screen door bang shut behind me. Then I latched it, just for good measure and for safety's sake.

The car horn blasted again, three times.

In the living room, Myra Sue lounged on the sofa with a pile of clean, unfolded towels all around her, as if she thought she were a princess and the laundry were velvet cushions. With her mouth hanging half-open, she had her eyes glued to the TV, watching *Days of Our Lives*. She didn't have anything better to do, I guess, because her two best friends, Jessica and Jennifer Cleland, were spending the summer with their grandparents in Hawaii.

I settled carefully into the soft, old rocking chair Grandma uses whenever she comes to visit, which, if you are interested, is every single day.

"Is someone outside?" Myra Sue asked, coming up for air during a commercial. My sister has wavy blond hair and bright blue eyes and thinks she is so all-fired gorgeous that it's like her feet are glued to the floor in front of the mirror. I bet she'd stare at herself 'til the Second Coming if Mama would let her. I even caught her kissing her reflection one time, and she like to pulled me bald-headed when I couldn't stop laughing.

"You could say that," I muttered.

Outside, Daisy gave another low, lazy woof. Someone squealed. A car door slammed loud enough to wake the dead in Cedar Ridge Cemetery eight miles away.

Myra Sue gave me her usual dirty look.

"Did you lock the screen?" she asked. "We don't want a lunatic or a salesman in the house."

With one foot, I set Grandma's chair to rocking and ignored her. I opened my book and plunged myself back into the world of *Oliver Twist*, which I like way, way better than that series about junior high cheerleaders all the other girls my age love so much.

"Hey in there! Girlie!" The man's voice came from outside, somewhere in the region of the porch steps.

Myra Sue didn't move, and neither did I.

"He's hollering at you," she said. That girl is so lazy she wouldn't move if the towels caught fire.

"Say! In the house! Hello in there!" the voice came again.

"Aren't you going to see what he wants?" Myra Sue asked.

"Nope," I said.

My sister's dirty look got dirtier. Then she blew an exaggerated sigh and heaved herself off the sofa just as *Days of Our Lives* came back on. Clean towels fell on the floor, and she kicked them out of the way with her bare feet. The TV remote was still clutched in her hot little hand, so I couldn't use it even if I wanted to. With the other hand, she smoothed her side ponytail in its blue scrunchie, patted her bright yellow T-shirt and stone-washed jeans in case wrinkles had invaded her territory, then went to the screen door.

"Are your parents at home?" the banker-looking man asked.

Myra Sue gave this oopsy little gasp and blurted out, "Ooo! I *love* your car! It's a Chrysler New Yorker, isn't it?"

So much for lunatics and salesmen. All they'd have to do

is drive up in a flashy car, and she'd invite them in to murder us or sell us a Kirby vacuum cleaner.

"It's a Cadillac!" the man snapped. "Now call off your dog. He's terrorizing my wife."

I figured I might have to call the TV station about this late-breaking phenomenon. You see, Daisy is fifteen years old. If she were an old lady, she'd be almost a hundred. Plus, she has lost most of her teeth. I scooched around in the rocking chair so I could look outside. Oh yeah, Daisy seemed ferocious, all right, sitting near the bottom of the steps, her tongue hanging out of her mouth sideways while her tail whacked back and forth in the dust. The skinny woman in the car looked like she was about to run for the hills.

"Go get 'er, Daisy," I whispered and turned away.

That goofy Myra Sue was still fluttering and panting over the man's dumb ole car when I went upstairs to renew my calamine lotion and sit in front of the fan.

Here's the thing: I'm pretty sure Myra Sue is adopted because she isn't like Mama or Daddy or me, or even Grandma. None of us cares about what people drive or what they have. If Myra Sue is related to anyone I know, it would have to be Queenie, Grandma's cat, because they are both such a pain in the behind and like to cause trouble for everyone else.

For instance, that very evening my dear sister announced right at the supper table: "April Grace was mean and rude to our new neighbors."

Well, everyone, including yours very truly, stopped chewing and stared at her. She was sitting so straight and prim, you'd think Mama had starched her drawers.

"What new neighbors?" Mama, Daddy, and I said at the same time.

"Ian and Isabel St. James."

Her tone of voice and her high-and-mighty expression said the rest of us must be from a planet far, far away.

"You mean that loudmouthed man and that skinny woman that looks like the ugliest boy in the world?" I said.

"April Grace," Mama said.

Here is something you should know. Mama is prettier than anyone in all of Zachary County and maybe in the entire state of Arkansas. She has shiny, curly red hair that touches just below her shoulders, and her eyes are green and sparkly. Everyone says her freckles are adorable. Not only is Mama beautiful to look at, but she's beautiful inside. Everybody says I look like her, but I don't see it. And my inside sure as the world isn't as pretty as hers. She never says anything bad about anyone, and she doesn't like us to talk bad about someone else, even if we don't know them personally, even if it's just somebody on the TV.

"I'm sorry, Mama," I said, "but it kinda hurt my eyes to look at her. Her face looks like the edge of a butcher knife, and her nose is so long . . ."

"Enough, April Grace, or leave the table," Mama said.

I looked down at my fried okra. "Yes'm."

"Were you rude to them?" Daddy asked. Daddy is all strong and muscle-y from working hard on our farm every single day of his life. He has dark hair, and his eyes look real blue because his face is so sun-browned.

"No, sir, Daddy," I said at the same time ole Myra Sue said, "Yes, sir, Daddy. She was plain hateful."

"I was not!"

"Was so!"

"Stop it," Daddy said in that Tone of Voice that makes us quit whatever we're doing. Like Mama, he's real nice, and he's soft-spoken, but he can get riled sometimes.

I took a deep breath, looked first at Daddy, then at Mama.

"I was not being rude," I said. "They were fighting and screaming at each other—"

"Oh, you are such a liar," Myra Sue butted in. "Mother, they had to raise their voices because she was in the car and he was on the porch, and Daisy set up such a ruckus—"

Well, that was too much for me to take.

"Daisy barked two measly little times." I jabbed my pointy finger in the air to emphasize my words. "Just two little woofs. And anyway, even if she did set up a ruckus—which she didn't, Myra Sue, and you know it—don't you want her to let us know when a stranger drives up?"

"April Grace," Mama said in a tone that made the hair on the back of my neck prickle, "were you rude to those people?"

"Yes, she was," Big Mouth answered. "She just walked off and left poor Mr. St. James out there, pitiful and confused." Suddenly my sister was Mother Teresa, but she lost the effect when she said to me, "You are so rude and crude wearing that ugly ratty T-shirt and shorts. I bet when you grow up, you'll be nothing but trailer trash."

"Myra Sue, leave this table," Daddy said.

She stared at him with her mouth hanging open. We all got a good look at her new braces, which she dearly hates.

"But April Grace is such a big, fat pain!"

Daddy leaned back in his chair and narrowed his eyes at her.

"One more word, Myra Sue, and you'll be helping me muck out the cow barn tomorrow. Right now you can get started on the supper dishes."

She pooched out her lower lip but didn't say anything else. Her sigh nearly heaved the shoes right off her feet. And the way she dragged herself toward the kitchen, you would've thought she was going to her own execution.

As soon as we heard water running in the kitchen sink, Mama slowly wiped her lips with her napkin. She and Daddy both looked at me for a minute or two. My food settled in my belly like a big, hard lump.

"April Grace, honey," Mama said, "there is no excuse for rudeness to strangers or to family."

"But Myra Sue just opened the door right up to that man and went right out on the porch. Mama, he could have been an ax murderer or a kidnapper or something." I looked at Daddy for a little backup on this logic.

Now here's something else you should know: Daddy and Mama are In Love. They went together since eighth grade, never dated anyone else, and got married the year they turned nineteen. Never in my life have I heard them contradict each other. Maybe they agree about everything. I don't expect them to change anytime soon.

"Of course, you should never open the door to a stranger," he said to me. "But you shouldn't just walk away when someone asks a question. Your mother and I have tried to teach you that the way other people act doesn't make a difference in how you treat them. You could have answered through the door. And now that we know they're our neighbors, we need to make them welcome."

"Remember what Jesus said about treating others the way you want to be treated, always." Mama added. "Do you understand?"

"Yes'm."

"So you will give these St. James people a person-to-person apology tomorrow?"

I thought my heart had already sunk, but I was wrong.

"But that woman said I had rural diseases, and she called us hillbillies, and . . . and . . ."

I could see this wasn't helping. I thrashed around in my head for something to tell my parents so they would understand how awful the St. Jameses were.

"And they were cussing and took the Lord's name in vain. And they insulted poor ole Daisy, and scared her with their loud car horn and their big mouths. You wouldn't want me not to defend Daisy, would you, or keep listening to them take the Lord's name in vain, would you?"

"No, honey, of course not," Mama said. "And I admire your loyalty to Daisy, I really do. But I'm sure Daisy would want you to apologize. And God wants us to forgive others, so no more excuses."

Well, if insulting our dog and using the Lord's name in vain wouldn't change Mama's mind, nothing would. I slumped back in my chair. The only comfort I got out of the whole situation was the sound of my sister in the kitchen, washing dishes and getting dishpan hands.

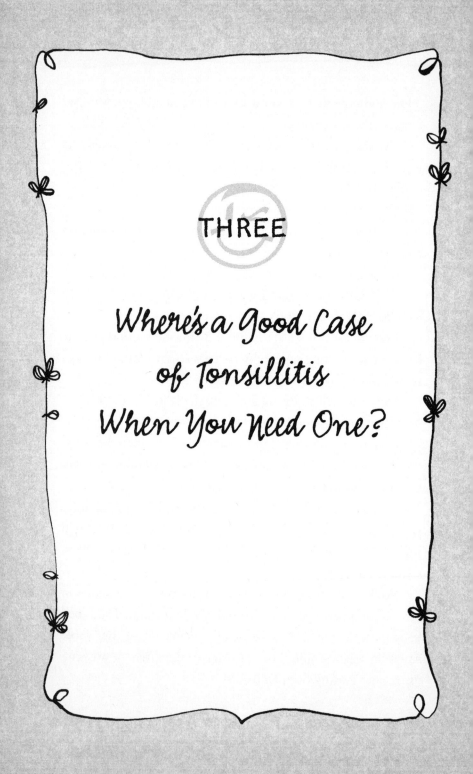

THREE

Where's a Good Case of Tonsillitis When You Need One?

☺

When I woke up the next morning, it took me a minute to figure out why I felt so depressed.

Mama was downstairs in the kitchen, singing the hymn "Rock of Ages." The sun shone, the birds sang. It was Myra Sue's turn to do laundry, and since we only used the clothes dryer in the winter or when it rained, she would have to hang the wet wash on the clothesline in the backyard. It was a job she dearly hated. All things considered, I had every reason to feel blissfully happy.

Then I remembered.

Today was the day I had to apologize to our new neighbors, the St. Jameses. As far as I was concerned, I'd done nothing wrong. But what Mama says is Law, so I'd just have to do it, even if I turned blue and fell over dead.

I lay there and stared up at the ceiling and wished I could suddenly get sick. Not cancer or the black plague or even the flu, understand. But a good case of tonsillitis would be helpful. If I had a sore throat, everyone would know I couldn't talk.

I practiced speaking in a pitiful, hoarse voice, and when Mama called me for breakfast, I dragged myself downstairs in my nightie. I left my hair uncombed and my face unwashed, hoping I looked puny. It was hard to do, let me tell you. You know as well as I do that it's hard to look frail and sick if you're hungry as a starving lumberjack and the aroma of bacon and eggs is filling the kitchen. Mama stood at the big, old stove in our yellow-and-white kitchen, breaking eggs into the cast-iron skillet. They sizzled as they hit the hot grease.

On the counter were a bunch of canning jars filled with fresh cucumbers, and on the back stove burners were two big pots of vinegar, water, and salt simmering for pickles. The vinegar and bacon smells mixed together real nice. Mama makes the best dill pickles you'll ever have the pleasure to munch.

Now, I should tell you that my mama isn't one of them low-fat cooks whose food tastes like packing peanuts or the boxes they come in. For instance, she uses bacon fat for flavoring. At least once a week she fixes fried chicken and mashed potatoes and gravy. In the summer we eat fried okra, fried potatoes, fried or baked squash, fried catfish, and fried corn fritters, and every bit of it will melt in your mouth. In the winter we enjoy thick, yummy soup made of brown beans and ham with corn-bread and fried potatoes on the side. We also eat meat loaf or pot roast with brown gravy and roasted potatoes. On Mama's hot, fluffy biscuits, we spread real butter, not margarine. We drink fresh, whole milk, and every single night, all year round, we have dessert. Everyone says Mama is the best cook in the whole county—even Grandma, who is her mother-in-law.

And in case you're wondering, none of us is fat, except Grandma, who is merely plump and prefers it that way. She says, "A layer of fat under an old lady's skin keeps her looking twenty years younger."

While Mama cooked my eggs that morning, I slumped down into a chair at the table and tried to look as pathetic as possible. She glanced at me and smiled.

"Wash your face, April Grace," she singsonged. That was a rhyme she'd made up a long time ago when I was little. I used to think it was funny. "And brush your hair and teeth."

Inside my head, I made a face, 'cause there's something I can't understand: what's the Big Deal about primping for breakfast? Mama and Daddy had eaten earlier, right before Daddy went out to do the milking, and it wasn't like the two eggs on my plate could see me. And I sure didn't care two hoots how lovely or revolting I looked to my dumb sister. Which was just as well because, as I went upstairs to wash up, she came clomping down with a basket of dirty laundry. She was all scrubbed and brushed with her blonde hair all big and curly. She probably thought she looked like Madonna or Cyndi Lauper or somebody like that. Lucky Mama wouldn't let her wear makeup or clothes like any of those girl singers, or we'd have a mess to look at around here.

"You look like dog poop," Myra Sue said to me as she passed.

I gave serious thought to sticking out my foot and tripping her so she'd fall face-first into some dirty underwear, but if she fell down the stairs and ended up breaking her head or something important, I'd be blamed for it. Plus, I'd have to do all her chores. So I just crossed my eyes at her and went to primp for breakfast.

"Why don't you act like you're eleven-going-on-twelve, instead of like you're three years old?" she hollered after me. Silly, silly girl. At least I didn't act fourteen-going-on-thirty.

Back in the kitchen a little later, I was all wound up to complain about a headache, stomachache, water on the knee, *and* poison ivy, but the back door opened and Grandma walked in. She lives in a little house on the other side of the hayfield. Her name is Myra Grace Reilly. My sister and I are named after her.

She goes by Grace. I never knew my other grandma, whose name was Sandra. That's all I know, because Mama won't tell me anything else about when she was a little girl, other than that her great-aunt Maxie raised her. Great-Aunt Maxie died the year before Myra Sue happened. One time I asked Grandma if she knew anything about Mama's mother, but she acted odd and quiet and told me never to talk about it to anyone again. So I haven't, but it sure makes you wonder, doesn't it?

Now here's the thing about Grandma: she is not like my friends' grandmothers. They all wear their hair short, and they usually dye it brown or red or blond, and they have jobs and go to aerobics at the gym and stuff. Daddy says my grandma is a "throwback to another era." She wears dresses, which she makes at home, and has wavy gray hair she wears in a bun. Her shoes are way ugly, but Grandma declares she's long past trying to show off trim ankles and pretty legs. She says anyone who wears high heels is out of her cotton-pickin' mind. That's how she ruined her feet in the first place, when she worked at the dime store during the war. She has this big blue vein on her right leg.

When Myra Sue starts whining for new shoes with heels, Grandma sticks out her leg with the vein, hikes her skirt up to her knee, and says, "Lookie there, sis. Is that what you're after? 'Cause that's what you'll get if you wear them kind of fool shoes."

"City girls wear high heels to the dances all the time," my sister told her one time, all uppity, as if she knows everything about dances in the city—which she does not, let me assure you.

Myra Sue made this profound announcement one evening a

few weeks ago when we were all sitting in the living room playing the latest craze, a game called Pictionary, where you try to
guess the answer by the pictures your partner draws. Everybody
stared at my goofy sister; then Grandma spoke.

"I've seen pictures of what girls wear at those discos.
Disgraceful."

Myra Sue had rolled her eyes like she does when she
thinks she knows Everything.

"Step into reality, Grandma. It's 1986, and disco is out.
Good grief."

Daddy had laughed. "Yeah, Mom. Break-dancing is the
thing these days."

I thought break-dancing was out, too, but what do I know?
I want to learn the Charleston.

"Break-dancing!" Grandma said. "What's that? No, wait.
I don't even want to know. It sounds painful."

That morning in the kitchen, for a minute after Grandma
came in, I forgot to try to look sick. I jumped up from my
chair and gave her a hug. She hugged me back and asked
about my poison ivy.

"Itchy."

"Looks itchy," she agreed, examining my arms and legs.

"Morning, Lily," she said to Mama.

"Morning, Myra Susie," she said to my prissy big sister
coming out of the laundry room. "Got your first load ready
to hang out already?"

Myra Sue gave her a pained smile. "Yes, and there's about
a million tons more to do."

"Ah, well." Grandma sat down heavily. "Doing the wash

is like politics. It's always there, always dirty, and there ain't no end in sight."

Myra Sue grunted and went outside with her basket of wet laundry. She probably thought politics were bugs that bite you on the bottom in the summer.

I buttered a biscuit.

"Coffee, Mama Grace?" Mama asked. She got out the special cup with *#1 Grandma* printed on it in big, red letters. She filled it before Grandma had a chance to answer.

"Thankee kindly, Lily." She took a noisy sip.

"Grandma?" I said.

"Woo?" Grandma always says "Woo?" like that. She says it in a high-pitched kind of way, kinda like she's making a train whistle. Everybody else's grandma just says "What?" or "Huh?" or "Don't bother me now."

"How do you drink your coffee that way, right out of the coffee pot without even blowing on it?" I asked. "Don't it burn your guzzle?"

Guzzle is another Grandma word I like to borrow. Aside from its real dictionary definition, I think it means anything inside you, from your lips all the way to your belly.

"Aw, April, I been drinking hot coffee since I was a squirt, littler 'n you. My guzzle is calloused."

Even on a day as hot as that one, steam rose from her mug. I watched her drink.

"I guess it is," I agreed. "Plumb calloused."

"Some eggs and toast, Mama Grace?" my mama asked.

"Had me some oats earlier, Lily, but thanks anyway."

Grandma put down her mug and tapped the rim for

a minute, as if she was gathering her thoughts. Then she announced right out loud, "I do believe old man Rance has got designs on me."

Mama had just poured herself a cup of coffee, and now she turned around so fast it sloshed over her fingers and onto the floor.

"Ouch!" She sucked in a breath, shaking the drops from her hand while she gave Grandma a big-eyed look. "Jeffrey Rance?"

"The very one."

Grandma swigged another drink, eyeballing my mama with her eyebrows raised.

"Well, don't look so stunned, Lily. I won't win no Miss Universe contest, but I ain't that ugly, am I?"

Mama kept staring at her. "You mean Mr. Rance from Texas? The man who bought the Fielding place this spring? The one who told us his wife died just last Christmas?"

"Yep."

"Designs? Like tattoos?" I asked, all agog. Which was the wrong thing to do because it drew Mama's attention.

"April Grace, go take a shower and get dressed."

"But, Mama, if Grandma is—"

"Right now."

She had that don't-give-me-any-sass look on her face, so I had to leave the room just when things were getting good. Believe me, my grandma getting a tattoo just about topped my list of Interesting Things. I left the kitchen, but I hung around out of sight in the dining room, straightening the knickknacks and stuff on the shelves. I kept real quiet, but I want to tell you something: I had met that Mr. Rance, and there was something about that man I didn't care for. Not that I knew him personally at that point, but I'd seen him at the store a time or two, and he came to church a couple of times. There was just something about the way he looked at people when they weren't looking at him, kinda like he was sizing them up or looking for their secrets or something. Then when they'd look at him, he'd smile real big and get all friendly. I wondered if anybody else had noticed these things.

"What makes you think Mr. Rance is after you?" I heard Mama ask.

After her? I stopped breathing and straightening. After her, like a stalker?

"Oh, he's been calling, bringing me things."

Grandma said this real casual. Too casual, if you ask me.

Mama must have thought so, too, because she said suspiciously, "What things?"

"Oh, some tomatoes he bought from a vendor at the farmer's market."

"We have plenty of early eating tomatoes in our own garden. You're welcome to as many as you want. Goodness knows you've done enough work taking care of them."

"And he brought me some peaches."

Mama didn't say anything for a second or two, then answered, "Well, that was nice. Peaches are kinda expensive this year since that late freeze."

"Yes. And he gave me a book on horses, and a little glass horse too."

"Well, Mama Grace, that doesn't mean . . . Well, that is, has he said, well, you know . . ."

I heard Grandma take a noisy slurp of coffee and set the mug back on the table. She sucked in a big loud breath and heaved it out.

"It's like this, Lily. He kissed me last night."

Well, I almost fainted right there on the dining room floor and nearly dropped the little ceramic elf I was holding. I love my grandma, so don't get me wrong, but . . . it kinda makes the tiny little hairs on my arms stand up when I think about her and some man kissing.

There was no sound at all from the kitchen for a minute. Then Mama said in a very odd voice that sounded as if she was choking, "Mama Grace, did you kiss him back?"

Well, this had gone way past my interest. I plunked down the ceramic elf and fled upstairs so I wouldn't hear the answer to that.

FOUR

Calling on
Ian and Isabel

♪

You have probably guessed that since our new neighbors impressed ole Myra Sue so all-fired much, she pitched a fit when she found out Mama was gonna drag me to their house without her.

"Myra Sue could go instead of me," I offered real generously. "She could apologize for me, like a lawyer or preacher or something, and she'd do a better job 'cause she's older and stuff."

"Yeah," my sister agreed, smiling all over herself. "I could—"

"No."

The word fell out of Mama's mouth like a rock.

Myra Sue pooched out her lower lip and frowned and looked as aggravated as I felt. One of the few times we were actually willing to cooperate, and you'd think it would've thrilled Mama. I had even *complimented* my sister. Sort of.

"How about if I don't read any books for a whole week?" I said. "That could be my punishment."

And if you know me at all, you know taking away my books is about the worst thing you could do to me. Mama gave me a look.

"Absolutely not."

Boy, oh boy, Mama sure could be unreasonable sometimes.

We went to the St. Jameses in the Taurus, our good car, which is usually saved just for going to church or Special Occasions. I guess since Mama'd put on a pretty summer dress and made up her face, and poufed her hair and mine— and forced me to change out of my loose scruffies—paying a visit to the St. Jameses was a Special Occasion. I hoped she wouldn't care if I threw up on the new shorts and shirt she'd got me for school next month, because I had a feeling that by the time I finished apologizing for something I wasn't sorry for, I'd 'urp up my breakfast. I toted along my book, just in case I had a chance to read.

Let me tell you something. Rough Creek Road is real pretty. Tall trees grow on both sides, so most of the road is shady and cool all day. If you drive on our road in the autumn with the car windows down, the spicy smell of fallen leaves as they rot into the earth is better than any perfume you'll smell at the counter in Macy's. But here's the thing: Rough Creek Road abused our Taurus, which was why we drove the car only on Special Occasions. The road mistreated any vehicle except maybe a tractor or a farm truck or the road grader—or maybe a mule. Mama drove about five miles an hour, doing her best to miss the worst of the tricky bumps, gaping holes, and pointy rocks. I tried to read as we trekked to the St. Jameses, but it was impossible.

"Do you think the St. Jameses live in Sam White's old house?" I asked.

"Well, they bought the place, so I assume they plan to live in it."

I thought about that abandoned old house for a minute or two.

"You reckon that roof leaks?"

"I'm sure it does." Mama bit her lower lip and eased over a particularly nasty boulder-type rock in the road.

"It's an awful small house. Do you think—"

"April Grace, honey, can you give me a minute, please? I need to focus on getting this car down the road." That was Mama's way of saying, "Be quiet and leave me alone."

So I kept quiet, but I tried to imagine Ian St. James parking that big, shiny black car in front of Sam White's run-down old house. My imagination just wasn't that strong, I guess, and that's saying something.

Mama turned off the road and onto the driveway leading to the St. Jameses. Weeds grew so thick you could hardly see the tracks of the driveway or much of the house. Even the front yard looked like a tangled jungle of chicory and sticker weeds and toe-jerkers. Last year, our fifth grade science teacher, Mr. McCoach, said those weeds are called plantain, *not* toe-jerkers. Well, I'll tell you, when they get to a certain age and size, they start growing long stems with an ugly little flower at the end. And if you're walking barefoot and one gets between your toes, it's so strong it'll like to jerk your toe off. Grandma calls them toe-jerkers, and that's good enough for me.

Right away, when I saw that black car wasn't there, a great swell of joy nearly swallowed me alive. Then I saw that scrawny Isabel St. James sitting on the top porch step, looking like a reject from a Saturday morning cartoon. Her short, dark hair was slicked back, and she was dressed all in black—skinny black pants and a sleeveless black shirt and black high heels. Like I'm so sure that's what people should wear out here in the country. Good grief.

When we stopped the car, she stared at us as if she'd like to throw us both in a black hole. She had big dark smudges around her eyes, and I wondered if the mister had hauled off and given her a couple of socks in the eyes. If he had, I figured we'd better haul his sorry self to the Zachary County sheriff and be right quick about it before he hurt her worse. But then I realized those smudges were nothing but smeared mascara.

"Poor thing," Mama said softly. "She's been crying." Trust Mama to feel sorry for that sharp-tongued ole gal who practically called me a louse-bound hillbilly just the day before.

Mama got out of the car and, with my book in my hand, I followed like molasses in January. By the time I reached the porch, Mama had settled on the step next to Isabel St. James, with her arm around those bony shoulders. "There, there," Mama said.

Isabel sniffled and blinked. When she saw me, she drew up her shoulders and backbone until she was as straight and wide as a crowbar.

"Does that child have something contagious?"

Her voice sounded nose-pinched, and her mouth was all smushed up into a pucker.

I gave Mama an I-told-you-so look, hoping she'd finally understand that Isabel was Rude to the Max so that we could go home. But you know what Mama did? She took out a little pack of Kleenex from her purse, shook out a tissue, and handed it to Isabel, who grabbed it without saying "bless you," "thank you," or anything.

"This is my daughter, April Grace Reilly. She got into some poison ivy, but it isn't contagious, so please don't worry." She patted the woman's arm. Isabel eyeballed my rash and nodded ever so slightly—I guess that was her way of apologizing.

"I'm your neighbor, Lily Reilly. The girls said you stopped by our house yesterday."

Luckily, Myra Sue had already told Mama the woman's name because Isabel didn't bother to introduce herself before she started blubbering again.

Through her sniffling, wiping, and hiccupping, she managed to say, "When I saw your house yesterday, I was horrified."

Mama's eyes widened. "Why?" She handed over a fresh tissue.

Isabel dabbed her eyelashes, smearing the raccoon effect. She blew her considerable nose.

"Because it's so old and . . . so . . . country."

Mama cleared her throat, glancing at me long enough to finally see my educated expression. She turned to Isabel.

"Well, Mrs. St. James, we're in the country. My husband's grandfather built that wonderful old house in the 1920s. It might be old, but it's clean and neat and solid. And it's our home."

So there.

"But *I* loathe old houses! And look at this!" She gestured behind her as she shrieked the final word. Sam White's old falling-down house was way worse than I realized. I'd never seen it up close and personal 'cause Myra Sue said it was haunted. I didn't believe her, of course, but the place sure looked like a rat haven to me. Gaps in the red shingle siding showed the tar paper beneath. The front windows that remained in place were cracked or broken, and no front door hung where one should be. The best thing about the whole house was the front porch, but most of its remaining boards had seen better days.

"I despise it," Isabel continued to rant. "And that ghastly, dusty road, and these weeds, and whatever wild animal is scratching around under this shack. I hate it all, I tell you, and I want to go back to California where I had a life!"

Mama glanced at the house and winced. I guess she hadn't realized it was so run-down, either.

"Well," she said, turning back to Isabel, "you certainly can't stay here until some work's been done. It isn't safe."

"Oh no!" Isabel screeched. "Not on your life. I will never live in this hovel, not if my very life depends on it!"

Mama and I looked at each other. To tell you the truth, I didn't blame poor ole Isabel for how she felt. I wouldn't want to live there, either. For a long time, nobody said anything, and the only sounds were the jar flies shrilling in the trees and Isabel snuffling into her soggy Kleenex.

Mama handed her the whole pack of tissues and said, "Well, what are you going to do? Where's your husband?"

Isabel stiffened as if she had been poked in the back-side with a sharp stick. Her tears stopped like a spigot being turned off, and her mouth thinned until you couldn't see her lips. Boy, oh boy, you could tell she was itching for a fight.

"I don't know where he went, that wretch, but I hope some banjo-picking, cross-eyed hillbilly gets hold of him and drags him into the woods."

"Surely he didn't just leave you here!" said Mama.

Isabel blinked about a hundred times in five seconds.

"I should say he did! He forced me to get up at the crack of dawn this morning, practically yanking me out of bed in that Starshine Motel in town. He refused—*refused*, mind you—to let me stay there for the day, even when I begged. Not that I harbor affection for dinky, low-class hostels, of course, but I certainly did not want to come back out to this backwoods shack again. Ian literally hauled me to this toxic dump. And then he had the unmitigated gall to ask which room we should start cleaning first." She shuddered. "Well, I told him what I thought of him, this hovel, and his bright idea to drag us out into the back of nowhere, where no one in their right mind would ever want to live."

By this time, she seemed to have forgotten about bawling her head off and was ready to knock her husband into the middle of next week.

I'll tell you one thing: Isabel St. James was no prize to look at the day before, when she had her makeup on. But after she'd been bellowing like a newborn calf for half the morning, it hurt my eyes to look at her. She'd do the rest of us a world of good if she'd wear a bag over her head.

I sat down on the bottom step, and before I opened my book, I looked out over the weedy yard. Two gigantic oak trees shaded the house. The lawn would look real pretty if someone would cut the grass and plant some flowers. A nice, gentle breeze blew against my face as I stared up at the trees, at the long-armed limbs stretching out and reaching up like they were so glad to be alive. The green, green leaves against the blue of the sky made my heart tremble. I bet those trees had been there a hundred years.

"Look at the oak trees, Isabel St. James," I said. "They ought to make you feel better."

Isabel's expression said I was something stinky on the

bottom of her long, narrow shoe. Then, without saying a word to me, she turned to my mother.

"That miserable cur bought this dump without ever having seen it. Can you believe it? After we . . . well, after we . . . after we had to sell our house . . . then he . . . and the only place we could afford was here in this wilderness. Then he had the nerve to say, 'Maybe it's for the best, lambkins. Maybe we can find our dream.' And then this morning, he abandoned me."

"Abandoned?" Mama asked, startled. "Surely not!"

"Well, he went somewhere without saying a word and left me completely alone in this wilderness!"

She squalled into her Kleenex and waterlogged about three more before taking a deep breath. "If he longs for nature, what's wrong with the San Fernando Valley, I'd like to know?!" she said, looking at Mama as if she blamed her for everything wrong in her life. "And you people here are so out of touch with the world. How can you stand being a hillbilly?"

I stared at her, amazed by her nastiness when Mama had been so nice. And let me tell you something right now: I couldn't just sit there and be quiet.

When I jumped to my feet, I guess Mama realized I was all wound up because she gave me a look, but by then I was so mad I didn't care. I refused to listen to that ole Isabel St. James one more second. But I never got a chance to say a word because right then, that slick, black Cadillac came skulking down the weedy driveway like an egg-suckin' dog.

"There!" Mama said in a cheerful voice. "Isn't that your husband? See? He didn't plan to leave you here for long!"

Isabel's tears dried instantly. She narrowed her eyes, pinched in her lips, and threw down all those soggy tissues.

"He's going to wish he had," she announced as she stood. "Because I am going to tear out his black heart with my bare hands."

Well, this I had to see.

FIVE

Isabel's Mortal Injuries

✳

As I watched Isabel in her high heels and fancy designer pants go charging through the weeds toward her husband, I got to thinking, and here's what I thought: what would happen when the St. Jameses met their next-door neighbors, the Freebirds? They are about as opposite as Ecuador and Iceland. To tell you the truth, I'd dearly love to be there when they finally got a load of one another.

Now, to fully appreciate this situation, you have to know about the Freebirds. For one thing, "Freebird" is not their real name. Their actual last name is Durwood. And her real name is not Temple; it's Estelle. And his real name is not Forest; it's DeWayne. She says she is the temple of her inner goddess, and he says he inhabits the souls of trees. So, okay. They are hippies—*old hippies*—and if you know anything, you know what that means.

Anyway, there went ole Isabel stomping toward Ian, and she was screaming at him before he even got out of the car. She called him names that I won't repeat, and he just stood there while his pink face turned the color of a ripe tomato, and his blue eyes looked like hot marbles. I figured she and her husband were probably about Daddy's and Mama's age, but it's hard to tell someone's age once they get old. Anyway, she sure wasn't acting like a grown-up.

Isabel waved her arms while she yelled, and at one point she stomped her foot. Then she fell down like a rock in a pond. But this time all her screaming and cussing was from pain.

By the time Mama and I reached her, she was holding on

to her foot like she was afraid someone planned to run off with it. Ian looked down at her as if she were an obnoxious skunk cabbage in his rose garden.

"My goodness, what happened?" Mama said, kneeling on the ground.

Isabel was screeching so loud and long, she wouldn't have heard a freight train coming, even if she'd been tied to the tracks. I saw what had happened, though.

"She stomped so hard throwing her hissy fit that she broke her shoe," I announced.

I figured all that hollering was more for the sake of her broken high heel than her injured foot, so I picked up the thin spike and held it out to her.

She yanked it from me and hurled it at Ian's head, calling him a you-know-what and a you-know-who. Ian roared like a mad bull, threw the heel back at her, and missed by a mile because he threw like a girl. He marched off toward the house, saying as he went, "I came home with good news, and you won't even let me talk."

"There is no good news," she bellowed after him. "There is no good news in this hideous armpit of the world!"

He turned. His face was nearly as purple as plums on Grandma's tree.

"Well, you can just—"

One time I saw a rerun of the old *Andy Griffith Show*, when Gomer Pyle got mad at Barney Fife and told him, "You just go up an alley and holler fish!"

Well, that was not what Ian St. James said to his wife, let me tell you.

I looked at her, real interested in what new cuss words I might hear, but Mama spoiled it.

"Mr. and Mrs. St. James! My daughter is only eleven."

Isabel blinked and squooshed up her mouth. "Well, I did not invite either of you here."

She started to stand, then squealed bloody murder and grabbed her leg.

Mama stayed just as sweet and nice as always, though in my opinion I thought she should have smacked Isabel a good one. Instead, she patted one of Isabel's skinny shoulders.

"Here, hon," she said. "You just sit still and let me look at your foot."

"I think I've shattered my entire foot and leg." Isabel's voice quivered like Jell-O in a windstorm.

"Oh, I hope not," Mama told her.

I knew good and well Mama didn't think for one minute that Isabel had seriously hurt herself, even though her skinny ankle was starting to swell some. She touched Isabel's long, bony toes with her fingertips, but Mama jerked back when Isabel screamed again.

"I'm sorry," Mama said. "I didn't mean to hurt you."

"It's quite all right," Isabel bravely answered, blinking rapidly. "Please, tell me how bad it is. Will I be able to walk again, do you think?"

"Of course. Now let me feel for any broken—"

Isabel shrieked at the mere words.

Mama did not touch her. "Can you at least wiggle your toes?" she said.

With her lips thinned to where you couldn't even see

them, Isabel wiggled all her little piggies with their bright red nail polish.

"How about your ankle?"

The woman sucked in air and cursed, but she moved it a little bit.

"Your knee?"

She flexed and bent it.

"I'm a dancer, you know," Isabel said. "Ballet, of course, not clodhopping."

Mama cleared her throat. "Mrs. St. James, is it all right if I call you Isabel?" The woman sort of nodded. "Isabel, I'm pretty sure you'll be dancing again soon. I believe you've only sprained your ankle."

Isabel narrowed her eyes.

"I'm in agony. Sheer torture. Something is broken, or I wouldn't feel this wrenching pain."

"If you broke something," I told her, "you wouldn't be able to move it, and you just moved everything."

She glared at me. Boy, what a d-r-i-p, drip.

"You should get your husband to drive you to the clinic in town," Mama said, "just to be sure everything is all right."

"When pigs take flight," Isabel said calmly, as if she weren't in agony, sheer torture.

"April Grace, run and get Mr. St. James. Tell him his wife needs medical attention."

Isabel sniffled loudly. "He'll only want to shoot me, like a wounded racehorse. I know Ian. He does not care about anyone except himself."

If that wasn't the pot calling the kettle black. Boy, oh boy.

"Go on, honey," Mama said to me.

So Mama stayed with Isabel while I went after her mister. I didn't know who I felt the most sorriest for, me or Mama. I found Ian inside that awful house, kicking a stained, stinky old mattress that must have been on the floor since before Noah sailed the Ark. He was still cussing up a blue streak. When he saw me, he snarled like a mean dog.

"What do you want?" he asked.

"My mama said to tell you that you should take your wife to see a doctor."

"If my wife wants to see a doctor, she can drive herself."

Well, I held no especial affection for either of them, as you know, but I'm not heartless.

"She hurt her foot pretty good, and I don't think she can drive," I said.

He glared at me a minute longer. "Is she really hurt, or is she just being dramatic?" he asked. "She's the queen of drama."

"Well, she's being pretty dramatic," I agreed, "but her ankle has done swelled up the size of a turnip." This was an Extreme Exaggeration, but I did not want to argue with him.

I watched as this bit of news sunk in. The glare and nastiness slid right off his face. He rushed from the house like Sir George out to slay a dragon. Imagine Isabel St. James as a damsel in distress. If a dragon met up with her, she'd scare it so bad, it would run for cover with its tail between its legs.

"Poor darling," Ian was saying when I reached them. "Is it unbearable, lambkins?"

"Horribly so, dearest," Isabel said. "It's unbelievable how much pain I'm suffering."

Oh, brother.

The year I turned six, I broke my wrist when I used a shovel as a sled on the north slope behind the barn, and even then, I didn't carry on as bad as Isabel.

Watching those two coo and twinkle at each other was almost worse than listening to them scream and swear. I figured they weren't going to hurl shoes at each other for a while.

With Mama's help, Ian got his wife into the backseat of their car amidst her crying and hollering, "Help me, I'm in agony," about thirty times.

After they closed the car door and Ian jumped into the driver's seat, Mama gave him directions to the clinic. Then she did something I really hated.

She said, "It's a small clinic, so you'll probably have a long wait and won't feel up to cooking. Come to our house for supper tonight."

"I'll be in the hospital for at least a week," I heard Isabel wail. "I'm sure of it."

"Well, if they decide to send you back home today, come by and eat with us. We usually have supper at about 5:30."

"Yes, yes," Ian said impatiently.

Without a "thank you" or an "excuse me" or a "see ya later," Ian rolled up his automatic window and blasted backward out of his driveway. It's impossible to squeal tires on the dirt of Rough Creek Road, but his engine whined, and gravel flew like rice at a shotgun wedding. He drove off in a dust cloud so thick I nearly coughed up my lungs.

"He'll tear up their nice car, driving like that on this road," Mama said.

"He's afraid 'lambkins' is going to die in the backseat."

Mama wiped the dust off her clothes. "Just between you and me, I believe they both think she's dying," she said.

We looked at each other, and I busted out laughing. Mama smiled real big and patted my head.

After they were gone, peace settled around us like the dust off Rough Creek Road. It was so quiet that for a few moments, Mama and I just stood there and listened as leaves rustled against one another and hundreds of birds whistled and sang. I reckon you couldn't actually call it *quiet*, but it sure was better than listening to the St. Jameses, or the noise of cars, and people talking, and radios and televisions blaring like you hear when you go to Cedar Ridge. Which is just a little town, by the way. I can't imagine the racket in an actual city, and I prayed to God I'd never have to find out because I love it in the country so much, right here on Rough Creek Road. The Ozarks is a fine place to live, I think.

"Isabel St. James is crazy to hate being here," I declared.

"Well, I agree with you, honey," Mama said. "Of course, I understand why she doesn't want to live in that house right now."

I eyeballed the house. "Me, too. It looks full of mice and spiders to me."

We stared at the old place for a bit longer.

"I like our house, Mama."

She put one arm around my shoulders and pulled me to

her. It didn't make my poison ivy itch too bad since it was Mama who was doing the hugging.

"I do too," she said.

Our peace was then broken by a thrashing, crashing, tree-limb-breaking, leaf-crushing commotion coming from the woods on the east side of that weedy yard.

SIX

There's No Hippies Like Old Hippies

*

Mama and I stared at the east woods.

"Think that might be the wild animal Isabel said was scratching around under the house?" I asked.

Before Mama could reply, Temple and Forest Freebird, three dogs, five cats, and two goats emerged from the trees and into the weed-infested yard.

Temple was thin and friendly. She wore her gray hair in a braid like mine, except hers hung way down past her backside. I've never seen her wear anything but faded old T-shirts, long, flowy skirts, and sandals in the summer, or overalls, flannel shirts, and heavy, scuffed brogans in winter. Forest was medium-tall and kinda quiet. The top of his head was bald as an egg, but a thin gray ponytail hung, wormlike, on the back of his head. He wore overalls and T-shirts all year round. And he hardly ever wore shoes.

Temple and Forest both had some highfalutin college degrees, but they preferred to live like hippies.

Neither the people nor the animals looked as if they'd bathed in the last couple of months, which is not unusual, and I was glad we were upwind.

"Hey, Lily, April Grace," Forest called as they approached. "What's going on over here? Sounded like someone being murdered. Scared us all."

He looked around as if expecting to see blood, mayhem, and body parts.

"Hi guys!" Mama replied cheerfully.

With a big smile, she walked through the overgrown yard

toward the Freebirds and Company. Leaving my book on the porch, I trailed behind with a lot more enthusiasm than I'd approached ole Isabel earlier.

"I've not seen either of you in so long," Mama said. "How are you?"

Mama loved everybody, and everybody loved her right back. Well, except the St. Jameses. I've never seen anyone act like those two rude knotheads.

"Please don't be concerned about the noise," she told the old hippies as she patted the heads of all three dogs and both goats. The cats were uppity and avoided her. "Your new neighbor fell and hurt her ankle, but she's all right."

"She only *sounded* like she was being murdered," I told Forest. "You never saw such carrying-on in your whole entire life."

Temple looked at me, and this spaced-out, mushy expression came over her face as if she'd just seen a litter of new puppies.

"My goodness, you sweet baby," she said. "How you have grown this summer!"

She put both arms around me and smashed my face into her front. My nose was right at her armpit, and I nearly choked to death right then and there. Isabel would have had a real excuse to scream and squall if she'd caught a whiff of that.

Now, don't get me wrong. I like Temple just fine. She's real nice, and so is Forest, but they are strange and weird and they don't believe in things like deodorant and toothpaste or having regular jobs. They farm, but not like everyone else on Rough Creek Road. What I mean is, they have this huge, organic vegetable and herb garden, and they grow everything you can think of, plus a few things you've never heard about. They eat everything they grow, but they don't eat animals, so all their goats and pigs and chickens and what have you are perfectly safe.

"Look at you," Temple said, pulling back.

I gulped fresh, clean air and resisted the urge to wipe the damp feeling of her sweaty pit off my face. Then she tightened her grip on my upper arms.

"Tootsie Roll, have you been wallowing in poison ivy?"

She almost always calls me Tootsie Roll.

"Grandma's cat got out again, and I had to chase her all over creation," I said. "I didn't see the poison ivy."

"Aha." Temple gave me a smile, like the kind you give to a little kid. "Now, if dear little Queenie escapes her prison again—"

"You mean *when* she escapes again," I said.

"*When* she escapes her prison again, you could get her back much easier if you centered yourself in the universe."

Then Temple folded her hands and closed her eyes as if she were praying. I wasn't sure whether or not I should do the same.

"You see," she continued, "if you had simply sat down and sent her patient, loving vibes, she would have come right to you."

Her eyelids popped open, and she looked at me.

"You felt you had to chase her, and her dear, little kitty instincts told her to run," she said, beaming at me like a new flashlight.

"But you don't know Queenie," I began.

"Ah, but I do know cats. I have six of them. And I know something else: how to dry up that nasty poison ivy rash and take away the itch."

She put an arm around my shoulders, and I breathed through my mouth.

Turning us toward the woods, she said to Mama over her shoulder, "I have just the cure at home."

Except for the funky odors wafting from Temple and Forest, I was more than willing to go with her. Their house was weird and messy, with incense and candles burning and lots of interesting books lying around.

"I'm sorry, Temple," Mama said as we started walking, "but we have company coming, and I need my little helper."

Temple crimped her mouth at me, but she smiled as if we were partners in crime and then turned me around to face Mama. Those two women smiled sweetly at each other as sunlight and the shade of the trees danced around in the breeze. Forest stood a few steps away, blinking in the hot sun at Sam White's old place, which was now the St. James's new place. The sweat beads on his bald head glittered in the sun.

"Say," he said, looking at Mama, "what was that bit about new neighbors? Sam sold this place?"

"That's right," Mama said. "To a couple about our age. Ian and Isabel St. James."

"From San Francisco," I added in what was a pretty good imitation of Isabel's snooty voice, if I do say so my own self.

Mama frowned and shook her head at me.

"Well, what d'ya know about that?" Forest sighed deeply.

"I tried to buy this place from Sam a dozen times, and he just kept telling me it wasn't for sale." He squinted at the house again. "It's really nice here."

He said it so sadly that I felt sorry for him. With his slow, deep voice, droopy brown eyes, and long, hangy-down earlobes, Forest always made me think of an old hound dog. I just sort of felt sorry for him all the time, for no reason.

"Oh well." He sighed again, then looked at me and Mama and smiled. "Tell Mike and the rest of your family I said hi."

"I will," Mama said. "It was good to see you both."

I ran back to the porch to get my book; then I headed toward the car. We were almost there when Temple yoo-hooed and trotted toward me and Mama.

"Since you're so busy, I'll just bring over some of my salve for Tootsie Roll's poison ivy," Temple said.

"Temple, that's very nice," Mama said. "But please don't go to any trouble—"

"No, no. I can't bear to see her this way, so I'm going to do it. She must be so uncomfortable. Are you, sweetie?"

"I itch like crazy," I declared.

She nodded. "That junk they sell at the drugstore is worse than useless. And it's full of toxins. I'll bring you some literature about that, Lily, so you can be informed. You don't want to poison your family."

"Oh, I hardly think . . . Well, you needn't go to so much bother."

Temple rested her hand on Mama's arm. "It's not a bit of trouble. And nature is so much kinder to our bodies than a laboratory. I'll fix you right up with the good stuff."

"Well, thank you," Mama said kind of helplessly, smiling and nodding and pushing me toward the car.

There were times when you might as well go visit with a fence post as try to talk to Temple Freebird, and I reckon Mama knew this was one of those times. I figured if Temple had some kind of magic potion to cure my poison ivy, I was willing to take a bath in it, even if it smelled like armpits.

Temple and Forest waved and turned to walk back home, their three dogs, five cats, and two goats in tow.

"Oh dear!" Mama said as we drove out of their weedy driveway. "We forgot your apology."

"That's okay, Mama. I'm sure the St. Jameses don't even remember anything about any of it."

She gave me a look. "It's not okay. You'll just have to do it when they come for supper."

Well, I was disgusted right down to the core. I could only harbor the hope that they might not show up to eat. That was a very small hope, indeed, so I shoved the whole mess out of my mind.

But I got to thinking again about something else: Temple and Forest and Isabel and Ian as next-door neighbors.

"Wouldn't it be something," I wondered out loud, "if Temple came by with her poison ivy cure while the St. Jameses are at our house?"

Well, just call me psychic.

SEVEN

Hot for Grandma

When Mama and I got back to the house early that same afternoon, Grandma was still in the kitchen. She had fixed tuna
salad sandwiches and baked brownies while we were gone. A
fresh pot of coffee was giving off its waves of coffee fragrance.

"You gonna run into town with me, April?" Grandma
asked as she put a sandwich and a warm brownie on a small
plate in front of me. Then she set down a tall, cold glass of
milk. "It's Tuesday."

Well, other than to be stuck with Queenie and Myra Sue
on a deserted island, or to have supper with the St. Jameses, I
could think of nothing I wanted to do less than ride into town
with Grandma at the wheel, and I'll tell you why: Grandma
drives about thirty miles an hour on the hills and curves of
the highway and about five million cars get stuck behind
her because they can't pass safely. Then, when she gets to a
straight stretch where folks can pass her, she mashes the gas
pedal, and we go flying along at about seventy miles an hour.
Boy, you should hear the horns honk when that happens. At
intersections, Grandma stops and looks both ways like she's
supposed to, but then she doesn't wait. She just pulls right
out whether it's her turn or not. She never uses a turn signal.

"I've been going to Ernie's Grocerteria every Tuesday
for forty years," she says proudly. "Folks should know that
by now."

And if you're a pedestrian in Cedar Ridge, get some life
insurance. Grandma says the streets are for cars, not pedes-
trians. She claims she can't watch out for everybody in town,

so they should watch out for themselves. Last spring she like to have run down Mayor Pangborn when he was crossing the street from city hall to the Koffee Kup. I didn't think mayors were allowed to shake their fists and yell at old ladies, but obviously I was wrong.

Your best hope, if you cross the street in Cedar Ridge when Grandma is driving, is to pray that the good Lord sends down about ten thousand angels to protect you.

Right after lunch, Grandma and I walked across the hay-field to her little house near the pine forest. Except when the field grass has grown high like it was that day, you can see her place from our kitchen window. Her house looks like a little storybook cottage with a dark red roof and matching shutters. I love it there because it usually smells like cinnamon and nutmeg and vanilla and other good things. She used to live with us, but I guess when I was born I took up too much room or something, 'cause right after that, Daddy and Mr. Brett, our hired man who lives up Rough Creek Road about a half mile, built the house for her, and she moved out.

Grandma says she likes having her own place, and there was no use in her and Lily sharing the same house. She said she wanted to move out while they still loved each other and got along. It worked out real well.

Other than sitting in the passenger seat of her car while she drives, I like spending time with her. It's like we're good friends, even though she's my grandma. She always listens when I tell her about whatever book I've been reading. She's smart and funny and makes me think of things I never thought of before. For instance, one time when we were walking around in the pine forest beyond her house, she started talking about turpentine.

She said, "You ever notice how good these pine trees smell?"

I breathed real deep. "Umm-hmmm."

She breathed in deep too. "Yep. I love to smell a pine tree, don't you? But, now, turpentine—why, it's enough to turn your stomach."

I reckon I must have looked as confused as I felt, because she said, "You know turpentine comes from pine trees, don't you, April?"

Well, I hate to admit to being a complete ignoramus, but I told her, "I didn't know that."

She stopped and looked me up and down as if something peculiar were oozing out of my skin.

"Do you mean to tell me with all the reading you do, you don't know about turpentine? What do you think comes from pine trees? Pine-Sol?"

"Don't it? All the commercials say—"

Grandma flapped her skirt-tail as though chasing away flies. "Phooey on that! TV has done ruined your generation. *The Cosby Show* is about the only thing worth watching other than *Murder, She Wrote*."

Now, don't let that fool you. Grandma and Myra Sue watch way more TV than I do. They watch the soaps as faithfully as they go to church, and they talk about those soap opera people like they and their troubles are real. You ought to hear them sometime: "I hope Kayla will come home soon!" or "That

Emma. She's plotting against Kim." Myra Sue even cried when someone died on that show *Search for Tomorrow*. She saved the Kleenex she wiped her eyes on. She has it in a baggie in her drawer with her underwear. How anyone can be that dumb and still be able to eat with a fork is beyond me.

Mama doesn't watch the soaps. She listens to NPR on the radio in the kitchen in the afternoon. She and Daddy do not encourage TV watching, of course, but sometimes they like *Masterpiece Theater* and *NOVA*. I'd rather read. But then, I'm a bookworm, so what do you expect?

That day, when Grandma and I got to her house, she went to freshen up and change her shoes. I plopped down on her sofa. A little glass horse sat on a doily on the coffee table. I looked at it, but I wasn't impressed with Mr. Rance's gift.

Grandma's cat, Queenie, sat on the dining room table and stared without blinking, like she was trying to cast a spell on me. I'll tell you right now, if I'd sat on the table, Grandma would have shooed me off there like a nasty fly. I gave Queenie a grim look. Grandma came into the room with a mess of jangling keys in her hand.

"I thought you was going to put on your good shoes," I said.

She bent from the waist a little and looked at her feet. "These *are* my good shoes." She straightened up and glanced around. "Have you seen my pocketbook?"

You have to know that my grandma can't keep up with her big black purse any more than I can sprout wings and fly to Kansas City. Three weeks ago I found it in the refrigerator crisper, on top of the lettuce.

"Why don't we just walk to town?" I suggested hopefully. "It would be real healthy."

Grandma stared at me like she thought I was nuts.

"It's eight miles to town, you silly child, and ninety degrees in the shade."

Hopes dashed, I slouched back against the sofa. Her purse was right on the small table next to the front door, but I wanted to put off getting in her car as long as possible, so I kept my mouth shut.

Just then, a big red pickup pulled off Rough Creek Road and into Grandma's driveway. Grandma was so busy looking behind the china cabinet that she didn't hear it arrive. I stood up to get a better look out the picture window.

"You got company, Grandma," I said.

"Woo?"

"Company. In the driveway. A red pickup." The truck door opened, and I grimaced. "It's that old man from down the road."

Grandma stared at me for a moment, then both hands flew up.

"Good gravy!" she yelped. "Jeffrey Rance is calling on me *again*."

She went trotting off to the bedroom, taking out hairpins and smoothing her hair.

"You gonna start kissin'?" I called after her. "'Cause there's some things a kid ought not to see."

She popped her head around the doorway between her bedroom and the living room and glared at me.

"Hush that, for heaven's sake!" She popped out of sight

again, and I heard bobby pins hitting the little glass tray on her dresser. "You oughta be paddled for eavesdropping, April Grace Reilly." A second later her bedroom door snapped shut.

I looked outside again. He was standing out there by his truck, a huge, old man in his black Stetson hat, bright red shirt, black jeans, and cowboy boots. He eyeballed the house like he was fixing to buy it. Then he walked around a bit, gawking up and down, right and left, as if he were looking for something. Then he came toward the house, so I right quick settled back down on the sofa and pretended I was somewhere else. His boot-steps thundered on the porch floor as he approached the door.

"Miz Grace, darlin', are ya home?"

The voice boomed into the house as what looked like a red-and-black grizzly bear passed the window and blocked out the daylight from the screen door like a solar eclipse. The odor of Old Spice came through the open windows and screen door and went right up my nose.

"Say, sugar plum," he yelled. "You here?"

Queenie shot down off the table and streaked into the spare room. He yanked open the screen door and walked right in, just like he'd been invited.

"Miz Grace!" he bugled like a lovesick moose.

I made a real admirable attempt to keep my hands off my ears. He didn't see me, and I sure as shootin' didn't let him know I was ten feet away. He stood for a minute, then walked kinda all quiet and sneaky-like over to the TV. He looked at it close, then bent over a little and examined the brand-new VCR sitting on top, which Daddy and Mama had given Grandma last Christmas.

Not many people had VCRs in 1986 because they were new and expensive gadgets. But they were real nice if you wanted to sit in the front room and watch a movie. Grandma was afraid of it, if you can believe that. She said she was afraid she'd push the wrong button and burn the house down or something, even though I've shown her a million times how to use it.

With his big ole pointy finger, Mr. Rance poked the little flap where the tapes go in, smiling as big as if he'd discovered gold in the backyard. He muttered something about that "nifty little item oughta be worth something." He straightened and looked around, but I sat quiet as a mouse, praying he'd never see me. And he didn't. Not right then, anyway.

What he *did* see was Grandma's purse, laying right out there on the little table by the door, plain as day. Boy, oh boy, did his eyes light up. He turned toward it, his hand out.

And he saw me. He gave a jump of surprise. I didn't know I looked so scary.

"Grandma is in the other room," I told him.

He stared at me a few seconds, then said, real loud, "Well, who are you? Wait! Don't tell me. Let me guess." He snapped his fingers. "You're Miz Grace's grandson."

I don't look like a boy, even if he couldn't see my long hair.

"I'm a girl!" I yanked my red braid over a shoulder and all but waved it at the old goofball.

"Why, blamed if that ain't so!" He laughed like an asthmatic hyena. "Blamed if that ain't so. What's your name, young'un?" He sat down right next to me. The air around us practically turned blue from all that Old Spice aftershave lotion he musta bathed in.

"April Grace Reilly."

"Ha!" he said so loud and quick that I was the one who jumped that time. "Named after your granny, are you?"

I nodded and wished that said granny would get back in here and take care of this thing.

"You like school?"

"I like summer vacation better."

He leaned closer and yelled, "How's that?"

I could see, plain as daylight, that he wore hearing aids, so why didn't he turn 'em on?

"I said I like summer vacation better," I repeated.

He snorted and laughed and slapped his thigh like that was the funniest joke since God created Myra Sue. Grandma finally came out of the bedroom, her hair all fresh combed and smooth. She wore her new, blue, just-for-church dress.

"You going to church, Grandma?"

Her cheeks got red, and I realized too late that she'd dressed up for Mr. Rance. He turned to face her and looked her up and down the way Daddy does to Mama when he thinks nobody is looking. Mr. Rance didn't seem to care that I was sitting right there.

"Well, don't you look a picture, Miz Grace?" He pushed both hands against his thighs and stood up, grunting a little.

"Thank you, Jeffrey," she said real soft. I doubted the deaf old man heard her.

Then he did the unthinkable. He gave her a big, loud, wet smooch you could have heard clear up to the Missouri state line. I squinched myself back into the sofa as far as I could and pressed my face with a green cushion embroidered with the Lord's Prayer.

Grandma mumbled something. "Whatsa matter?" Mr. Rance boomed. "Ain't she never heard of kissin' before?"

I kept the cushion over my face and pretended I was in the Outback of Australia, away from Rough Creek Road, Myra Sue, the St. Jameses, Queenie, Mr. Rance, and Grandma.

"April and I were fixing to go into Cedar Ridge," Grandma said. "It's Tuesday, you know. Double coupons at the Grocerteria, and one percent off regular prices for seniors."

Then Grandma yanked the cushion away from my face and looked like she wanted to swat my behind.

"Well, what a coincidence." Mr. Rance grinned so big, he like to have split his face. He had a mouthful of teeth, and he was showing every one of them. I hoped they were real, because I sure didn't want to see dentures fall out of his head. He continued, "I was on my way to town myself, so I come over here to see if you wanted to go along, maybe have lunch at the Koffee Kup."

"Oh." Grandma looked about half-pleased and half-nervous.

"We've done had lunch," I told him, hoping he'd go home. "Grandma made tuna sandwiches with little pickles in them."

"Oh, April," Grandma said, laughing all funny-peculiar. "That was just a little snack. And actually, Jeffrey, I was going to take April into town—"

"Bring 'er along! The more the merrier." He turned

to me. "Whatcha say, kid? I'll buy you a hamburger at the Koffee Kup."

Now, I was of two minds about this. While I was downright overjoyed that I might be safe from Grandma's driving this week, I really, really did not want to sit in a café with those two senior citizen lovebirds. What if they started smooching right at the table in front of God and everybody?

I gulped. "Mama needs me to help her get ready for company," I said. I looked at Grandma. "If you're going to go with Mr. Rance, you won't need me."

"Well." She seemed to think it over real hard. "Well, all right, then. But you and me will go next Tuesday. How 'bout that?"

Next Tuesday was a whole seven days away. Maybe she'd misplace her driver's license by then.

"Okay." I scooted off the couch. "See ya later."

I ran outside and raced toward our house before either of them had a chance to change their minds and call me back.

Mr. Rance had moved from Texas to Rough Creek Road early this spring, and according to my daddy—who makes it a point to welcome all the newcomers and see if there's anything he can do to help them settle in—the old man used to have a big ole ranch and lots of thoroughbred horses. He said Mose Fielding sold Mr. Rance that twenty-acre parcel of dirt that his hogs had ruined. You know how hogs root around, upturning rocks while they snuffle and snort, looking for something to eat. It takes forever for the grass to grow back where hogs have rooted. Well, you don't have to be a rocket scientist to know thoroughbred horses couldn't live in such a place.

When he first moved here, Mr. Rance had bought a little trailer to live in, but I didn't think he stayed there very often. Maybe he was bored or something, because I saw him in that red truck, driving up and down Rough Creek Road about ten times a day. Plus, every blessed time we went to Cedar Ridge, there was that same red pickup parked at the Koffee Kup.

Here's the thing: that morning I was about halfway across the hayfield when a thought hit my brain and made me stop dead in my tracks, so I could give it serious and detailed consideration. Why would someone with a lot of horses leave a big horse-raising state like Texas and come to the rocky hills of Arkansas and live on a hog-rooted twenty acres where nothing would grow? Why would anyone do something that dumb?

And here's another thing: with his own wife dead just a few months, why was he suddenly hot for Grandma? Maybe he wanted a brand-new wife, the thought of which made me swimmy-headed.

Boy, oh boy, thoughts flooded through my head so fast it was hard to keep up with them. A particular remembrance, though, seemed louder and bigger than the rest, and it was this: he'd been kinda sneaky in Grandma's living room, looking at her stuff like he wanted to swipe it. And what about her purse? Would he have picked it up if he hadn't seen me? It sure looked like it from where I sat.

"I bet he's a crook," I said aloud. "He's probably wanted down in Texas and came to the Ozarks to hide from the law." I've seen cop shows on the TV, and an awful theory rose up in my brain. "Maybe he's a horse thief. Or worse, maybe he even *killed* his wife."

Now, there's a notion. I have to admit, though, there was no reasoning behind it. Of course, being just a plain, ordinary crook . . . well, that was possible. That's why the Ozarks have so many criminals and weirdos, you know. They come here from everywhere else and think they can hide in the hills and hollers. Well, maybe they can, 'cause there sure seem to be a lot of them.

You better believe Rough Creek Road has its own oddballs. For example, there's Uncle Melt and Auntie Freesia Mahoney, who like to say they've raised three kids, one of each. One of each what, I'd like to know? A girl and a boy and what else? They talk to and about their fixed poodle, Pancake, as if it's a kid. Maybe that's what they mean. And then there's the Todds. They've lived at the end of the road, right on the edge of the Ozark National Forest, since the early 1960s. They don't talk to anyone—especially not the locals—and they sure don't want anyone talking to them. If you try, you might get your head blown off. Like I said, we got our share of weirdos around here.

Anyway, the more I thought about Mr. Rance being up to no good, the more it all made sense. The way the old man eyeballed the TV and VCR, he probably thought she was loaded. I'd heard about men who sweet-talk nice ladies into giving them everything they own, but Grandma don't have much—just her home furnishings and her Social Security checks.

Well, he better not try to sponge off my grandma. He better not be a crook. Or an old lady's purse snatcher. Or a wife murderer.

"Boy, oh boy," I said as I started walking again. "You don't want to mess with the grandma of April Grace Reilly. If I find out he's up to mischief, I'm going to fix him good."

I sort of felt like John Wayne or Clint Eastwood. If either one of them had been a girl, I mean.

EIGHT

The St. Jameses Are Coming, Hurrah, Hurrah

That night I set the table for company supper. Myra Sue came into the dining room. She stared at the table, then squawked like a strangled goose.

"You dumb little kid! Don't you know *anything*?" she said to me. She began stacking up the plates I'd just laid out.

"Mama told me to set the table, and you're messing it up. Stop it!" I reached out to take the plates back from her.

"Stop it yourself, you toad!" said Myra Sue.

She yanked backward. The top two plates slid from the stack and crashed to the floor.

"What in the world?" Mama came out of the kitchen, looking from the plates on the floor to us. Her face was pink and damp from the hot stove.

"Mama, she unset the table—" I began.

"Mama, she was using these old dishes—" Myra Sue butted in.

"Quiet!" Mama hardly ever raised her voice, so when she hollered we both hushed. She glared at us, then said, "I told you to set the table, April Grace, and you, Myra Sue, are supposed to call Grandma and tell her to bring ice."

Usually, Mama never gets flustered, but I had a feeling she was all nervous and jumpy because those snotty St. Jameses were coming. She rubbed a spot above her eyebrows.

"What happened, April?" she asked in a voice that sounded as if she were tired enough to lay right down.

I shot a triumphant look at my sister.

"I set the table, eight places, just like you told me to. Then Myra Sue sticks her stupid head in here—"

"April Grace." Mama's voice held a warning.

I cleared my throat. "Myra Sue sticks her head in here and starts hollering and unsets it all, then she goes and dumps them plates on the floor."

"You are such a big fat liar. Mama, your youngest daughter used our old dishes instead of our good ones, and Mr. and Mrs. St. James are extra special guests."

"Oh brother," I muttered.

"They deserve the very best," she added.

Suddenly we're the Hallmark card people. I was afraid I might upchuck, but from the expression on Mama's face, I decided standing there and gagging probably wasn't the smartest thing I could do.

"They are from *California*," Myra Sue continued, as if that were the cherry on top of her sundae.

"So what?" I said.

"What about these broken plates on the floor?" Mama pronounced each word real slow and precise, and her voice got louder with each word.

"I guess I picked up too many," Myra said. "They slid off."

Mama stared at her real hard, then at the plates, then at me. She took in a breath so deep, both sides of her nose pinched in.

"All right, Miss Myra. You want to set the table so much, set it. Use the good dishes, not because the St. Jameses are from California, but because they are our guests. And you." She turned to me, and I shrunk a little inside my skin. "Get the broom and sweep up these broken plates. I'm sure your sister would not deliberately dump them on the floor. *Then*"—she turned back to the sister—"you quit stalling and call your grandmother."

Myra Sue's expression said she was dying by bits and pieces.

"Why does *Grandma* have to come?" Myra Sue said. "She is so . . . uncouth. She has no class."

Mama's mouth flew open, but before she could respond, I said, "You are mean, Myra Sue Reilly! Grandma is the best grandma is the whole entire world!"

"But, Mama, she'll show up in one of those awful home-made dresses and her Dr. Scholl's shoes and use bad grammar and tell some stupid story about when she was a girl during the Great Depression. It will be absolutely humiliating."

Mama unclenched her jaw. "For shame, Myra Sue Reilly! What's got into you, anyway? She's coming. That's that."

Another sigh from the dark depths of Myra Sue's soul.

"And you better be nice to her," Mama added.

"I'm always nice to her. But face it, Mama, Grandma is a hillbilly. A hick. She'll disgrace us all."

I wanted to smack that girl square on the head, but Mama would've come unglued. She closed her eyes again and clamped her mouth real tight.

Mama took a deep breath, willing her patience. "Tonight, after our guests are gone, you and I, Myra Sue, are going to have a talk. And you *will* see the light. Do I make myself per-fectly clear?"

Then Mama looked at me, and I lost my grin right quick.

"Why are you still standing there, April? Get the broom and sweep up these broken plates like I told you to."

I shot off to the broom closet without pausing to blink.

🐶

Now, I'm just a kid, so supposedly I don't know anything, but here's what I think: if you're invited to supper at 5:30, you got a lot of nerve to show up at 6:57 without calling to say you'll be late. But those St. Jameses. I tell you what. They must never have learned good manners out there in California. Grandma got here at 5:15, and she dragged old Mr. Rance right along with her, but at least they were here on time.

I just happened to be standing at the front door when Ian and Isabel drove up. I guess Ian saw me through the screen because he rolled down his window and hollered, "Is that vicious dog tied up?"

I didn't know where Daisy was, but she's never been tied up in her whole life. Probably she was asleep next to her food dish in the backyard. But I said "yep" and watched him stop the car near the front steps.

Ole Isabel took her sweet time getting out of the car all by herself because her mister didn't give her any assistance. He was flapping his handkerchief across the windshield of their car, like that was going to do something about the dust from Rough Creek Road. He held a little purse in one hand. I assume it belonged to his wife, but I wasn't too sure. Maybe men in their social circle carried purses. Isabel wobbled to the front porch steps on crutches.

Mama, who'd been keeping supper warm, saw Isabel through the screen. "Oh my goodness!" Mama said, and she went running outside. She was down the front steps before the screen door shut behind her.

I followed more slowly and hung around near the edge of the porch to watch what promised to be a real circus. Myra Sue was in the kitchen washing the pots and pans for the second time, since she didn't do it right the first go-round. She didn't know that the Emperor and Empress of the Isle of Rude had arrived.

"My stars!" Mama said to Isabel. "You injured it that badly?"

"Those quacks at that hick clinic are a bunch of fools. They told me I had barely twisted my ankle."

"And they put you on crutches?" Mama said.

"Isabel insisted," said Ian. His lips hardly moved. Well, how could they? His jaws looked clenched tight enough to crack walnuts. So much for *darling* and *lambkins* and *snookums* and whatever other names they came up with while Isabel was dying on the way to town.

"Of course I insisted," Isabel snarled. "They were just going to wrap it, give me an aspirin, and send me on my merry way."

"They took X-rays," Ian said.

Isabel snorted. "That contraption was ancient. I'm sure I have radiation poisoning now."

"Well, if you start to glow in the dark, I'll let you know," Ian snapped.

Mama interrupted this precious gem of a conversation. "It can't be comfortable for you, standing here," she said.

Isabel whimpered and looked pitiful. "So you come on inside where you can sit down. I have supper ready."

"How am I supposed to get to the door?" Isabel asked.

Mama shot a glance at Ian. "Why, your husband looks strong, and you're just a little mite. He can carry you. Here, I'll take your crutches."

"Ian can't lift me, let alone carry me," Isabel said.

"Of course he can," Mama smiled. "I bet you don't weigh more than a hundred pounds."

I looked at Ian. I bet the preschoolers in T-ball could beat him up.

"Well," Ian said, staring at Isabel. He took in a deep breath and blew it out. "Let's get you inside."

Pulling a face that involved squinching his eyes and dragging down the corners of his mouth, Ian picked up his lambkins and staggered around like it was midnight in an ice storm. Isabel shrieked the whole entire time.

Mama followed with the crutches, and I stood where I was, disgusted to the very bone. Inside the house, Mr. Rance—who had invited himself to come along with Grandma—told a long-winded horse story, and he was telling it so loud that I walked clear to the end of our long driveway to see if I could still hear him. I could. Honest.

I stayed outside until my sister came out on the porch.

"Oh, April," she sang out. I looked at her standing on the edge of the porch, all prissy and sweet. "Mama says it's time to eat!" She bounced every word as if reciting a poem about a basket of kittens.

I stared at her, wondering if her sweetie-pie smiling-ness

was supposed to fool me into getting close enough so she could whomp me upside my head. She's been known to pull that trick before. But I guess she didn't plan to do it right then, because she whirled on one foot and went back into the house.

Myra Sue might have planned to be all sweetness and light, and maybe she thought that evening was going to be something out of an old black-and-white Fred Astaire movie, but it wasn't. It turned out to be something closer to *A Nightmare on Elm Street*.

NINE

Home-cookin' and the St. Jameses

☀

Everyone was seated at the supper table by the time I washed my hands and went into the dining room.

Isabel sat in a chair at one end of the table, her foot propped up in another chair nearby with every pillow and cushion in the house under it. Boy, I hoped her skinny, stinky foot wasn't on the pillow where I lay my own personal head.

Isabel's crutches leaned against the wall behind her. Ian sat on her right, and next to him sat Grandma and Mr. Rance. Daddy sat at the head of the table with Mama on his right. Myra Sue came next. Lucky for her, she got to sit on Isabel's left. She patted the empty chair between her and Mama.

"Here, sis," she said happily.

"What's wrong with you?" I asked her as I sat down.

She smiled as if I'd given her a compliment; then she turned that dopey grin to Isabel, dazzling the woman with all her braces-covered teeth, including the lower ones.

"Time to give thanks," Daddy said. "Mr. St. James, as our guest tonight, would you?"

Ian looked at him. "Would I what?"

"Ask the blessing?"

The man's eyes bugged, then settled back in his head.

"Oh, well, I—"

"We are *not* religious," Isabel piped up in a tone of voice that said they weren't cannibals, either. Then she plucked up a fork and looked at it as if she'd never seen one before.

"Almighty God!" yelled Mr. Rance, and everyone but him jumped about three feet. Isabel's fork clattered to the table.

I saw the old man had his eyes closed and realized he was hollering a prayer, not swearing. He thanked the Lord for everything from summer rain and good food to paved roads and high-steppin' horses. Then he asked for a blessing on the world, the United States, Texas, the "group gathered here today to eat of the bounty which looked fit," and "Miz Grace, who is one of yer own dear angels, dear Lord." I thought he was done, but he kept rambling, and I like to have passed out from starvation.

As Mr. Rance droned on, I breathed in the wonderful smell of Mama's crispy fried chicken. I opened my eyes while the old man prayed without ceasing and eyeballed the platter of corn on the cob in front of me. Butter dripped off every piece. I imagined biting into it, how it would taste all sweet and smooth and salty. Next to the roasting ears, a bowl of fluffy mashed potatoes sat like a snowy mountain, and there was thick, creamy gravy right next to it. There was big salad with everything taken from our garden that day and a bowl of seasoned, fresh green beans with pieces of bacon and onion. The fried okra came next, then a platter of red tomatoes, sliced thick and fresh, with long slabs of cucumbers and little green onions around them.

I heartily wished God would tell Mr. Rance, "Enough, already."

I cut a glance from the food to see if anyone else were dying of hunger and over-blessedness, but they all had their eyes closed—except Isabel. She was staring at the fried chicken like she thought it might roost on her plate at any minute. Then her eyes darted nervously from the bowl of gravy to the fried okra to the heaping basket of Grandma's hot, homemade yeast rolls, for which she is famous.

I looked at Mr. Rance to see if he were about finished, and what do you think I saw? He was talking all that big prayer to God, but he was looking around the dining room to beat the band. He even picked up the serving fork next to the chicken, flipped it over and studied the writing on the back, all without taking a pause in all that thanksgiving. He never did see me looking at him 'cause I closed my eyes again before he had the chance.

When he finally yelled, "Amen!" there was silence. Nobody moved for a minute. I wanted to say something about the total inappropriateness of looking around during prayers, but I supposed I was a bit guilty myself. Anyway, I was too hungry to get sent from the table for speaking out of turn.

"Well, dig in, folks," Daddy said. "If you don't see it on the table, just ask for it. Lily, my sweet, it all looks mighty fine, as usual."

"Apple cobbler for dessert," Mama told him. They gave each other that gooey look, which I dearly hoped didn't lead to a kiss. Mr. Rance might think kissing at the table was a habit in our house, and he might decide to lay one on Grandma again.

My daddy looked tired. He had rushed his chores when he could probably have taken his time. As you might know, summer is the busiest time of year for dairy farmers. But do you think the St. Jameses thought of that? In California, they probably never ate their supper until eight or nine.

Before anyone could pass him the fried chicken, Mr. Rance reached out and stuck his fork in the biggest piece. He commenced to whoop and holler about how good it looked. Pretty soon, the food made the rounds with folks serving themselves. Except for Isabel, who took nothing. Myra Sue held out the bowl of potatoes to her, and the woman curled back as if it was full of worms. Ian finally reached across the table, grabbed the bowl, and served himself a little.

I thought Isabel would scream when the gravy reached her. Ian took it from Myra Sue and dabbed a bit on his potatoes.

"Isabel," Mama said, looking concerned, "you don't have a thing on your plate. Aren't you hungry? Are you feeling poorly?"

Isabel's long blade of a nose curled as her skinny lips puckered into a tiny, wrinkled circle. Boy, could she make herself any uglier?

"I *cannot* eat this," she said.

All of us looked at the big bunch of food Mama had worked all afternoon to prepare.

"We eat very little fat," Ian said.

"And everything here is swimming in grease," added his lovely wife.

"Swimming in grease?" Mama repeated weakly.

"Butter, gravy, fried," Isabel said. "In California, we don't eat any of it."

Ian shook his head. "Never."

I figured there were plenty of folks out there who ate fatty foods—they have McDonald's out there, don't they?—so I didn't believe them. Mama looked as if someone had slapped her. I glared at Isabel and wanted to hit her in the head with one of her crutches, then smack Ian with the other one. Not that I'm violent, but boy, oh boy. Being nice doesn't seem to work with some people.

"Oh, I'm so sorry," Mama said. "I never even thought . . . I'm so used to my way of cooking . . ."

"Your way of cooking is the best in the whole world," I declared. Daddy patted her hand. Grandma had pulled in the corners of her mouth, aiming a sour expression at some of our company.

"Well, I meant no offense," Isabel sniffed. She blinked rapidly about twelve times. "I just don't want to develop that corn-fed look you country people have. I guess you can't help it, Lucy, if you always eat like this. I simply refuse to put on the extra pounds. Sorry."

"I understand," Mama said quietly. "Here's a nice salad."

"Her name is Lily," I told that nasty woman. But she acted like I wasn't at the table. She brightened as the salad reached her. I guess she'd rather look like a hollowed-out scarecrow than soft and pretty like Mama.

Mr. Rance had been wolfing down his supper like he was the only one in the room. He looked up and saw that everyone watched Isabel put salad on her plate.

"Try some of this here chicken," he yelled, shoving it her direction. "It's larrupin'."

Boy, do I hate that word. It sounds like a disease. Couldn't he just have said the chicken was tasty?

Ian pushed it back, and Mr. Rance shoved it toward them again.

"Feed that poor woman!" he hollered. "She looks half-starved."

The platter tipped, and a great big chicken breast slid off to land smack-dab on top of Ian's wee blob of mashed potatoes and gravy.

Ian looked down at his plate and back up at Mr. Rance. "My wife does not eat fried foods," he responded.

No way the deaf old man heard that, and his next words proved it.

"Give 'er some of this here chicken. You'd be surprised how much better she'll look with a little meat on 'er bones."

After the chicken fell onto his plate, I reckon Ian must have given in to temptation because he scooped out a big serving of potatoes, asked for the gravy, then got a couple of roasting ears, some beans, and a hot roll. Before you had time to turn around twice, his plate was as full as Daddy's. Isabel looked like she was gonna divorce him. She grabbed his arm with her bony white fingers.

"What do you think you're doing?" she asked.

"Eating," Ian said. "This food is great."

Isabel squawked like an old laying hen. "Do you have to talk with food in your mouth?" She pinched her lips together and turned back to her salad. She ate it one tiny bit at a time and kept blinking as if someone threw sand in her eyes every few seconds.

I cut a sideways glance at Myra Sue to see if she watched this nonsense, and what do you suppose I saw? That girl had pushed aside all the good stuff and was nibbling on her salad, one small piece at a time. And blinking her eyes.

"Ian, are you going to renovate the old house, or are you going to build a new one?" Daddy asked.

Isabel sat up straight. She leaned in, and you could practically see her ears grow as she listened to Ian's answer.

"Well, I'm not sure that old house can be saved—" Ian began.

"At last you see reason!" Isabel announced, curling her lips in what I figured was her version of a smile. It looked to me more like she smelled something foul, but what do I know?

"Termites may have done a lot of damage," Ian continued, as if she weren't there. "And the roof has a lot of leaks. The decking is probably completely ruined. We'd be better off not moving into the house just yet."

"So you're going to build?" Daddy asked.

"Not exactly. We can't—"

"What do you mean, not exactly?" Isabel interrupted—quite rudely, I might add. "We will *not* live in that hideous old shack, and the housing we saw in that pathetic little town is absolutely out of the question. There are no decent hotels. We will have to go elsewhere, and that's that."

Isabel sat back as if she'd just recited the entire Declaration of Independence and half the Constitution.

Ian acted like he was deaf. "We'll have to make do for a while, so I went into town this morning to look at used mobile homes—"

"*What?!*" Isabel screamed and stood up, sore foot and all. "What? What?"

When I pictured that prissy, stuck-up woman living in a trailer house when she so obviously believes she belongs in a gold-encrusted mansion, I like to have exploded my face and lungs trying not to laugh right out loud.

TEN

The Way
to Make Friends.
Ahem.

"You and your roots might be trailer trash, Ian St. James, but I am not! My father was a California state senator!"

Ian finally turned and looked at his little woman.

"I am talking." He bit the head off of every word.

"I don't care." She bit right back.

"Mobile home living isn't so bad, Isabel," Mama said. "There actually are some very nice ones."

Isabel gave her a look that would make a blackjack tree drop its thorns. Mama just smiled at her, but I could see the smile no longer reached her eyes. In fact, it hadn't reached her eyes all evening.

"You might want to live in one, Lucy, but I refuse!" said Isabel.

"We have to live somewhere, Isabel," Ian said.

She leaned forward and hissed like a snake. "If you hadn't lost all our money in Las Vegas—"

"We will not talk about that in front of these people." Ian said this through clenched teeth.

Boy, oh boy, the St. Jameses were itching for a fight, and I wasn't sure I wanted to see it. On the other hand, I wasn't sure I'd want to miss it, especially if it was going to lead to throwing punches. But after they glared at each other for about ten seconds, Ian turned from his little woman and ate a big forkful of fried okra. Isabel blinked a bunch of times in that way she had, then picked up her glass of ice water and sipped.

Don't misunderstand and think Isabel blinked to hold

back tears. No sirree, not for a minute. I'm pretty sure she was trying to keep her eyeballs from bursting into flames like those pictures you see of Satan.

Here's the thing: If she didn't want to live here, why didn't she just go back to where she came from? Or failing that, somewhere else? It was plain as day she and the mister had problems. And it wasn't like she couldn't get a job. I figured she could get work real easy as one of the "before" models in the before-and-after ads you see in those dumb tabloid newspapers at the supermarket. She could even pose for the alien photos they sometimes print on the cover.

They must have had a good reason to leave California and never return, because ole Isabel was homesick, good and proper. I was itching to ask why they left and why they stayed, but the atmosphere at the table rendered me wordless. Now, that's saying something.

Ian and Isabel snarled under their breath at each other, cussing quite a bit, so Mama spoke up. "I do believe these are the best rolls you've ever made, Mama Grace." She was trying to get things back to normal.

"I used a different brand of yeast," Grandma announced quickly, reaching for a roll and breaking it open. "They are nice and soft, ain't they? Have another, Mr. St. James?" She held out the basket to him, and he took one.

Just about that time, Mr. Rance said to Daddy, "I hear tell this here is just about the biggest farm in these parts. How many acres you farmin'?"

"A little under four hundred."

"'Zat all? Why, this ain't but a flyspeck to what I ranched

down in Beauhide County in Texas," the old man bragged. "Just my backyard was a couple a hundred acres."

What was this, anyway? Be Rude to the Folks Who Feed You Night?

But my good ole daddy just laughed and said, "Well, I hear everything's bigger in Texas."

Mr. Rance's loud laugh drowned out everybody else. While the old man snorted and heehawed, Daddy asked Ian about the weather in California this time of year. Mama tried to talk to Isabel, but the ole gal didn't talk back. She blinked a lot, though, with her mouth all pushed into a wad.

Mr. Rance bellowed some information about some kind of new horse breed and would have bored everyone stiff, not to mention shriveled our eardrums, if Grandma hadn't kept putting food on his plate to keep his big mouth busy that way.

Grandma said to Myra Sue, "I hear they're gonna add some new subjects to the high school curriculum this year. Maybe some foreign languages. I heard tell they was gonna have some kind of performing arts classes. That'll be nice, won't it? You'll like that, won't you?"

Myra Sue, that rude toad, just shrugged and kept gawking at Isabel and Ian like she'd never seen people before.

Mama had no luck getting Isabel to speak, but Myra Sue did. She started saying things like, "What kind of eyeliner do you use? It makes your eyes look so dramatic!" and, "Is that a designer blouse? It's gorgeous!" and, "How do you keep your hair in place? It's just so perfect!"

I nearly choked, but Isabel started to thaw, and Myra Sue kept telling her how beautiful she was until pretty soon that woman told my dumb sister that pink fingernail polish was not fashionable.

"Blood red, darling. And long. Remember: passion and glamour, *always*." She held out a scrawny claw so Myra Sue could gush over it. "I'll show you how to do yours properly yourself, if you don't go to a manicurist. There probably isn't one within a hundred miles of here, anyway." She sniffed and pursed her mouth for a few seconds. "Of course, avoid harsh detergents, like dish soap or bathroom cleaner. They are murder on your nails. And always remember: they are adornments, *not* tools."

Myra Sue looked at her short, frosty pink nails and curled her fingers out of sight.

"I so totally agree," she sighed. I bet she was thinking right then of ways to get out of even more chores, most especially the supper dishes, so as not to ruin her nails.

Isabel and Myra Sue smiled at each other, then nibbled on bits of lettuce. It occurred to me all of a sudden that since I'm pretty sure my sister is adopted, her real mother is probably Isabel St. James. Maybe that was why they had come to Rough Creek Road, to claim their child.

"Did you ever have a baby, Isabel St. James?" I asked.

The woman jerked like she'd been poked with a sharp stick. "Most certainly not! I refuse to ruin my figure. And what business is it of yours, anyway?"

"Don't listen to her," Myra Sue said. "She's a mere child. By the way, how's your poor foot?"

"Dreadful, darling!"

Well, just when I thought I'd seen it all, Isabel pulled the ugliest face yet, this time with her eyeballs rolled back in her head and the ropey places on her throat all tight and sticking out more than usual.

"It throbs," Isabel said, "and the pain shoots all the way to my head."

"Shall I get you an ice pack, or maybe a heat pad?" Myra Sue moved to the edge of her chair, ready to fly to get whatever Isabel wanted.

"How about both?" I suggested, but they ignored me.

Isabel touched her hand. "Dear girl. No. Nothing more can be done, so I'll just bear it as best I can."

"Didn't the clinic give you anything for the pain?" Mama asked.

"Tylenol. I wanted Darvocet at the very, very least. And some Valium for the stress. But . . . Tylenol." She groaned and then sighed. "With nothing but a bunch of ignorant quacks in charge, what do you people do when you get sick?"

Daddy spoke up. "It's hard to get quality healthcare in a small town like Cedar Ridge, but the clinic's not so bad. And we're all pretty healthy. Hard work, good food, family, and friends work toward keeping a person in good health and good spirits."

"See? See?" Ian crowed. "What did I tell you? Get back to our roots, I said. Out of the pollution and the rat race and you'll feel better, I said."

"I'll *feel better* if we—"

"You'll feel better if you'll eat somethin' besides that gall-durned rabbit food," Mr. Rance yelled.

Isabel shifted in her chair and gave the old man a look,

but he was scraping the last of the beans out of the bowl and onto his plate, so he didn't see her expression.

"Well, I'll just go get the dessert," Mama said as she got to her feet.

"I'll help you, Lily." Grandma went into the kitchen with her. They stayed in the kitchen for a while, and when they were out of the room, Isabel leaned toward Myra Sue.

"Be a darling and retrieve my purse from wherever it has been taken."

She made it sound like a bunch of thieves and pick-pockets ran our house. Of course, after the way I saw him eyeball everything, I wasn't too sure about Mr. Rance. . . .

"It's laying right in there on the sofa where Ian put it when you came in," I told her. So much for my notion that California men might carry purses. She gave me a tight little smile that wasn't friendly, not even an itty-bitty bit.

Myra Sue nearly broke her neck in a mad dash to get the pocketbook and bring it to Isabel.

"What line of work are you in, Ian?" Daddy asked.

"Banking," he said shortly. "I was a banker."

Ha! I knew he looked like a banker.

Daddy nodded. Either he had nothing to say to that, or he saw as well as I did that Ian didn't want to discuss it. Apparently Mr. Rance failed to notice or care.

"Banks around here ain't hirin', I'm told," he said. "You'd best put her t'work." He pointed his fork at Isabel.

Her face turned frosty, and that's putting it warmly. I figured this was my chance to ask a question without seeming nosy.

"What do you do, Isabel St. James?" I asked. "I mean, for work."

For a minute I thought she would ignore me. But finally she sniffed primly and said, "I've done some acting. But by profession, I'm a dancer. A prima ballerina, actually. I had to leave all that behind, along with everything else."

"I remember you saying you danced," I said, "but I didn't think you meant you actually did it for a *living*."

"A ballerina?" Myra Sue clasped both hands to her chest and leaned forward, all agog. Boy, it doesn't take much to impress her. "You can be one here!"

"Good grief, Myra Sue," I said. "When's the last time you saw a ballet around in these parts?" To Isabel, I said, "The only nutcracker around here is the one we use after the black walnuts dry."

Isabel whimpered, and Mama and Grandma came out of the kitchen right then. Grandma toted a carton of ice cream, and Mama carried a big pan of flaky apple cobbler, steaming hot with plenty of cinnamon. It smelled the way I think heaven smells. No matter how full I am, even if I think my stomach will explode, I will still eat Mama's apple cobbler.

Isabel gave the dessert one of her looks and didn't even try to keep the snooty expression off her face. She made a big show of looking away from the food as Mama began to scoop out huge servings into dishes.

Isabel opened her little slip of a purse, pulling out a pack of cigarettes and a fancy silver lighter. She tapped a cigarette against the table a few times, then lit the stupid thing. Myra Sue watched like she was hypnotized. I looked at Mama and

Daddy just in time to see them exchange a glance. They saw all this, but I reckon they were going to be polite. Grandma heaped a big plop of vanilla ice cream on top of a bowl of cobbler, but she was frowning right at Isabel St. James, who either didn't notice or didn't care.

Mama passed a goodly serving to Ian. "Would you like some nice, warm apple cobbler, Isabel?" Mama asked. "It isn't greasy."

The ole gal had sucked in a big lungful from her cigarette and blew the stinking smoke out of the corner of her mouth. I hacked and wheezed a few times, but she didn't seem to notice.

"I never eat sugar," she said. "It's pure poison." She took another deep pull and heaved it out, further stinking up our dining room.

"What do you think cigarettes are?" I asked. "Vitamin C?"

She looked at me through the fuzz of smoke around her head. Her eyes were little slits.

"Don't be dumb," Myra Sue piped up. "She smokes so she won't get fat."

Isabel looked at her and smiled as if my silly sister was a sweet little baby.

"Bingo, darling." She knocked off the ash right smack dab on Mama's good china, which Bingo-darling had insisted we use.

Isabel stared at her water glass for a minute, then said, "Don't you people have anything to drink?"

I'm not stupid. I knew she meant booze, but before anyone

else could reply, I piped up and said, "We got milk, coffee, tea, and water. Or I could make you some red Kool-Aid."

I think she wanted to slap me, but I just grinned and pretended like trotting off to the kitchen to make it for her pleased me to no end. Myra Sue reached under the table and pinched my thigh.

"Stop it!" I yelped and pinched her back.

She screeched. "You stop it, you brat! And she doesn't want milk or water or tea or Kool-Aid. She wants something like . . ." Her face got all dopey and slack from the effort of thinking. "Sherry!" she announced in triumph. "Would you like some sherry, Isabel-dear?"

We don't have alcohol of any kind in this house, and besides, Myra Sue wouldn't know sherry if it bit her pinky toe.

Isabel gave a snotty little laugh. "No, my dear. Not sherry. Never sherry. I was thinking more like—"

"Cherry Coke!" I hollered. Myra Sue pinched me again.

"Girls," my daddy interrupted from the head of the table. "What's going on?"

The adults stopped talking and stared at us.

"Nothing, Daddy," we both said, sweet as baby lambs.

As soon as everyone started talking again, Myra leaned over. "You better quit being stupid," she said from the corner of her mouth.

I started to cross my eyes at her but got interrupted. "Greetings and salutations, Reilly family!" someone shouted from the front door.

A moment later the screen door opened and in walked

Temple Freebird. She came into the dining room with Forest trailing along. She was all dressed up in a grimy floral prairie skirt and a dingy blue tank top. And there was good ole Forest, his crusty bare feet making a dark contrast against Mama's clean floor. Their body odors followed like a pack of faithful dogs, and old man Rance's Old Spice did nothing to mask a bit of it.

I looked at Isabel. She pulled back as if she thought she could escape the sight, sound, *and* smell. Ha! Temple is everyone's chum, and there's no getting away from her.

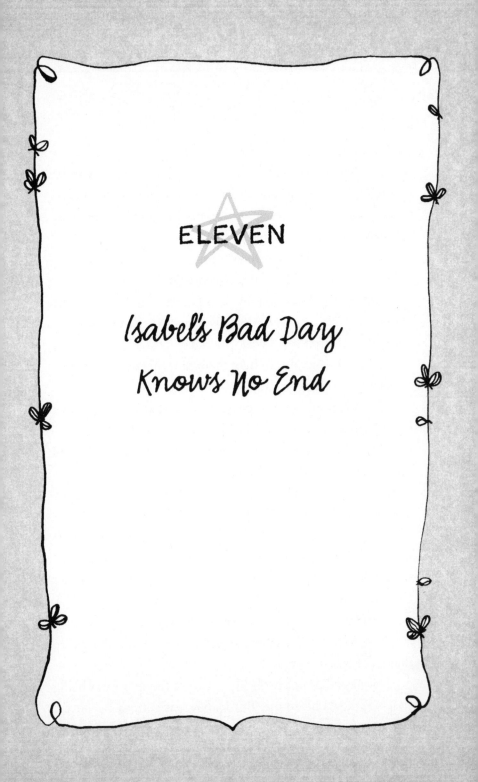

ELEVEN

Isabel's Bad Day Knows No End

☆

Daddy got to his feet. "Temple! Forest!"

Mr. Rance was too busy gulping down his cobbler to be polite. Ian seemed stunned and unable to move. Or maybe no one ever told him a man is supposed to stand when a lady enters the room. It's called Good Manners.

"Come in and have some supper," Daddy invited.

"Yes," Mama said. "There's plenty. Have a seat."

Daddy introduced Temple and Forest to the St. Jameses, who looked like they'd accidentally opened the outhouse door. Ian finally cleared his throat, nodding slightly at the two of them. Temple smiled at both of them, showing where a couple of her teeth were missing.

"I thought all you hill people howdied at the door to be let in," Ian said, stifling a belch behind his hand.

"Well, Temple and Forest came here from Boston," I told him, "and anyways, they know they're always welcome to come right on in. But us hillbillies always knock or ring the doorbell. What do you West Coasters do?"

Ian gave me a look that said he was trying to figure out if I were all innocent or if I were just a smart-alecky kid. I figured if he were too silly to know the difference, I wouldn't educate him.

"We knock or ring the doorbell, of course."

"You fool, Ian," his little woman snapped. "Can't you see that child is baiting you?"

Daddy and Mama probably would've thought I was being rude—if they'd heard me. But Daddy was getting a chair for

Forest to sit in, and Mama was getting another couple of plates from the china cabinet, so this enlightening conversation totally passed by them. On the other hand, Grandma fixed a real hard look on me.

"You got a lot of your great-grandma in you, Miss April," she said.

I knew my great-grandma had been a sassy flapper girl, so I grinned real big. "Thanks!" I said. But the way Grandma shook her head, I knew that it had been no compliment in her eyes.

In the meantime, Forest settled down on Daddy's end of the table, and Temple pulled a chair up beside me. Myra Sue shrank away and shuddered.

"I brought the poison ivy salve for you, Tootsie Roll." Temple held up a pint Mason jar with greenish-brown goop in it, then set it on the table for us all to see. She had used a crinkledy piece of old aluminum foil for a lid. The stuff inside sort of looked like something Daisy or Queenie might have yoirked up, so I tried not to look at it again while I ate.

"Help yourself to the food, Temple," Mama said, handing her the plate and silverware. She didn't seem to notice that our neighbor hadn't bothered to wash her hands, and she smelled pretty ripe. I'm not sure which was worse, Isabel's cigarette smoke or Temple's armpits, but someone should have called the Environmental Protection Agency. Next to me, Myra Sue hacked pretty loud.

"How about some cobbler and ice cream?" Grandma asked.

She knew as well as I did that the Freebirds wouldn't eat

it because they ate only raw fruits, vegetables, and nuts. At least good ole Temple and Forest weren't rude about it. They took the plates.

"I'll just have a little of that yummy salad after Forest gets finished serving himself. Don't take it all, honey," she joked. "Oh, Lily! Do you have any pine nuts or radish sprouts?"

"'Fraid not," Mama said. "We got some ranch dressing, though."

"This is fine just as it is." Temple heaped her plate, and giving Isabel a big smile, she said, "I understand you're our next-door neighbor."

Isabel looked as if she'd just swallowed rat poison while sitting on a rusty nail.

"You'll have to come over to our place real soon," Temple continued. She glanced at the foot resting on its throne. "When you're recovered, I mean. Meantime, I'll just pop over to your place, and we can get acquainted over a cup of red clover tea."

Isabel made more funny little whimpering sounds down in her throat.

"Yeah, Isabel St. James," I said. "You and Temple both like salad, and neither one of you will eat sugar or fat, so I bet you have a ton of other stuff in common."

Isabel's whimpering got louder as Temple put down her fork and rested her grubby hand on Isabel's scrawny, pale one.

"Diet is so important for our health, isn't it?" Temple said. "You should eat lots of raw spinach."

"Excuse me?" Isabel choked out, staring at Temple's hand.

"To build up the iron in your blood, of course. Plus, it would get rid of that pallor." She squeezed Isabel's fingers.

"*Excuse me?*"

Ole Isabel's eyes couldn't have got any buggier. She finally yanked her hand away and began scrubbing at it with her napkin.

"What are you talking about?" Isabel asked.

Temple was chewing a mouthful of lettuce and tomatoes, but she stopped to gaze at Isabel. She put down her fork again and reached out. Isabel reared back.

"Oh goodness," Temple said, leaving her hand stretched out in midair. "It's just that you're so thin and fair-skinned, and your plate looks as though you've barely eaten anything . . . Oh dear." Temple dropped both hands to her lap and looked at all of us as if she were about to bust out bawling. "I've really made an awful gaffe, haven't I?" She pinned a really pitiful look on Isabel. "I am so sorry."

Isabel, true to her rude self, looked back with her long, pointy nose wrinkled up.

Words just sorta sailed right out from between my lips without me even thinking about them.

"If you'd get out in the sunshine, maybe folks wouldn't think you're sick," I said.

"April Grace!" said Mama, Daddy, and Grandma, as if they'd been practicing all day.

Isabel's mouth flew open like she was a baby buzzard waiting for a fresh piece of roadkill. She didn't get a chance to tell me off, though, because old man Rance yelled, "If she'd put on about twenty-five pounds, she wouldn't look like death on a cracker."

Isabel's face got redder and redder, and her mouth snapped open and shut. Finally she choked out, *"I am leaving! Ian!"*

My mama, ever the peacemaker, just like the good Lord wants us to be, said, "Now, everyone be fair. Remember poor Isabel is hurt. Anyone would look pale. Myra Sue, run and fetch Miss Isabel some more ice water."

Myra Sue almost killed herself in her rush to fill the woman's glass. I knew Mama and Daddy and probably Grandma were glaring at me, but I was real intent on drinking my own water and couldn't look at them.

"Well," Isabel finally spluttered, "thank you for understanding, Lucy."

"It's Lily." Mama smiled at her. "Now, I have some nice apples in the kitchen. Would you like one?"

Isabel wagged her head no and looked at Ian, who was grinning down at his cobbler with its mound of ice cream dribbling down the sides to mix with the warm, sweet cinnamon. She shook another cigarette from the pack and frowned at her mister while she tapped it on the table.

"Oink, oink," Isabel muttered as she planted the cigarette between her lips and lit it.

Temple again stopped chewing, this time to sneeze and cough. Her eyes turned red and weepy.

"Please," she gasped. "Tobacco smoke makes me ill. Would you please put out your cigarette?"

Isabel held on to what she'd just inhaled and looked coolly at Temple. Then she blew it out, long and slow, as if she wanted to prolong poor Temple's agony. She took another deep drag before stubbing the cigarette out on her plate right next to the first butt. She looked at Ian, who ate his dessert like he thought a nuclear holocaust would start in thirty minutes.

"Would you stop poisoning yourself, and let's get out of this place?" Isabel asked him.

The look he gave her would have iced over Rough Creek in August, if it'd had any water in it. She glowered at him before she turned away and leaned toward Myra Sue.

"My dear, *please*," Isabel asked. "Are you positive there is no liquor in this house?"

"Nope," I replied cheerfully. "Grandma would have a fit if we even had rum cake on the farm."

"Ian, will you hurry up?" Isabel snapped.

"Our grandmother is nothing but an ignorant hillbilly," Myra Sue declared in a whisper that no one but me and Isabel heard. "I wish anyone but her was my grandmother."

Well, let me tell you, it felt right good when my foot smacked into the lower half of my sister's leg. Myra Sue screamed bloody murder and grabbed for me, but I was quicker, and I was mad.

"Take it back!" I grabbed a big fistful of her blond curls in one hand and part of her nose and cheek and lips in the other. Somehow she got ahold of my neck and hair and yanked almost as hard as I did.

"Stop it, you little—"

"*Take it back!*"

I yelled and yanked while she screamed and pulled. We both started kicking and I'm not sure what else, but somehow we tumbled to the floor, our chairs lying sideways. Some dishes crashed, and above all that racket came Isabel's voice hollering that someone better do something.

The next thing I knew, both of us flailed and kicked nothing but air 'cause Mr. Rance had hold of Myra Sue, and Daddy had hold of me.

"Take it back, you frog wart," I screamed at my sister.

Daddy turned me around to face him. "Stop it right now! You, too, Myra. Right now!"

Little by little, we both quit trying to kill each other from twenty feet apart. But we didn't stop glaring and snarling like tomcats.

"Go to your room, Myra Sue," Daddy told her.

Mr. Rance let go of her real slow, like he was afraid she'd murder us all once she had her freedom.

"But, Daddy, April Grace—"

"Go! Now."

Myra Sue looked at the St. Jameses.

"Sorry, truly devastated!" she squealed out to them. Then she fled from the room. She thundered up the stairs so loud and heavy that the cobwebs down in the cellar probably fell off and the spiders all had heart attacks.

Daddy kept hold of me, even after Myra Sue stormed out. He gave me a teeny little shake I hardly felt and said, "Apologize, Miss April." Well, it took me a minute to speak without my voice shaking, I tell you. And it wasn't the easiest thing telling those people I was sorry, but I managed it, all prim and proper and not like a crying nanny goat the way my sister did.

I looked at the St. Jameses and said, "I apologize for my

rude behavior to guests in our house." I reckon that took care of it 'cause Daddy finally let me go.

"Now, you. Go," he said.

I was still so mad, I shook all over. Everyone else at the table was real quiet and looking at me, except Isabel. She sat real straight and stiff and made funny little mewly noises, like a cat.

Somehow, in all that ruckus, me or my rotten ole sister had managed to knock the bowl of gravy off the table and onto Isabel. She sat there whimpering with big globs of gravy trailing down her scrawny chest and out of sight. Next to her, Temple began to wipe the mess off Isabel's designer blouse.

I photographed that whole picture in my head, then went upstairs.

TWELVE

An Invitation
to Die For

☺

Well, as you probably have guessed by now, me and Myra Sue got punished. Of course, as soon as everyone went home, we had to clean up the mess we'd made.

"You should tan the seats of their britches," Grandma advised.

But, thank the Lord, Daddy and Mama do not believe in spanking. What they came up with, however, was far worse. In fact, I believe I'd rather have had my britches tanned every day for a week. We had to write a letter telling why we loved each other. Oh, brother. It wasn't easy, let me tell you, but we managed to do it.

For instance, I said I loved how Myra Sue didn't snore in her room at night and keep me awake. She said she loved that I did a good job when I washed the dishes.

Mama read my letter while Daddy read my sister's. Then they exchanged them. When they finished, they looked at us as if we were both alien children. Mama sighed. Daddy groaned.

"I guess these will do," Mama said after a while, and Daddy added, "But we never want to see a fight like that again, in front of company or in private."

We understood. But I'll tell you one thing right now: if ole Myra Sue ever again says anything bad about my grandma, I'll snatch her bald-headed, in front of company or not.

A few days later, Daddy came in from the field for lunch at noon just like always. Instead of going back to work after he ate, though, he showered while Mama freshened up and changed her clothes. Then they loaded a couple of baskets with tomatoes, corn, onions, beans, and other stuff picked from our garden that very morning, along with a baked chicken, a big salad, and fresh bread, which I thought Mama was fixing for our supper.

"What are you doing?" I asked, sniffing all those flavorsome odors and following Mama and Daddy outside as they toted away the baskets of food. "Where are you taking our food?"

"We're going over to the St. Jameses' to see what we can do to help them settle in," Daddy told me as he hoisted his basket into the back of the pickup. He put Mama's basket right next to it while she went back to the house. Half a minute later she came out with a gallon jug of iced tea. The ice clinked invitingly against the sides. He opened the passenger door for her, then went around the cab to the driver's side and got in.

Before he started the engine, he gave me a look. "Mama wants you girls to pull the weeds from her flowerbeds in front of the house. We'll be back after a while."

I watched them drive away and thanked my lucky stars I didn't have to go along.

Back in the house, I delivered Mama's order, and Myra—who was brushing and fluffing her hair in front of the bathroom mirror—blinked her eyes about a zillion times.

"I am not getting my hands in that dirt." She strolled into the living room and flipped on the television.

"If Mama finds out you didn't do it, she'll probably make you do the whole thing by yourself the next time. Maybe the whole garden."

Myra Sue drew in her lips and scrunched up her nose. "I have to do *everything* around here! I hate this farm."

I walked away. "Poor you," I said over my shoulder as I went.

"Hush. My stories are on." She turned up the volume, and I heard a deep voice intone the familiar words: "Like sands through the hourglass . . ." Ho-hum.

I went outside. Now, to tell you the truth, I'd rather be sitting under a tree or on the porch, reading *Jane Eyre*, but I had my orders. Jane and Mr. Rochester would just have to wait. I think I liked that story even better than *Oliver Twist*, which I really, really liked.

I'd only knelt by the marigolds—all alone—for about thirty seconds when Mama and Daddy drove back up the driveway.

"April Grace," Mama called. "You come with us."

Well, now, I have to tell you, I'd rather dig in the dirt until I reached burning hot magma than go to the St. Jameses', but I had no choice. I got to my feet real slow, trying to think of an excuse to stay home, but Mama said, "Go wash your face, hands, and arms, and put on some clean clothes. Be quick about it."

You better believe I was as quick as a snail riding shotgun on a turtle, while Myra Sue sprawled on the floor in front of the television, watching her stories. I looked at her dopey face resting against her hands and thought about just letting her get caught, but sometimes you have to be the bigger person.

"Mama and Daddy came back," I said. "They're outside in the truck, waiting for me."

"Liar." She didn't even take her eyes off that show.

So be it. She had her chance.

"Slow as Christmas, Miss April," Mama said when I got into the pickup cab.

"Sorry. My poison ivy slows me down."

Temple's poison ivy goop had dried my rash right up, just like she said it would, so Mama just looked at me as if she could read my mind and saw I was trying to pull a fast one.

"Sorry, Mama," I said.

Daddy said, "Why isn't your sister weeding the flower beds?"

"She will after *Days* is over."

Instead of slamming on his brakes and marching into the house to drag that girl out by the scruff of the neck the way she deserved, he said, "Well, she better get on the weeds before we get back, or her *Days* will be numbered."

Mama laughed. "That's funny, Mike," she said, smiling at him. Then she rested her head on his shoulder for a second or two.

"I'll weed the flowers," I offered. "Myra Sue can go with you guys."

"There's that little matter of an apology that you forgot to deliver in all the excitement the other day," Mama said. "From the first time you met the St. Jameses, when you were less than polite. Remember?"

"But you forgot to remind me!" Again she just looked at me. I pulled down the corners of my mouth, knowing I was defeated. I brooded about it all the way to our destination. Boy, oh boy, this whole thing seemed unfair. I mean, that whole business was almost a week ago. Isabel St. James probably already forgot about it, but trust Mama to do the Right Thing.

"What about ole Myra Sue?" I demanded.

"What about her?" Mama said.

"She started the whole fight the other night. Why don't she have to go apologize for that?"

"If you recall, you both apologized as you were leaving the room. You were sorry, April Grace, and so was Myra Sue," Mama said.

Oh, brother! As if. The only thing Myra Sue was sorry for was being a knothead in front of her idol, but far be it from me to correct Mama.

"Anyway, this isn't about that," Mama continued. "This is about that first day, when they got into town, and you were not very kind to our new neighbors."

I stared out the window as we drove down that old road. Boy, oh boy. I sighed deeply, but I don't think anyone cared.

When we got to their house, I saw what needed to be weeded: the St. Jameses's rotten old driveway, that's what. Everything there was growing like weeds, hardy, har, har. But when we got to the house, you could have knocked me over with a dry Q-tip. There was Ian, wearing a pair of blue shorts and a fancy, pale yellow polo shirt, and he was pushing a red lawn mower. His face was so scarlet, the pale blue of his eyes seemed glassy. Through his thin blond hair, his scalp looked ready to catch fire.

"He's going to have a heat stroke," Mama said in alarm.

"Maybe we should have brought water," Daddy said. "Now that I think about it, I'm not sure the pump in that old well even works."

"Where's ole Isabel?" I asked.

"Call her Mrs. St. James, or Isabel," Mama corrected. She glanced around. "She's there. Standing in the doorway."

Daddy looked at the woman. "Well, maybe the house isn't as bad as we thought. Last I heard she was refusing to go inside."

There was sudden silence when Ian turned off the roaring lawn mower. He pulled a handkerchief from his pocket and mopped his face.

"Hello," Daddy called as we all piled out. "You look a mite overheated."

Ian wiped the back of his neck with the kerchief and blotted his face again. He actually gave my dad a little smile.

"Yeah. You could say that," Ian said. "I've not mowed the grass since I was fifteen—and it was nothing like this! In California everyone either uses a riding mower or hires it done."

Oh brother. I'm so sure.

"We brought some iced tea," Mama said, carrying the cold jug. She held up a Walmart bag. "Hope you don't mind Solo cups. They aren't exactly fine crystal."

"That tea looks good, and those cups will be fine. Come on inside," Ian said. He actually sounded like a real person instead of an uptight twit. Maybe Mama's good cooking the other night shook loose his human-being-ness.

I tagged along behind everyone, dodging the weak, rotted places on the steps and the porch floor. The inside of the house was hot, and it smelled like mildew, cigarette smoke, and old mice nests. A few boxes and two or three sacks from Walmart were strewn about. A yellow-handled broom stood in the corner where the old pink-and-yellow wallpaper had peeled loose. That broom looked like it had never been used. Two webbed lawn chairs seemed to be the only furniture in the place.

Isabel, all hunched into herself, stood back from everyone, puffing a cigarette like she was an old steam engine. Her crutches were nowhere to be seen. She wore her preferred garb, all black. This time she was wearing shorty-shorts and a halter top. She was a sight, I tell you. You could see her ribs, and all her knobby ole bones were sticking out in plain view. Apparently, she hadn't combed her dark hair for days, and now it stuck out every which way in short, pointy wisps. I might've screamed at the frightful sight if I'd come up on her unexpected in the woods or in the middle of the night in a cemetery.

"How's your foot?" I asked, looking at the ankle that didn't seem any bigger than the other one. In fact, they both were so thin and sharp, they looked like razor blades beneath her pasty skin.

"Fine," she muttered, puffing her cigarette.

"I'm so glad you're feeling better," Mama said, smiling, to which Isabel did not respond. She could have been a mountain in the Blue Ridge, the way clouds of smoke hovered around her head.

"Look, darling," Ian said. "Our neighbors brought some iced tea." The way he said *darling* wasn't exactly endearing, and from the way she looked at him, Isabel knew it. She glanced at us as she puffed and blew and said nothing.

"Where's your furniture?" I asked.

Ian and Isabel glanced at each other, so did Mama and Daddy, then Mama hissed at me to hush.

"Let me pour you some tea," she said, setting the glass jug on a nearby box. She handed me the sack of cups. "April Grace, honey, open these for us."

"And while you're doing that, I'll bring in the baskets," Daddy told us all cheerfully.

"Baskets?" Ian echoed.

"Of food," I said. "I thought it was gonna be our supper, but . . ."

I caught sight of Mama's expression and let my voice fade.

"Food?" Isabel finally had something to say. "Really, Lucy—"

"Her name is Lily!" I hollered for probably the five millionth time.

"April," Mama said, and I hushed. She looked from me to Isabel. "Isabel, *Lucy* is a very lovely name, and many women are blessed to have it. But it does not belong to me. My name is *Lily*. Please be kind enough to call me *Lily*." She met Isabel's eyes and didn't even crack a smile. I wanted to do cartwheels all over that old house.

Isabel blinked about three dozen times. "Pardon me for making a mistake," she said, all prissy. "And I have to tell you that we do not want your food. After that meal the other night, Ian could not get to sleep until after two thirty in the morning."

"My inability to sleep had nothing to do with that meal!" Ian snarled. "It had everything to do with your whining—"

"We figured you're tired of eating in restaurants, so everything we brought is fresh from the garden," Mama said a little loudly, putting a halt to their exchange. "Except the baked chicken and the bread. We just thought you'd probably not feel like cooking when you're so busy getting your house fixed up."

Ian gave Mama a smile. "That's kind of you. And it will be a help. We—"

"This house does not have a refrigerator or dishwasher or even a microwave. And besides that, I do not cook." Isabel lit another cigarette from the one she'd just smoked down to its filter, then added the butt to an oversized, overflowing ashtray. She might not cook, but she sure was barbecuing her lungs fit to be tied.

"Maybe Lily will teach you," Ian said.

You should have seen the look Isabel threw at him. I figured fists were gonna fly next. In fact, I wondered if the fists hadn't been flying for a while. They acted like they'd like to lay into each other the way me and Myra Sue had done.

Mama cleared her throat. She put both hands on my shoulders and propelled me to where I faced the couple, who continued to glare at each other. She cleared her throat again.

With her fingers right firm against my shoulder muscles, she said, "My daughter has something she wants to say to you both."

Boy, oh boy, I wished I'd written a speech and practiced it, because I felt real dumb. I shifted around a bit, but Mama kept her hands on me. "I'm real sorry for being rude when you were at our house needing directions to Sam White's old place, where you now live," I finally blurted.

Ian looked at me, and for a minute I don't think he even saw me, but then his face kinda cleared and a little smile came to his lips.

"Thank you. We accept." He shot a glance at the missus. "Don't we, darling?"

Isabel crimped her mouth. I wasn't sure if it were a smile or gas caught crossways. She didn't say anything, but she puffed on her cigarette like it was the last one before execution sunrise.

Daddy came in with the baskets. As he settled them on the floor, he said, "Ian, that chicory and buckbrush and all the rest of it is too dense and too tough for you to cut with a lawn mower. Why don't I bring over my tractor and Bush Hog and take care of it for you? Won't take hardly any time—"

"Don't you bring any pigs to us!" Isabel screeched. "It's bad enough around here without smelly, disease-infested swine running loose."

"A Bush Hog is a piece of machinery," I told that ignorant woman.

"It's a big cutting machine," Daddy explained. "I'll have all these weeds and small brush cut in no time. Then your yard will be manageable. But you'll have to keep it mowed; otherwise, it'll look like this again in another week or two."

Ian nodded. "I can do that. I bought that mower yesterday at Walmart."

Isabel snorted. "Sure. You can spend money on lawn mowers but none on furniture."

"Fifty dollars won't buy furniture," Ian said through clenched teeth. "It barely bought a cheap lawn mower!"

Mama gave a Solo cup full of iced tea to Ian, then handed one to Isabel. I hoped it would cool them down and shut them up. Their loud fussing made my head hurt all over again.

"Not a bit of sugar in it," she assured them.

I don't see how anyone can drink iced tea without sugar, but then I don't pretend to know everything.

Ian drained his cup in practically one swallow. Isabel just looked into hers as if she'd rather drink that Mexican booze with the worm in it. Mama refilled Ian's cup, and you probably won't believe this, but he actually thanked her and smiled real big.

"I want to go home!" Isabel shrieked so suddenly that I jumped and grabbed hold of Daddy. "Look, Lucy—I mean, Lily!" She rushed to Mama, caught her hand, and pulled her across the room. She didn't even limp. She pointed through a door. "That's where I've slept the last three nights. Right there on that air mattress, on the floor. And I'm telling you, I hear wild animals skittering and scratching and eating all night long. I can't live like this. I'm not a hillbilly!"

The hillbilly remark gave me a severe pain, but Mama overlooked it. "Why, I had no idea you were living in the house. We thought you were staying at the Starshine Motel in Cedar Ridge."

"We were! For three days. Then Ian put a stop to all semblance of comfort and civility." Isabel pointed to her mister and screeched, "He says we can't afford to stay there anymore. He's a beast! An insensitive lout who thinks of no one but himself!"

Then Isabel burst into tears, crying so hard, I thought she'd break all her skinny bones. Mama gaped at her with her mouth open; then she gently pulled Isabel into her arms and let the woman cry all over her.

"I can't live this way," Isabel kept saying every little bit, which only made her wail even louder. "I miss my home and my friends and my dancing!"

"I know, I know," Mama soothed, patting her bony ole back.

Well, I'll tell you something you might not believe, but I felt sorry for ole Isabel. If I'd been hauled away from everything familiar and everything I loved, I'd squall my eyes out too. And I wouldn't have wanted to stay in that falling-down house, either.

When it seemed the woman had cried herself dry, she let go of Mama and pulled back.

"I'm sorry," she said, prissier than ever. "I'm not given to displays of emotion."

Now, while I sympathized with her homesickness, I nearly hooted out loud at that remark. Practically every time I'd seen her, she was either in the throes of some kind of fit or on a crying jag. However, my own personal self, I wouldn't have wanted to live in that falling-down house and sleep on the floor, either, so I completely understood what ole Isabel was saying.

"It's perfectly reasonable," Mama said. "You shouldn't have to live without the things you need. When will they be arriving?"

Isabel looked at her. "They won't."

Mama blinked. "What do you mean?"

"Our stuff—our lovely furniture, custom built in Europe last year—will not be arriving, ever. Neither will any appliances, lamps, pillows, nor anything else that makes life worth living. Most of our clothes are gone, as well!" So that's why she was dressed in that dumb outfit. But her next words ruled out that notion. "What I'm wearing and the few things in those boxes are the clothes I simply could not part with. But my furs. My jewelry. Most of my shoes . . . oh, *my shoes*!" Here came another nonemotional display of sobbing and whimpering.

"What's the deal?" my daddy asked Ian in his quiet voice. Isabel's face was buried in her hands, and I doubt she heard a word over her own wailing. "Did you folks have a burnout?"

Ian shook his head. He stared up at the ceiling, took in a deep breath, and blew it out.

"We lost it all."

Lost it? My mind clicked. They had been living in San Francisco, where earthquakes happen. But I hadn't heard of one in the last few months.

"Was there an earthquake like the one back in 1908?"

Ian looked at me in surprise. "You know about that?"

"Well, if you go to school and pay attention in history and social studies, you learn about things."

"No earthquake," Ian said. "Bad business investment, actually."

I wasn't sure what that meant, but Daddy seemed to get it. "Well, I'm sure sorry," he said.

Ian looked out the window, but you could tell he didn't actually see anything. He went on, "I worked for twenty-five years trying to build our fortune and support Isabel's career— which, by the way, never has taken off to any degree." She growled at him, but he ignored her. "Almost overnight, we lost it all, every bit of it."

"Yes," Isabel said, coming up for air. Her bloodshot eyes stared meanly at him. "We had to sell what was left for legal fees to keep Ian out of prison."

There was dead silence in that rickety old house for what seemed years.

"Oh my," Mama said at last, faintly.

"It wasn't my fault," Ian said. "Isabel, you *know* it wasn't my fault, and that was proven in a court of law, so I wish you'd just get over it." To Mama and Daddy, he said, "We all thought the guy was on the up-and-up. Instead, he misled me and my partners with false information and phony documents. That was proven in court."

Isabel wasn't about to let it go. "Well, it was your fault when you sold my Mercedes and my jewelry and my clothes—"

"I sold my stuff too," he snapped.

"—then took that money to Las Vegas and proceeded to lose it there playing blackjack and poker and who knows what else—"

"You know I was trying to win back our money!" Ian shouted. "You know that!"

"Ha! You still have your ring, Ian St. James! I notice you didn't sell that thing." He curled that hand—the one with the diamond pinky ring—right into a fist just about then.

"My mother gave me this ring," he snarled, "and I'm not selling it. Ever!"

She hissed like a snake. "You and your mother!"

"Don't you say a word about my mother. She's in her grave."

"And let me tell you something else, you mama's boy. It's

your fault we can't go home again. It's your fault no bank will ever hire you—"

"Isabel!" he shouted.

"Oh! You miserable . . ." Then she said names that I'd get into trouble for mentioning, so just use your imagination.

They glared and glowered and snorted and stomped and shouted for a long time. It was a regular rodeo in their house. Mama and Daddy looked at each other like they didn't know what to say or do. After a bit, when Ian and Isabel had wound down a little, Mama drew in a deep breath.

"Mike, take those baskets back to the pickup. April Grace, you get the iced tea and the cups and go with your daddy."

Each and every one of us stared at her. I would never in a million years have thought Mama would've turned her back on anyone, but boy, oh boy, it sure seemed to be happening.

"Isabel, Ian," Mama said. "Pack your clothes and gather anything you want to bring. You two are going to come and stay with us so you can get some rest and relax a little. You've been under too much pressure."

Good grief. I thought I'd die right there on that dirty floor.

THIRTEEN

Mike Reilly's Bighearted Idea . . . and Lily's Too

♡

Ian just stared at Mama for a minute while he appeared to search his brain for some wits. Finally he spoke.

"It's kind of you to offer, but we cannot—"

Isabel let out a strangled sound. "Oh, yes, we can, Ian St. James! I refuse to spend another night on that hideous air mattress, and you refuse to let me stay at a decent hotel—"

"We are broke, *darling*." The way he said *darling* indicated he was thinking she was anything but darling. "How many times . . ."

He stopped speaking all of a sudden, glanced our way, and gave us a sorry excuse for a smile. He took a deep breath and turned his back on the little woman. Maybe not such a good idea, given that she was sending him murderous looks.

"As you can see, Mr. Reilly—" Ian started.

"I'm Mike," Daddy said. "Mr. Reilly was my dad. And my granddad."

"Yes. Well. Mike, then. As you can see, it is going to take time and money to get this place to a level that suits our standards. We can't intrude on your hospitality for that long."

Amen to that, I agreed silently. In my worst nightmares, I couldn't dream of living under the same roof with Isabel St. James. Unfortunately, my mama must never have had any such nightmares.

"Of course you can," Mama said. "Your wife needs a comfortable bed so she can rest. And so do you. You've both been under far too much pressure in the last few weeks."

"Lu—Lily is right," Isabel said. "You listen to her."

I felt downright queasy.

Daddy looked around and seemed lost in thought for a bit. "Wait a minute," he said.

He walked through the house. As we watched, he knocked on the walls and looked real close at the doors and windows and ceilings. He kinda heaved his weight up and down in a few spots. At one point, he took out his pocketknife, hunkered down, and stabbed the scarred old floor. With the rest of us trailing him outside like a pack of dogs, he went and eyed the roof from one end to the other. For a while, he disappeared into the crawl space beneath the house.

Ian sipped his iced tea, and Isabel smoked. Mama just stood there and smiled faintly. No one spoke.

Daddy finally wriggled out from under the house and stood up. He dusted off his good jeans and nice blue shirt. "Lily, honey, can I talk to you?" he asked.

They walked as far as the pickup's tailgate and stood there whispering for a while. Mama nodded, and knowing how my folks treat people in need, I kept getting queasier and queasier. Ian and Isabel ignored me while I found the shade beneath the nearest oak tree and sat down to cool off.

Mama hadn't given me any of the iced tea she'd made for the St. Jameses. If I'd asked for it, she would have told me Ian and Isabel didn't have any at all while we had plenty at the house. Sometimes, I'm not so sure it's a blessing to have such kindhearted parents.

When Mama and Daddy walked toward Ian and Isabel again, I got up and sauntered over to them.

Daddy stood with his hands in his hip pockets and leaned

back against his thumbs, the way he usually did when having casual conversation with friends.

"I'm not trying to pry, Ian," Daddy said, "but I've got an idea how to get you out of this fix you're in."

"Oh yeah?" Ian seemed skeptical, but interested.

"You plan to fix up this house and live in it, right?" Daddy asked.

Isabel drew her scrawny self up straight and tall and opened her mouth, but Ian shook his head at her. She snapped her mouth closed with a splat. She blinked a dozen or so times, but she kept her yap shut.

"That's right," Ian said to Daddy

"Do you have any resources at all?" Daddy asked.

Ian made a face like someone had stomped on his foot. "Not a one," he said. "As I said, we sold everything except for a few clothes and our car. This place seemed about as affordable as we could find. Of course, I've wanted to move out here for a while, so I didn't mind the transition. But I didn't know the house—"

"Of course he didn't *see* this place before he bought it. Once again, he took someone else's word for something." Isabel spat this out for the edification of us all, then closed her lips real tight again.

Daddy looked at that shiny black car, which actually wasn't so shiny with all the dust on it. That car would never be shiny again except when it came fresh out of the car wash.

"What d'you reckon is the market value for that Caddy?" Daddy asked quietly.

"*What?!*" Isabel sounded like an old laying-hen.

Ian eyeballed the car. "Mike, we need a car, even out here in the sticks."

"It doesn't have to be that particular car, does it?"

Ian winced again.

"No, I guess not." You could tell it was like pulling his toenails up through his gizzard just to say it. "But it's not even a year old."

"Why don't we take 'er into Larry's Auto Sales in town and see what fair market value is? Then let's visit the lumber yard and see what you can get for the same money."

"But how are we supposed to get around if we sell our car?" Ian said. "How am I going to look for work?"

I took a gander at ole Isabel and wondered if she ever worked a day in her life without wearing a tutu and funny-looking shoes. Given the shape, length, and design of her fingernails, not to mention her general attitude, how could she have? Oh brother.

"Well, that's what I want to talk to you about," Daddy said.

Ian looked at him without blinking for a long minute. Then he stuck his hands in his back pockets and leaned against his thumbs, just like Daddy. Maybe getting back to his roots as a farmer wouldn't be so hard for him.

"I'm listening," Ian said.

I glanced at Mama, who was smiling. Then I looked at Isabel, who just stood there and said not one blessed word. But she listened so hard her ears practically stuck out.

"I'm willing to make you a trade," Daddy said. "I'll give you this old truck right here straightaway, plus my muscle and hard work fixing up this house, traded for your muscle and hard work on our farm this summer and fall. Not only that, but I'll talk to the other farmers around here, and if you're willing to help them some, I'm sure they'll lend a hand to work on the house too. It's a good old house, structurally sound, and there's no termite damage. I don't believe it'll take as much money to fix up as you might think."

Ian's mouth wagged between open and half-shut like the loose door on our mailbox during a windy day.

"Now, you have to understand that none of us can do anything on your house until summer work is done," Daddy continued. "My wife can always use extra help in the house this time of year. Our garden is producing more than we can eat, so your wife's help to put up the harvest would be a blessing. Then come winter, when the work on your place is all done, you'll have yourselves a cozy little house, just as snug and tight as all of us can make it."

"Oh, and you'll be staying with us until this house is ready for you to move into," Mama added. "What do you say?"

Nobody asked me, but I'd say, "Run! Run, Reilly family! Run for your lives!"

Neither of the St. Jameses said a word. Instead, they looked like someone had either given them an early Christmas present or had pulled down their drawers in front of the preacher. With them two, it's hard to tell.

Sometimes I wished Mama and Daddy didn't have such bighearted ideas.

FOURTEEN

Ian and Isabel Move In

❄

Having the St. Jameses move in was *not* the most fun I have ever experienced, let me tell you. Not only did my bighearted parents give their room to those two West Coasters, but my sister had to move into my room with me so Daddy and Mama could have her room. Good grief.

Maybe the two of them thought they didn't have a lot of clothes and stuff, but they like to have never stopped bringing in suitcases and wardrobe bags. And I'd hate to see how many shoes Isabel left behind, 'cause she sure as the world brought a million pairs with her into our house.

Where'd they plan to wear all that stuff, anyway?

The next day was Sunday, and you should know that we Reillys always go to church on Sunday unless we're sick.

At the supper table that evening, Mama invited the St. Jameses to go with us the next morning. Well, remembering how they acted at the mere mention of saying grace at the supper table, I knew how this was gonna turn out.

Isabel sucked her own used cigarette smoke back into her big mouth and nearly choked to death. That was her reply.

Ian bugged his eyes, then squirmed and shifted on his chair and said, "Er . . . er . . . no, thank you. We aren't church people."

"I understand," Mama said.

"Yes, of course, we understand," Daddy added, "but it would be a good way for you to meet some of the other folks in the community. A lot of the men who'll work on your house go to church with us. I'm sure they'd like to meet you."

"Well . . ." Ian glanced at his missus, who'd have shot him dead if her eyeballs had been a pair of six-shooters. "Maybe another time," he finished, and he didn't look at Isabel again for a good while.

Here's the thing as I saw it: Ole Ian sat at that table and scarfed down hamburgers and fried potatoes and baked beans and Mama's good-neighbor chocolate cake like there was no tomorrow. Daddy was giving them our good ole pickup, which he dearly loved because he bought it new a long time ago, and now he'd have to buy another one—and they got to sleep in Mama and Daddy's king-size bed. Now, after that, wouldn't you think the Very Least those St. Jameses could've done was go to church and meet some of the people who were going to help them even more? Didn't their folks ever teach them how to be grateful, for Pete's sake?

When we were getting ready to leave for church the next day, Isabel and Ian were both snoring away.

"They're just exhausted," Mama said.

Baloney.

Wouldn't you know Myra Sue pitched a fit to stay home on Sunday too? When Mama told her no, she started whining, "But someone needs to be here when they wake up. I can fix their breakfast and coffee and make their bed and everything."

"Oh brother," I hollered. "You don't even make your own breakfast. And have you ever in your life made coffee, pray tell?"

"Don't be dumb!" she snarled, pinching me.

"Girls," Daddy said. "It's Sunday. Act like it."

Well, I'll tell you something. I'd rather go to church and live there full-time, even when it's empty and spooky, than be at home one day with the St. Jameses there. I was not offered that option.

As that week passed, however, it turned out that the deal Daddy made with Ian worked out well, because ole Ian was outside and away from the house most of the day. It was kinda funny to see him in Daddy's jeans and work shirts instead of his tailored trousers and spiffy shirts. After a day or two of the sun scorching his face and his bald spot, he took to wearing a billed cap from the Farm and Tractor, where Daddy buys his farm supplies. Every time Isabel looked at him, she sort of shuddered. One thing for sure, he didn't look like a slick banker man anymore.

Isabel turned out to be pretty worthless. That woman's main activity besides sleeping late and smoking and griping about the heat and putting down the intelligence and class of people who live here—most of whom she has never met, by the way—was stretching and bending and doing twirly dance steps out on our big front porch.

Myra Sue joined her the very first day, and those two knot-heads would have jumped around to Jane Fonda's workout videos and exercised every waking hour of the day to tapes of Wham and Rick Astley and Blondie if Mama didn't break it up and assign some chore to my sister. She didn't say much to Isabel other than a gentle hint that some help would be appreciated.

Let me tell you something. People like Isabel St. James don't take hints. She dragged herself out of bed at the crack of noon quite frequently, and let me tell you, she was *not* a sight for sore eyes. Then, when she took a bath, she was in there so long it was like she was determined to drown herself. Her and her mister quarreled a lot. There was one day when I overheard Mama and Daddy talking to the St. Jameses in voices that were supposed to be private. Now, I couldn't hear exactly what was said, but the gist was this: Stop all that fussing and cussing in our home. I'm sure my folks said it in nicer terms than that.

That little conversation worked—for a while, anyway, 'cause them two fightin' St. Jameses got along for a little bit. Or they pretended to. Either way, it was a break for my ears.

All this nonsense went along for another week; then one morning, Mama said to me, "Better get scootin' on over to Grandma's, April Grace. It's Tuesday."

I was wolfing down cinnamon toast and scrambled eggs.

"But, Mama, Mr. Rance has took her to town a million times lately," I said.

"He has *taken* her to town," she corrected.

"I know! So she don't need me."

Mama was washing jars because she planned to can beans that day. The gigantic pressure cooker sat on the stove like Old King Cole. She looked at me over her shoulder.

"I declare, I'll be glad when school starts again. You talk as if you've never heard proper grammar. As much as you read, it seems to me you'd pick up on language rules."

I sighed, then shoved in the last bite of toast.

"Grandma doesn't need me," I said. "She has him. Or is it 'she has he'?"

Mama gave me a look that clearly said she did not appreciate my attempt at humor.

"And where's ole Myra Sue, anyways?" I asked. "Doing stomach crunches and twirly-toes on the porch with Isabel?"

For a minute, I figured I was in trouble for being sassy again, but what she said was, "April, why are you so cranky? Are you feeling all right?"

I shrugged. I'd probably never feel all right again for the rest of my life, or until Ian and Isabel moved out, whichever came first. I like excitement and fun as much as the next kid, but I have to tell you, those past two weeks with all the ruckus had been rough on my world.

"Your sister is picking beans," Mama told me.

I brightened. "All by herself?"

"Yes," Mama said. "She dillydallied about getting her chores done yesterday, so today she picks beans. And I don't want you helping her. This is her punishment."

Aw, shucks. And I was hankering to pick beans from the itchy, old bean vines out in the broiling hot sun.

Just about then, the door to Mama and Daddy's bedroom opened, and you could hear the *scuff-scuff* of Isabel's feet as she shuffled down the hall and into the kitchen. Boy, oh boy, she looked spookier than she had that day Mama invited her and Ian to live with us. This morning she wore a slinky robe that she hadn't bothered to tie and a nightie so sheer you could practically see her gallbladder and spleen. In one hand, she clutched her cigarettes and lighter.

"April Grace," Mama said, pouring a cup of coffee. "Better get a move on. And bring in that basket of green beans on the porch, will you, honey?" She put the coffee in front of Isabel and said, "Isabel, have you ever snapped beans before?"

The woman drew herself up straight. "I have not," she said, looking outraged that she had been asked such a question.

Mama smiled grimly. "Well, this is your lucky day. I'm going to show you how. There are enough to keep you and Myra Sue busy until tonight, if not tomorrow, as well."

Some things are worth seeing, but Mama said, "April Grace, your grandmother is waiting for you."

I was about halfway across the hayfield to Grandma's house before I stopped laughing.

FIFTEEN

Going to Town When Crawling in a Hole Is a Better Idea

Mr. Rance's pickup truck, as big and red as sin itself, sat in Grandma's driveway. For a minute I was glad to see it because that meant I wouldn't have to ride while Grandma endangered the drivers of Zachary County.

The old man stood in the yard, big black Stetson hat pushed back, arms akimbo, eyeballing Grandma's yard and house like the place belonged to him. As I got closer, I saw that he squinted up into the branches of the humongous old oak tree where my swing hung.

Daddy had made the swing for me and Myra Sue a long time ago. He said it was just like the one his daddy had made him. It hung on a thick, stout rope and had a broad, wooden seat. I loved that swing and dearly hoped Mr. Rance wouldn't decide to park his broad carcass in it, because he'd not only break the swing but probably uproot the whole tree while he was at it. He turned and stared at the field that stretched out all wide and grassy.

I paused right where I was, 'cause I didn't want the old feller to see me, let alone talk to me. I needn't have worried. He was busy eyeballing Grandma's house again. It looked to me like he was trying to see through the windows without actually going to the house. Then he went slinking around the side of the house to the little carport where Grandma parks her 1977 white Corolla.

I followed at a distance, like a coyote watching the rancher. He didn't see me, 'cause if he had, I don't think he woulda opened the passenger door real quiet-like or dug around in the glove compartment like he did.

So I, April Grace Coyote, decided to approach the scent of Old Spice.

"Whatcha lookin' for?" I asked from about six feet away.

He jumped so high and so hard, he knocked that black Stetson right off his goofy old head. He turned to look at me, his face red, eyes flashing. Right quick, he grinned real big.

"Wal, howdy there, young'un!" he bellowed, grabbing up his hat from the backseat where it had fallen. "Lemme see, now, your name is . . . uh . . . Tommy! No, it's Joe! Wait a minnut, now. It's George Henry, ain't it?"

By then, I knew he believed that acting as if he thought I were a boy was the greatest joke of 1986.

"Ha-ha!" I said. "So what are you looking for?"

He blinked, then looked down at the bunch of papers in his hand. He pulled out an Arkansas state map and waved it around and stuffed the rest back in the glove box. He closed it good and tight.

"Got it right here! Lookin' for a road map 'cause your granny and I might want to take a little drive."

It was a likely story in the biggest imaginary way, and it wasn't anything I could argue with, especially since he had the map in his chunky old hand.

"Where you planning to go?"

He guffawed. "Now, if I told you, you'd tell her, and it wouldn't be a surprise."

I just looked at him. He grinned like he was as honest and

trustworthy as our preacher. I wanted to go inside, but I knew better than to walk away while someone was talking to me. The last thing I wanted to do was apologize to Mr. Rance the way Mama had made me apologize to the St. Jameses.

"Well, let's go inside." He got out of the car and closed the door nice and quiet. "Now, don't you say a word to your granny, or you'll spoil my plans for her. Okay?"

I hated to agree with him because it went against everything I felt inside, but there was really no reason not to, and I didn't want to ruin a nice outing for Grandma.

"Okay," I said. But it wasn't easy.

"Now, lemme see," he said as we walked to the house. "Is this here swing yours or yer granny's?"

"It's Grandma's. It's her favorite thing to do after we finish playing with the hula hoop."

I thought he'd bust a gut laughing, and I hurried into the house before he could call me Paul or Jason or Billy Bob. The old man thundered in right behind me, and it was like he filled up the whole entire house. His voice sure did. In fact, his voice nearly knocked the picture of Jesus in the Garden right off the wall.

Grandma sat at her kitchen table, going over her grocery list.

"I'm thinkin' about apples!" he boomed before I could say, "Top o' the mornin'," or even "howdy-do."

"I believe there's a couple in the icebox," Grandma said.

"I don't mean them kind of apples. I mean apple *trees*. An orchard."

Grandma looked up, kinda puzzled. "Woo?" she asked.

"I thought maybe about twenty or so acres in apple trees right out there." He pointed toward the east.

Grandma looked at his pointy finger and frowned.

"I got a couple of plum trees, and that's enough," she said. "I don't want to fool with any more fruit trees. Not at my age."

He grinned, great big and toothy. "*You* won't have to fool with 'em. That'll be my job."

"Why would you do that?" I asked him.

"That's what I'm wondering," Grandma said.

"What?" he yelled at me. I don't think he even knew Grandma spoke.

"Why not plant trees on your own place?" I said real loud.

"'Cause the number one crop on my place is rocks. That there land right out there is good soil, not so rocky."

"Jeffrey!" Grandma said, trying to get his attention.

"I'll order 'em right away from Stark Brothers," he told us, "and they'll send 'em at planting time. We'll dig a water line out there and—"

"Jeffrey!"

"—I'll put in a irrigation—"

"Jeffrey Rance!" Grandma hollered loud enough to stop traffic on Highway 542.

This time, he actually heard her. "You say somethin', Miz Grace?"

"I don't want any apple trees out there."

"What's that?"

"Turn on your hearing aids!" I screamed at him. "You're gonna make Grandma hoarse."

He dug the thing out of the hairy recesses of his right ear

and fiddled with it, then did the same on the left side. When they quit buzzing and whining like a couple of sick wasps, he shook his head at me.

"I didn't say a word about your granny raising a horse. I was talking about trees. Apple trees."

"And I said you're making her hoarse because she has to yell all the time just so's you can hear her."

"Oh."

"And she don't want no apple trees, either!" I added.

He frowned. "How's that?"

"April Grace," Grandma said, "run and get my pocketbook off the dresser like a good girl." As soon as I was out of the room, she said to that old man, "We'll discuss apple trees another time."

"Well, if we wait too long, won't be any use to order 'em." He sounded sulky, but here's the thing: if he knew my grandma at all, he'd know that pouting wouldn't get him a blessed thing.

You reckon that old goat was buttering up Grandma so's he could use that back field for an apple orchard? Couldn't he see Daddy used it for pasture? Did he think he could flirt with Grandma and get apple trees? Boy, oh boy, he didn't know what he was up against with the Reilly family. We raised cows, not apples. And he better not try any funny business with my grandma.

Well, given that said grandma never puts her purse in the same place twice, it was not on the dresser like she said, or beside the dresser, or even under the dresser. It was nowhere in the bedroom or bathroom or living room. I thought about Mr. Rance and him going through the glove box of the car and going after her purse that time, and I wondered if he'd already stolen it. I went back into the kitchen to spill the beans, and that's when I saw the strap dangling out of the cabinet by the stove. Sure enough, when I opened the cabinet door, there was her purse next to the salt and baking soda.

I knew perfectly well that she's been misplacing her purse for a million years, but the notion occurred to me that she might be hiding it from Mr. Rance. But, I have to admit, if she had the least notion he'd steal her purse, she'd have told him to get lost the first time he tried to lay a big wet one on her.

To tell you the honest truth, I don't know why she didn't tell him to take a hike anyhow, him being so loud and bossy and obnoxious and sneaky. Like Mama and Daddy, my grandma is always kindhearted, but she also speaks her mind. The only reason I saw for her to let that old man hang around was that she was blinded by love—the mere thought of which makes my stomach want to barf up last Tuesday's breakfast.

I decided I'd just have to open her eyes, but I knew declaring that he was obnoxious, loud, and bossy probably wouldn't do the job. I figured I needed something specific to show her as solid proof. And there was that little incident that just happened out in the carport. Should I mention it or not? Maybe if I hung around with the two of them a little while, I'd figure it all out.

"So . . . I reckon Mr. Rance is going to take you to town today, huh?"

"Yes, honey," Grandma said. "You want to tag along?"

"Sure," I replied.

Now, I know what you're thinking, and as for my own personal self, I could hardly believe I agreed, because as

Grandma would say, I'd rather crawl in a hole and pull it in after me. But there are things you'll do for your grandma that you wouldn't do for all the gold in the world.

Besides, if I didn't go with them, I'd have to go back home—and you-know-who was staying there.

Grandma wrote something else on her list. Probably apples. At that very exact moment, Mr. Rance was peeling one with his pocketknife. I guess all that apple talk made him hungry, but it looked to me like he could live at least six months without another meal.

As the peel came off all in one long piece, he held it up and crowed like he'd won first prize in a turkey shoot. Then he cut off a hunk of apple with the same grungy knife and held it out to me. I eyeballed the knife and figured he'd used it for everything from skinning rabbits to cutting his toenails.

"No, thanks," I said.

"Ha!" he barked and popped the chunk in his mouth. "You don't know what's good," he mumbled while he chewed. "I bet I know what you'd like." He stood up and dug in the front pocket of his black Wrangler jeans, then pulled out something and offered it to me with his closed fingers hiding it.

With Grandma watching, I knew what I had to do, even if I didn't want to. I held out my hand, and he put a small object in it. I looked. It was a Kraft Caramel still in its wrapper, but it was all squishy and flat. Worst of all, it was warm from being in his pocket. He'd probably sweated all over it. I held it back out to him.

"No, thank you. I'm not hungry."

Now, you have to know that Kraft Caramels are my most

favorite candy, so it just goes to prove how disgusting it was to have one and not be able to eat it because it came warm and squooshy out of Mr. Rance's pocket.

"Don't like apples, don't like candy. What do you like, young'un? Cheeseburgers and french fries?"

Somewhere, way in the back of my mind, where unwanted thoughts and notions creep into my brain when I least want them to, came the idea that the old man was trying to be nice to me in his own weird way.

"Yes, sir," I answered.

He grinned real big. "Well, then. It'll be cheeseburgers and french fries at the Koffee Kup. Are you ready, Miz Grace, honey?"

"Almost," Grandma said. "I need to put on my good shoes."

I would have preferred McDonald's or Ruby's Place, but the closest McDonald's is twenty-five miles away in Ava or in Blue Reed sixty miles away in the other direction. Cedar Ridge only has the Koffee Kup, Ruby's Place, and the Rootin' Tootin'. The Koffee Kup is where all the old men go to slurp coffee and swap tall tales. Ruby's Place is super, but it's tiny, and Mr. Rance's big mouth would probably run off all her customers.

The Rootin' Tootin' is a beer joint that looks like someone pulled it out of a junkyard. Daddy says it's a blight on the landscape. Mama says it's a sad, sad sight, and Grandma says it's a disgrace to the crickets and ought to be burned—except where would all the roaches go? Because the good Lord knows nothing will get rid of roaches.

As we went outside to his pickup, I thought roaches and Mr. Rance probably had a lot in common.

SIXTEEN

Hard-to-Swallow Advice

☆

We went to Cedar Ridge in Mr. Rance's bright red pickup—which he announced was a 1986 Dodge Ram and less than six months old. And, if you recall, that is almost the same amount of time his wife has been dead. I've seen *60 Minutes* and cop shows. I may be a kid, but I've heard about life insurance and the money a person gets from it when someone passes on.

But right then, all I knew was that the seat was way high off the ground. You should've seen Grandma trying to get in that thing. With her short legs and chubby body, she made me think of a duck looking for something to eat in the pond. I pushed against her rump, and she kicked and squirmed and grunted and finally got herself on the seat, where she panted like Daisy on a hot day.

Mr. Rance sat behind the steering wheel, grinning the whole entire time like he thought she was putting on a show just to entertain him.

"Reckon I ought to build you that little stairstep," he said.

Grandma fanned her face with her hand for a few seconds.

"Yes, Jeffrey. You said the same thing last week. I think you better build it before I ride in this truck again."

"Yeah," I added. "With her old bones, Grandma don't have any business heaving herself into your red pickup all the time."

Mr. Rance leaned forward a little to look at me. He was grinning with his mouth hanging open.

"How's 'at?" he asked.

I started to repeat myself, but Grandma caught my eye and shook her head.

"Get in, April." She started to slide across the seat, then stopped. "Or would you rather sit in the middle?"

Now, one thing I did *not* want to do was sit next to Mr. Rance. He'd probably yell in my ear the whole entire way to town, and I'd be stone-deaf by the time we got there.

I pulled myself up the two miles it took to get into the pickup.

"You sit by him, Grandma. He's your boyfriend." I nearly choked on the word. Her face turned bright red.

All the way to town, Mr. Rance talked about that dumb truck.

"This here is the fifth Dodge I've owned. Ain't nothin' like 'em. This'un here's got a 318 motor, a five-point-nine liter Magnum V-8 engine and a Ram Trac shift-on-the-fly transfer case. Yes sirree, finest thing on the road. But I'll tell you one thing about a Dodge truck. The old'uns drive like new."

Now, I had to admit I liked being way up high where I could look out. And the big seat was comfortable. But Mr. Rance like to have driven me crazy with all his truck talk, talk, talk.

"Why don't you still drive the very first one you ever had, then, if they're all so good?" I asked, showing off my ability to be smart.

Grandma gave me a little pinch on the elbow. Not hard and mean the way Myra Sue does, but firm enough that I knew I better stop being smartmouthed to my elders. Her lips were in a tight line where you could hardly see them, and she shook her head at me again.

"How's 'at?" He cupped his hand around his right ear and leaned sideways toward us.

"Never mind," I yelled back.

When we got into town, we drove to the Koffee Kup first instead of the store, so Grandma's groceries wouldn't spoil out in the sun while we ate.

Mr. Rance, who didn't bother to take off his Stetson, bellowed our order to the waitress standing about two feet from him. I wanted to crawl under the table when everyone in the café looked at us. I suppose, though, the cook and waitresses were used to him since he went there every blessed day.

Right about then was when I decided Grandma must be losing her hearing, too, because his big mouth didn't seem to bother her in the least. She smoothed her hair and straightened her skirt and fluffed her sleeves, all with a little smile on her face.

"That's another pretty new dress, Grandma," I said. "I didn't see you sewing that one."

Most of the time she waved off compliments, but that day her cheeks turned pink.

"I ordered it from the JC Penney catalog," she said.

Used to be that Grandma wore plain homemade dresses with little round collars and shiny buttons, and she always had her hair combed back in a plain ole bun. Lately, she'd taken to wearing pretty dresses and broaches. She braided her hair before she pinned it up. She had quit using bobby pins and instead kept her hair in place with pretty combs with sparkledy things in them.

Anytime I do something peculiar, someone says I'm going through a phase. I started to ask Grandma if she was going through a phase, but Mr. Rance spoke up.

"You look right pleasin' to the eye, Miz Grace."

Her cheeks got redder, and it finally dawned on me that she didn't get so dolled up lately because of any old lady phase she might be going through. The sad and unvarnished truth was that she made herself all spiffy and glittery for that goofy old man.

I sighed as this soaked in. If she wanted to take up with some man, why hadn't she taken up with Reverend Jordan, who had been a bachelor his whole entire life and lived in a neat little house near the United Methodist Church and drove a snazzy little Mustang? Or Ernie Beason, who owned Ernie's Grocerteria? He was a nice old widower, and always real friendly. Or there was old man Watson who mowed yards and cut firewood for folks. I mean, there must have been more than two dozen old men available in Cedar Ridge, and she picked the loudmouthed newcomer who wouldn't let you get a word in edgewise, even if you were dying of snakebite.

Right then, he was yammering on about the Dallas Cowboys. If he knew anything at all about my grandma, he'd know she didn't like football, not even a little bitty bit. But there she was, listening to him, nodding her head as if touchdowns and tight ends were the most thrilling subjects she could imagine.

There came a point that day when God finally must have looked down on us and took a little pity, because Mr. Rance stopped talking all of a sudden and announced he had to go see a man about a horse. As he walked toward the men's room, Grandma watched him with a dreamy little smile. I looked to see what she found so fascinating. Besides that dumb hat, he wore a bright blue cowboy shirt, black jeans—over which his belly hung—and pointy-toed cowboy boots. After one quick glance, I looked away.

"Why didn't he just say he was going to the men's room, or just plain ole 'excuse me' like a normal person? Saying he had to see a man about a horse . . . that's dumb."

Grandma fiddled with her empty coffee cup and looked at the waitress, who pretended we weren't there.

"Well, people say things," she told me. "Maybe he thinks saying he's going to the restroom is crude. On car trips, when your grandpa had to go, he'd pull off the road and say he had to kick the tires." She glanced at our waitress again, who never did look at us. "People just say things."

"But don't he get on your nerves?" I asked.

"Who? Your grandpa? Why, I—"

"No! Mr. Rance," I said. "Don't he about drive you buggy and nearly bust your eardrums?"

She frowned a little bit. "I don't think he knows how loud he talks."

"And them dumb jokes. And all that talk, talk, talk. Don't he drive you buggy?" I asked. "He drives me buggy."

Grandma finally quit staring a hole through the waitress and looked at me.

"April Grace, you listen to me." There was a sharp edge in her voice that I didn't like. "You know I love you dearly, but honey, you just got to quit finding fault with everyone, and that includes Jeffrey Rance. There ain't never been but one perfect person in the world, and they killed Him. If you keep looking at the things you don't like about folks, you won't ever have any friends. Or any fun, neither. Folks don't act the way they do just to annoy you. They act the way they do 'cause they're people."

"But—"

"No buts about it. Jeffrey Rance lost his wife about Christmastime last year, and he don't have any kids, so he's lonesome with no one to talk to. And he can't hear thunder. He don't know how loud he talks."

"But he's so pushy," I said.

"Piffle! He ran a big horse ranch down in Texas. He's used to being in charge. But now all he's got is a little, bitty, rocky piece of dirt down the road from us. It don't hurt to let him feel a little bit needed."

"But why'd he move here in the first place?" I asked. "If he's a horse rancher, why isn't he still in Texas where he belongs?"

Grandma took a deep breath. "Well, his wife was sick for a long time. He had to sell his horses and his ranch to pay for her care. He said he just couldn't stand to live there without her anymore after she passed on. All the memories were just too hurtful. So he decided to move to the Ozarks."

I let all that information soak in. Then I chewed on my bottom lip for a while and pondered my theory of why he was so all-fired determined to be Grandma's boyfriend. I thought about how he eyeballed her stuff as if it belonged to him, and that sure as fire didn't have anything to do with his wife dying and him being lonesome.

"Well, I think you ought to know he was poking around in your living room the other day when he didn't know I was sitting right there," I said.

She frowned. "Oh, April." She said it like she was disappointed in me.

"He was looking at your TV," I explained, "and that new VCR."

"So?" Grandma said. "He probably don't know how to work one of them things any more than I do. He was just curious."

"Well, then, today when I was coming over to your house, he was pawing through your glove compartment," I said.

"He was? Why?"

I gave her a Look, but she didn't get it. "He *said* he was looking for a map, but I—"

"Then I'm sure he was looking for a map," Grandma said.

"Grandma! Don't you think—?"

She interrupted me before I could tell her anything more. "April Grace, tell me something, child. Who do you admire more than anyone?"

"You mean besides Jesus?" I knew I had to say Jesus in case this was a trick question.

"Yes," Grandma said.

"Mama and Daddy and you."

She smiled a little bit.

"Leave me out of it," she said. "You ever notice how your daddy and mama don't go around trying to find fault with folks? You notice how they hardly ever have anything bad to say about anyone?"

"I know! And how can they not say anything when them St. Jameses are Living With Us and driving us all crazy?"

"Can you think of one nice thing to say about them?"

"You mean Ian and Isabel?"

She nodded.

"I can't think of a thing," I said.

"Try real hard."

I sighed and thought. Real hard.

"Well," I said, after a bit, "Ian is actually not as bad as you might think." But I had to add, "Ole Isabel is as lazy as a toad in the sun except when her and Myra Sue are doing their workout. Plus, she's always whining and complaining and saying they don't have money anymore. Well, why don't she go get herself a job, then? They might hire her at Walmart or something. And she's supposed to be helping Mama, but she don't. She just expects Mama to wait on her hand and foot. And Mama does!"

Something flickered across Grandma's face, but all she said was, "Your daddy and mama do the Christian thing by folks."

Well, she was right about that.

"Isabel and Myra Sue are supposed to be snapping beans today," I said. "Can you picture ole Isabel breaking green beans with her long, red fingernails in the way?"

"At least she's doing something. Give her credit for that. You'd do yourself a real service, April Grace, if you was to take a page out of your folks' book. You'd be a lot happier."

"But Grandma—"

"If anyone in the world has a reason to feel distrustful and pessimistic about folks, it's your mama."

This was news to me. My ears perked up. "Why?"

She moved her coffee cup around on the table again. I could see she was debating with herself whether or not to give me an answer.

"Grandma, I'm old enough to know some things." When

she just looked at me, I added, "And I can keep my mouth shut about them."

"I've never known you to keep your mouth shut at the right time."

"Grandma."

She studied me a minute.

"Well, I'll tell you a little, and if your Mama ever wants you to know more, she'll tell you herself."

Afraid she might change her mind if I moved a fraction, I sat perfectly still. Deep inside my head, I could feel my eardrums twitch.

"The thing is, your other grandma did not want Lily."

Well, I knew that. Sort of. My other grandma is alive, I think. I asked Mama about her once, and she said that her mother hadn't been ready for her or for motherhood, and for me to please never mention it again. So I didn't. But I thought about it sometimes.

Grandma looked out the café window, but I could see she looked at nothing but her thoughts. In a bit, she dragged her gaze back to me.

"Sandra Moore—your other grandma—was not a nice person, and that's putting it mildly."

"Why?"

"She just wasn't, that's all."

"But why? Grandma, you keep fiddling with that cup and spoon, and you're twitching around in your chair. Is it so shameful you can't speak of it?"

She waved a hand. "It ain't scandalous or anything. And none of it is your mama's fault, but it does hurt me to remember."

"Remember what?"

"That Lily's great-aunt Maxie didn't want her, either."

I frowned. Great-Aunt Maxie had raised Mama, but she never said much about her one way or the other.

"She gave her a place to live, but that's about all," Grandma said. "First time I saw your mama was at church during Vacation Bible School. She was the scrawniest, dirtiest, pitifulest little thing you ever saw. Back in those days, the state didn't step in and take care of kids the way it does now. Mike said the kids at school picked on Lily something awful, and he did his best to stand up for her. 'Course, he wasn't always there to watch out for her." She paused a second or two. "I'll tell you one thing. That little redheaded girl had the most beautiful, shining smile you ever saw."

"She still does," I said.

"Yes, ma'am, she does. And you should've seen her eat the snacks during refreshment time at VBS. Of course, the church folks did everything they could for her as time went on, but Maxie didn't like that. Made her look bad, I guess, and after a while she wouldn't let Lily come to church anymore. Then, when Lily was about ten or so, her mama came back to town. Said she'd had a change of heart, so she packed her up, and off they went to God knows where. A couple of years later, she brought Lily back, dumped her on the old aunt again, and skedaddled for good." Grandma stopped talking for a few seconds. "Maybe I shouldn't have told you anything," she said.

"No. I'm glad you told me," I said. "But why won't Mama ever talk about this? Like you said, it wasn't her fault. She didn't do anything wrong."

"Well, that's the thing, honey. Lily Reilly lives by First Corinthians, chapter thirteen. You know that Scripture?"

"I think so."

"It says something like, love is patient and kind, and it doesn't get easily angered or keep records of wrongdoing. That's not an exact quote, but you've been to Sunday school. You know what I'm talking about. Your mama believes in that Scripture, and she lives her life by it."

"She sure does."

"The year Sandra Moore brought Lily back to Cedar Ridge was the year Lily and Mike became good friends. And you know how that turned out." She smiled. "And when the old aunt had a stroke a few months after they got married, you know what your folks did?"

I shook my head.

"They took her into that tiny apartment they lived in up in Branson while they went to the college up there. Yes sir-ree. Took that ole gal right into their home, and your mama dropped out of college to take care of her. She waited on her and treated her like a beloved member of the family, while your daddy got his agricultural degree at the School of the Ozarks. It wasn't easy on either of 'em, but they did it because Lily thought it was the right thing to do. Mike, he went along with her on it. You know, he has always thought your mama hung the moon."

Grandma stopped talking for a bit. I waited for her to finish her story and tried not to fidget. I hoped that old man who'd been seeing a man about a horse for a long time stayed away for a while longer.

"Mebbe I shouldn't have told you any of this," Grandma said at last. "But I wanted you to know that if anyone has a right to feel hard toward anyone, it's your mama. And she don't. She loves 'em all, so you just think about that and see if you can't be more like her and less like some other folks."

I sighed.

"It's a lot to take in," I said.

And it was pretty hard to swallow too. But I'd think about it. I wanted to think about it, but I sure didn't get much of a chance right then 'cause Mr. Rance came clumping toward the table in his loud, old cowboy boots. He was grinning like a monkey. I sighed again.

"Wal, now!" He sat down, looked at Grandma's empty cup, and glanced around until he saw our waitress busing a table across the room. He hollered like he thought he was at a hog-calling contest. "Missy! We need coffee."

While everyone turned to look at us again, and while the red-faced waitress hurried to our table, I forced myself to remember what Grandma had just said. I had to admit she was right. I really ought to be more like Mama and Daddy. Look at how nice they treated the St. Jameses, even when Isabel was lazy and rude and never said thank you for a blessed thing. She must never have even heard the word *gratitude* in her entire life. And whenever Temple and Forest dropped in, Mama and Daddy pretended they didn't stink at all. Mama always gave Temple a big hug. If Temple brought some of her bark bread or nature cookies, Mama took one and ate it right then and there—even when Temple looked like she hadn't a bathed in a week or three, and the cookies or bread were made without flour, sugar, eggs, or milk and tasted like dry cardboard.

Mama and Daddy were happy too.

I'm gonna start acting like them, I told myself. I'm gonna try to be nice to everyone, no matter what.

Then I looked at Mr. Rance. I looked at his big red face below that black hat and his big dumb grin and his sticky-out ears with their hearing aids poked down amongst the hairs in his ear holes. I wondered if Mama and Daddy ever felt queasy when they were being nice to certain people.

Well, I thought, *I'll just have to like him 'cause it's important to Grandma.*

I'll tell you one thing, though. I still had all my suspicions about him, and I was gonna watch him real close. But for the time being, I'd try to be nice. I sat up real straight.

I said, "I'm sorry your wife died last year about Christmastime."

A weird look came over his face, like he'd swallowed something he didn't mean to. He sort of nodded and poured about half the sugar from the dispenser into his coffee. He stirred it so hard and fast it sloshed onto the table and his fingers.

"How long were you married?" I asked. Not that I cared, but it seemed like a nice question.

"A while," he said.

"What happened to her?" I asked.

He took a big gulp of coffee. "She took sick."

I didn't have time to ponder this because Grandma nudged me under the table. She gave me a little frown and shook her head, so I figured this was one of the subjects the old man didn't want to talk about.

"You like to read?" I asked him.

"You mean books?"

"Yep," I said. "Good, big, fat books with stories."

He shook his big ole head. "Nah. Readin' is a pure waste of time."

Well, I tell you what. I'd never heard such an awful thing come out of the mouth of a grown-up.

"Are you kiddin' me?" I hollered. Grandma nudged me under the table again, and I swallowed down my outrage. It took me a minute to think up something new.

"What about horses?" I asked.

Sure enough, his face lit up.

"What about 'em, young'un?"

"How come you like them so good?" I asked.

Unfortunately, the subject of horses kept his mouth going through the rest of lunch, during the grocery shopping, and most of the way home. I wanted to jump out of the truck and walk, but I knew Grandma wouldn't let me. Besides, I'd have to help her get out of the pickup without splatting to the ground. And besides that, I sat between them going home, because I thought it would help me in my quest to be a nicer person and like that old man. So I just sat there in a cloud of sweaty Old Spice and suffered. Of course, I had no idea what was about to happen, or I might have been happy to ride in that truck 'til dark-thirty.

SEVENTEEN

Queenie, Queenie, You're a Weenie

☺

That day, while Mr. Rance drove us home from town, I did my best to close out his voice while the three of us bounced down Rough Creek Road in that red pickup. We were almost home when, without warning, Grandma screamed at the top of her lungs and like to have scared me to death. Mr. Rance slammed the brakes so hard that the truck slid sideways in a cloud of gravel and dust. I clunked my forehead on the dashboard. For a few seconds I saw stars and wondered if I'd see Jesus next.

"Miz Grace! What's wrong?" Mr. Rance hollered.

I was still blinking, trying to clear my head, when Grandma gasped, "Oh! Oh! Did you see?" Grandma said, pointing to the side of the road. "My Queenie, my kitty. How did she get out? Oh, there! *There she goes!* Here kitty, kitty!" She opened her door, hollering, "Oh, Queenie, come back to your mommy!"

She fumbled around and unfastened her seat belt, then jumped out of the pickup and stumbled down to the dry bed of Rough Creek.

Leaving his truck cattywampus on the road, Mr. Rance got out and started yelling, "Come back here, you blasted cat! Here!" He whistled as if he thought Queenie were a Bluetick hound.

I scooted across the seat and leaped to the ground.

"She won't come to you when you're screaming at her like that," I said.

But, of course, he couldn't hear me over the racket of his own big mouth. Grandma did her best to get up the embankment on the other side of the road, but she couldn't make it. I ran toward her. Before I got there, she skittered backward on the loose dirt and rocks and fell flat on her backside. Then she started to cry. I'd never seen her do that before.

"Don't worry, Grandma." I patted her head. Beneath my hand, her gray hair was as soft as cotton. "I'll find Queenie and bring her home. Don't worry. Don't cry."

She sat in the ditch, her new dress dirty, her stockings torn at the knee, and her shoes all scuffed. She hunched over her legs, breathing hard while tears poured down her cheeks and left tracks in the face powder I didn't even know she used. Her skin looked all gray and pale. I stared at her a minute, then got up and ran to Mr. Rance, who was crashing around in the brush on the opposite side of the road.

"Come 'ere, you ill-begotten feline!" he roared.

I had to grab his arm and jump up and down just to get his attention.

"I'll find Queenie," I shouted at him, "but you need to take Grandma to the house and calm her down. She's all upset."

Mr. Rance stood with his arms hanging loose at his sides and stared at me.

"How's 'at?"

I repeated my instructions. He nodded and went to where Grandma was trying to claw her way up the embankment again.

"Now, Miz Grace, your little'un will get your pussycat back for you," Mr. Rance said. "Let's you and me go get us some sweet tea and cool off. You look tuckered."

By the time I got up the other side of the embankment,

he was brushing the dirt off Grandma, patting her shoulder, talking a mile a minute, and leading her back to the truck. I took one last look at the two of them, then ran into the woods to find that Queenie, who is the Weenie of the World.

I was quite a ways into the trees, hoping I'd not step on a copperhead and die a hideous death all swole-up and purple with a black tongue hanging out of my mouth, when I saw that Dumb Cat several feet away, just standing there, looking at me and twitching her tail like I annoyed her.

As I got closer, she stood real still, and I thought, well, this is gonna be easier than I expected. When I was almost close enough to catch her, she ran off again, diving over a fallen tree and some brush. She got about fifty feet when she stopped and looked back at me.

"Come here, Queenie," I said quietly so she'd not run again.

Just about the time I reached her, she took off. This time she darted halfway up a small tree. She hung there like the dried-out shell of a jar fly, then let go, hit the ground, and started running and bounding over brush again.

"Come here, stupid!" I screamed at her, which was the wrongest thing to do because she hissed and yeowled and dashed off like the devil was after her. I knew chasing the fool just kept her going, but I didn't know what else to do. As I ran, every little once in a while, I'd see a fuzzy splotch of white.

Then she wasn't there anymore. I called until my throat hurt. I hunted in those trees and bushes, and twice I fell over rocks I didn't see under the fallen leaves. At one point, a black snake came sliding past me, and I about had a heart attack on the spot.

Now, I know you're thinking: why didn't you just go home, you silly little girl? Well, I'll tell you. When you see your grandma sitting in a ditch, crying because she lost her cat, you don't ever want to see her like that again.

So I searched the woods and fields and called, "Here, kitty, kitty, kitty," 'til I was dizzy. Finally, I dragged myself back home, so thirsty I was about to croak. All sweaty and dirty and scratched-up from running through woods, I crossed the back porch and went into the kitchen, figuring snooty Isabel would screw up her mouth and nose when she caught a look, but I didn't care. I grabbed a glass from the cabinet, ran to the sink, and got a long, cool drink of water. Then I turned around. That's when I saw an empty kitchen. Empty of people, I mean.

On the table sat a bushel basket about half-full of un-broken beans. The other basket was on the floor beside the door, and it was full. On the cabinet was a big blue enamel pan of broken beans. Mama, Isabel, and Myra Sue were nowhere to be seen. That was weird, let me tell you.

In summer, except when she goes to church or has to run into town for something, Mama is busy in the kitchen, pre-serving, canning, pickling, or freezing something. I've never known her to go missing. A scared feeling poked me, and I shivered.

"Mama?"

She didn't answer. She wasn't in the living room or din-ing room. I was just about to go upstairs when I heard voices coming from behind the closed door of her bedroom.

I ran down the hall and without pausing to knock, I threw open the door. Isabel jumped, screeching with fright, and so did the dark-haired girl with her. The girl wore a silver, spangly dress and strappy high heels. Her makeup was so thick, she looked like a clown.

"What are you doing here, you dumb little kid?" she screamed at me. "Did you ever hear of knocking?"

I stared at Myra Sue until my eyeballs nearly fell out.

"Mama is gonna kill you," I said.

I flinched as she approached, but instead of smacking the daylight out of me, she reached behind me and slammed the door shut.

"Hush your big mouth!" she hissed. "What are you doing here? You're supposed to be in Cedar Ridge with Grandma."

I was so stunned, I couldn't speak for a minute.

Her blond hair was now black. Blacker than black. So black it sucked the light right out of the room. Not only that, but it was big. Big like the girls in high school wear. Her idol, Her Isabel-ness, sat without moving or speaking.

"Mama is gonna kill you," I said again. "K-I-L-L-Y-O-U. And where'd you get that dress? It looks like aluminum foil." I reached out to touch it, but she smacked my hand away.

"Your sister has chosen to rise above her circumstances and embrace her inner goddess," Isabel said.

I looked at Isabel and said, "*Inner goddess*? You've been hanging out with Temple, haven't you?"

Isabel curled her thin nose. "That vile creature?"

"She is not!" I said. "And where's my mama?"

Isabel blinked. "My husband broke the tractor, and your

father had to go to that ridiculous little town to get a part. If anyone can tear up anything, that foolish Ian can. He's a master of destruction." She sniffed. Then, "Lily said she wanted to go with him." She flipped one hand airily. "And off she went."

Mama must have needed a break big-time to take off for no reason in the middle of the day with all those beans in there. "When she gets home and sees those beans aren't ready to be canned, she's—"

"*Why are you home?*" Myra Sue yelled. When she opened her mouth like that, you could see her new black hair did not go well with her braces. I wonder if Isabel had told her that.

I finally decided to quit gawking at this nightmare and get on with business. "Queenie got out again. Have you seen her? Has she been over here? Grandma's fit to be tied."

Isabel stiffened. "You mean that vicious dog your family owns?"

I looked at that ignorant woman.

"I mean Grandma's white cat."

"I haven't seen her," Myra Sue said. "How long has she been out?"

"A while. Grandma saw her run across the road just before we got home, and I saw her a few times in the woods, but she wouldn't let me catch her."

"She gets out all the time," Myra Sue said. "Who cares?"

"If you'd seen Grandma all upset and crying, you'd care. I'm going over to her house right now."

"Grandma was crying?" Myra Sue asked.

"She sat in the ditch on the side of Rough Creek Road and bawled her eyes out."

Through all that makeup, my sister looked worried. Even though Myra Sue insulted Grandma at supper that one time, I knew she loved her.

"Poor Grandma. I'll come with you," said Myra Sue.

I nodded, and she turned to Isabel, who leaned her head weakly against the back of an antique wicker chair. One hand was thrown across her eyes like she was a heroine in a cheesy old movie.

"I'll change my clothes and go with my sister now," Myra Sue said to her.

Isabel dropped her hand. She sighed.

"If you must. But tomorrow we'll continue our lessons." She smiled.

Lessons in what, besides exercising until your tongue hung out?

The two of them touched fingertips. Then, with her face beaming like the angel Gabriel just kissed her, my sister went out of the room with a stiff, uppity walk. Maybe her drawers were riding up her bottom under that slinky dress. She nearly fell off her high heels.

Isabel exchanged her smile for a hard look when she turned to me. She reached for the cigarettes and lighter.

"You could benefit from lessons yourself," she said as she started to shake out a smoke. "Or maybe not. I rather doubt lessons would do you an iota of good. Some people are simply born to be—"

"Mama's gonna have a cow when she sees my sister's hair. She'd flat-out keel over if she saw that aluminum foil dress. And if she knew you were smoking in her bedroom . . ."

The woman gave me tight little smile and put aside the pack.

"No offense, dear, but your mother could do with a make-over herself. She and her homespun ways would be laughed out of our circle back home."

Boy, oh boy, what a drip.

Honest, I tried to remember the little talk Grandma and I had shared earlier. I thought about it real hard, but Isabel had just insulted my mother, and there are some things I can't abide. All my good intentions flew right out the window.

"That would never happen," I said.

She twitched a little and sneered. "I beg to differ with—"

"Because Mama would never join your circle *back home* in the first place. She's picky about what groups she joins."

She narrowed her eyes. "You little . . ."

I won't tell you what she called me, but it sure wasn't "little darling."

Myra Sue, wearing her T-shirt and jeans shorts, came back into the room, hopping on her bare left foot while trying to put her right one in a sneaker. She had wiped off most of that gruesome makeup.

"April Grace, you better be nice to Isabel, or I'll tell Mama."

"If you do, I'll fill her in about your spangly dress and all that makeup."

Isabel followed us into the kitchen. She looked down at the beans as if she faced a brain transplant.

"I'll help you with those beans as soon as I get back, Isabel dear," my sister said.

"Will you, darling?"

"Of course!" She went to the woman, and they kissed the air on both sides of each other's cheeks.

"Good-bye, darling," said Isabel.

"Good-bye, dearest Isabel," said Myra Sue.

"Good grief," I said.

About the time we reached the edge of the hayfield, I asked, "Why'd you do that to your hair?"

She sniffed and didn't reply for a minute. Finally, she said, "Because I put a color on Isabel's hair, and she wanted to repay my kindness."

I stopped walking. "Are you kidding?"

"Well, her roots were showing! And . . . and she had two boxes of color, and they were the same, and I thought my hair would look like hers . . . Well, it was supposed to be rich chestnut brown."

"Yeah," I said, "But the thing is, now it's blacker than a moonless night in a cave."

She touched it with the fingertips of her right hand, looking dismayed. I shook my head and started walking again.

"I'd hate to be you when Mama and Daddy get home."

She drew in a deep breath that shuddered, but I didn't look at her. I actually felt kinda sorry for her. Kinda. I mean, not only was her hair ruined, she was in such Big Trouble, she'd be 104 years old before things got back to normal. And just when she had finally shown some real feelings for poor Grandma.

We crossed the hayfield while the sun beat down on our heads like we were loaves of bread in need of baking. At least Daddy kept the little track for going back and forth

to Grandma's mowed short. Otherwise we'd have been bat-
tling all that field grass 'til we passed out. Daddy or Mr. Brett
would mow that hayfield in a day or two; then everything
would look all clean and flat out there for a while.

Right when we got to Grandma's yard, we saw Queenie
lounging in the shade of the oak tree. She was right on top of
Mr. Rance's bright red Dodge Ram.

"There she is!" I hollered, making a dash toward the
house. "I'll tell Grandma."

Myra Sue was right behind me, and when we got to the
porch, we raced to the door, both of us trying to be the one who
got to announce the good news. I reached the door first, but
Myra Sue grabbed me by the arm and yanked me backward.

She opened the screen door and yelled, "Queenie's on top
of the pickup!"

I went inside, slammed her a dirty look, then shouted,
"Right out there, right on top of it."

Grandma had been lying on the couch, something she
didn't do very often. She had a wet cloth on her head, and she
looked pale. But when she heard us, she got up right quick,
exclaiming, "Kitty, kitty, kitty!"

Mr. Rance snored in the recliner with his mouth wide-
open. He didn't move a muscle. Looking at him, I thought I'd
just about seen all the human ugliness I could stand that day.

"Open the door, April," Grandma said. Then she called,
"Here, kitty, kitty," a couple more times. "Is she coming?"

I looked outside. That dumb Queenie was licking her tail.
She stopped and looked toward the house; then she just sat
there while Grandma called again. Finally, Queenie stood up,

real slow. She stretched herself so long you'd think she'd pull her body into two pieces. She sat down again, as if she were the Queen of Sheba, then wrapped her tail around her legs, stared at the house, and yawned so big you could practically see her gizzard.

How could Grandma love such a fool?

"Come on, Queenie," I said. "Grandma needs you."

She stared back at me, blinked, and began to lick her chest. I sighed and turned away.

"Grandma, she won't come," I said.

Grandma headed to the front door, but switched directions. "I know what'll work," she said, and went into the kitchen.

She returned with a little square box of Kat Kibble. At the door, she shook the box, and the treats rattled. Queenie leaped off the pickup like a flying squirrel and streaked through the open door. Grandma gave her a treat, and the minute that cat had swallowed it, my grandmother picked her up and cuddled her like a newborn baby.

"Ooh, oo ittle bad puddy tat, wunning off wike dat and scaring you mommy to def!"

"If me or Myra Sue had run off that way, we'd be in trouble 'til Doomsday," I said, purely disgusted.

"Oh, hush," Grandma said, smiling at Queenie and rubbing noses with her. "You're not a defenseless little animal."

And neither is Queenie, I thought silently. *Boy, oh boy.*

EIGHTEEN

The Magical Influence of Isabel St. James

*

I uttered not one mumblin' word to Mama and Daddy about the scary makeup, the strappy high-heeled shoes, or the shiny dress because ole Myra Sue got in such trouble for dyeing her hair black, it wouldn't have made any difference.

Instead, I decided just to tuck away those little tidbits for such a time in the future as they might be useful.

Here's what happened. It was late afternoon, that very same day. Me and Myra Sue and Isabel were in the kitchen, going at them beans like there was no tomorrow. And yes, I was helping, because Grandma's little talk kept playing over and over in my head.

We heard the truck door slam when Mama and Daddy arrived home from town, and ole Isabel jumped up and trotted off to the bedroom like a big coward. Myra Sue looked like she'd been caught in a rabbit trap, but she just sat there and broke beans so fast my eyes blurred watching her.

Mama and Daddy walked in the door, laughing and talking about something they'd just heard on the radio. Mama seemed more relaxed than I'd seen her for a few days, but their jolly mood evaporated the second they got a gander at my sister's hair.

She and Daddy just stood there, each holding a couple of brown paper sacks from Ernie's Grocerteria.

"What in the world?" Mama finally managed to say. Daddy's mouth opened and shut without a single sound coming out.

Myra Sue broke beans as she said, prim as the Queen of France, "Isabel and I colored each other's hair."

You could've heard the ice dripping off the glaciers in Alaska.

"Isabel put black dye on your hair?" Mama's voice was kind of strangled.

"The box said 'rich chestnut brown,'" said Myra Sue.

Snap, snap, snap went the beans. There was a soft rustle as she pitched each one into the nearly full bowl.

"It should have said 'coal dust black,'" Daddy said. "Good grief, girl."

I just about barked a laugh, but I thought better of it.

Mama swallowed hard. I guess it was a shock to see your golden-haired daughter turn into a coal-dust-black brunette. At least she hung on to the grocery sacks she held. Daddy put his on the counter, then took hers.

"Lily, honey," he said, "you know I'll abide by whatever decision you make about this. Right now, I better change clothes and get out to the barn to give Brett a hand with the milking. Ian's no good at it. He's afraid of the cows." He shook his head, kissed Mama, and hurried from the room.

Mama just stood in the middle of the kitchen. I don't think she even heard him. She stared at my sister for another long minute. Then, without a word, she marched to her own bedroom door and rapped on it. I followed her to see what would happen. But when she went inside, she shut the door right in my face.

She opened it immediately and snapped, "Go take a bath, April Grace," and shut the door again.

Well, what did *I* do wrong? I had been good as gold, searching for Queenie and later sitting right there at the kitchen table, snapping beans. I had nothing to do with Myra Sue's hair or the fact that another bushel basket of beans still needed to be broken.

The next morning, which was Wednesday, Mama called Faye at the beauty shop in Cedar Ridge and told her it was an emergency. Faye said she was sick with a stomach virus, but when Mama told her about Myra Sue's blond locks being dyed black as night, Faye got right up out of her sickbed and told Mama to come in immediately.

I was getting a glass from the cabinet when they got back home. Myra Sue's eyes were all swole up and red. The black had been stripped from her hair, leaving it an orangey-yellow. She looked right colorful with red eyes and that hair. Actually, she made me think of Mrs. Winkler, who works behind the counter at the dry cleaners, except Mrs. Winkler is about fifty years old and has wrinkles all around her mouth from smoking every other minute of the day.

"Nice hairdo," I muttered as I got the milk from the refrigerator and poured a glassful. She snarled at me like a rat terrier. She tried to stomp off upstairs, but Mama wouldn't let her. Then Myra Sue tried to run to Isabel, who still hid out in my folks' bedroom. Mama put a stop to that too.

"You have spent entirely too much time with Isabel lately," she said, "so you just stay in here with me and your sister and help us finish these beans. Your beautiful blond hair." Mama shook her head. "Do you realize how many girls want to have hair like yours? Or like yours was before you dyed it?"

Myra Sue blinked her eyes rapidly and tightened her lips for a few seconds.

"Mother," she said prissily, "you have absolutely no taste whatsoever. In fact, you could do with a *major* makeover yourself."

Mama's mouth dropped open in what I'm sure was pure astonishment.

Ole Myra Sue sealed her fate by adding, "Oh, how I wish I lived in California instead of this hideous hole of a farm!"

Mama recovered right quick. Myra Sue's attitude and her big mouth earned Kitchen Duty not only that night, but every night for a week. I'm not sure what Mama had said to Isabel when they talked the day before, but the woman stayed in her room all morning. I can tell you, I did not miss hearing her whine and complain.

Anyway, that night after we went to bed, Myra Sue lay beside me, sniffling and snuffling. She blubbered about her sad lot in life. I lost count of how many times she muttered, "I wish I'd been born anywhere but here."

"I wish you had been too," I told her fervently.

Given the notion that she was undoubtedly an adopted member of this family, she probably had been born somewhere else. You understand, don't you, that no one ever actually said Myra Sue was adopted. It's just my theory, but boy, oh boy, all signs point to it.

Thursday morning, I dawdled over my biscuits and gravy, while Myra Sue sulked her way through a piece of dry toast and half a glass of skim milk. She flat-out refused eggs, bacon, biscuits, gravy, grits, oatmeal, Malt-O-Meal, Cheerios, Corn Flakes, or Lucky Charms. Until the last few weeks, she'd always wolfed down any of it like a starving truck driver. I could only conclude that Isabel St. James, who smoked her breakfast on the front porch with a cup of coffee, encouraged, if not created, my sister's new menu.

Myra Sue regarded her last bite of toast with disgust, and I observed, "Your hair is the same color as my scrambled eggs."

She stood up so fast, her chair nearly toppled backward.

Mama looked up from ironing Daddy's shirts. "Myra Sue, sit down, please. You are not leaving the table until you finish your milk. April Grace, that was rude. Apologize to your sister."

I sighed, then remembered what Grandma said about Mama and Daddy being nice to people who did not always deserve it.

"Sorry, sis. Your hair doesn't look so bad."

Myra Sue just rolled her eyes, then glared at her milk.

"I will not stay where I am being insulted," she muttered.

Mama pursed her mouth. "Sit down, young woman," she said in That Tone.

You'd think Myra Sue, with all the punishments she'd piled up yesterday, would avoid further disaster, but she seemed to have a death wish, 'cause she met Mama's gaze without batting an eyelash.

Myra Sue just stood there. Mama turned off the iron without taking her eyes from my sister. "I said, *sit down*."

For a minute it seemed ole Myra Sue would stand forever by the table. I wondered if Mama might get a paddle and use it, but finally, Myra Sue plopped back into her chair. With pinkie extended, she picked up the glass as if it were covered in slime. She took a delicate sip.

"Thank you." Mama's voice seemed thin. Her cheeks

were red and her eyes were bright, but she held her temper. She turned the iron on again and picked up the final shirt from the basket.

Myra Sue sipped a thimbleful at a time until the milk was gone.

"May I please be excused from your table and your kitchen?" she said, all snooty-like.

"You may take the laundry basket outside and take the sheets and pillowcases off the line. Then you may iron them."

"Iron the sheets?"

"Yes."

I waited for ole Myra Sue's eyeballs to pop right out of her orangey-yellow head.

"March!" Mama said. "By the time you're back, I'll be finished, and you can have the iron."

"Oh, goody. Your generosity is boundless."

"No *Days of Our Lives* for three weeks," Mama said casually as she spray-starched the shirt collar.

"What?!" Myra Sue exclaimed. "Have I not been persecuted enough?"

"A month, then," Mama said.

"A month! Are you crazy?"

"No *Days of Our Lives* until Labor Day," Mama said calmly. That meant that school would start before my goofy sister was allowed to watch her favorite daytime TV. Those people on her soap would just have to do without her until Christmas vacation.

Myra Sue's lips flew apart, and I could see she was fixing to keep on running her mouth.

"Boy, you just don't know when to stop, do you?" I blurted. She looked at me right quick.

"Be quiet!" she screamed, then ran from the kitchen, blubbering like a spoiled brat.

Mama just kept ironing as if she weren't as mad as a wet hen. Pretty soon she put the last shirt on a hanger and started to carry them all away. I stopped her.

"Mama?"

"What is it, April Grace?" Her voice sounded normal, and her cheeks weren't so bright pink anymore.

"Mama, when you were pregnant with Myra Sue, were you ever bitten by a weasel, or maybe a rabid possum?" I asked.

She looked at me from the doorway. "What a question! Of course not."

I sat at the table after she left. Of course not, I thought. 'Cause she'd never been pregnant with Myra Sue. But something awful must have bitten Myra Sue's real mother to cause her to give birth to such a bratty kid.

I had just come up with my next question when Grandma walked in the back door.

"Yoo-hoo, Lily," she called; then she saw me. "Good morning, April," she said, all big smiles.

"Hey, Grandma," I said. "Queenie still in the house?"

"Oh, sure. But chasing after her did me in. I need to lose some weight." She patted her round tummy and slid her hands down her thighs.

"If you did that, you wouldn't look like Grandma."

"Piffle! I could use some fixin' up. Time was when I was right pretty." She poured herself a cup of coffee and sat down at the table just as Mama came back into the kitchen. "Mornin', Lily," Grandma said.

Mama greeted her, but it was easy to see she was distracted. Grandma looked at me, then back at my mother, who began to wash beans in clear, cool water.

"Reckon you weren't none too happy with Myra Sue's new hair," Grandma said, then took a noisy slurp of coffee.

"Did you ever!" Mama burst out, throwing a handful of beans into a colander to drain. "What in the world got into her?"

As if whatever had gotten into her wasn't snoozing until the crack of noon right down the hall.

"It's her age, Lily. Be grateful she hasn't pierced something. I hear that's all the rage nowadays. In fact, I saw a girl at Ernie's Grocerteria the other day with something pinned in the side of her nose that looked like a growth the doctor burned off mine years ago." She took another good swallow of coffee.

"But she's becoming so hateful, Mama Grace," Mama said. "Sarcastic, you know. Short-tempered. And she's suddenly taken on this . . . this superior tone of voice that makes my skin crawl—"

"Just like Isabel St. James," I muttered, but they ignored me.

"—and she's all but quit eating. Why, a couple of days ago I caught her staring at herself in the mirror, saying something about her huge butt. Where does she get that notion?"

"Isabel St. James," I said even louder, but they didn't even glance my way.

Grandma sighed. "I reckon every fourteen-year-old girl

thinks she's too fat, or too skinny, or her nose is too big, or her eyes are too small. I reckon all of 'em are sarcastic and temperamental at least part of the time. I sure was. 'Course, my mama whupped the daylights out of me whenever I was sassy-mouthed."

Mama nodded while she packed a quart jar with broken beans.

"Aunt Maxie made me suck on a bar of pine tar soap when she thought I was impudent." She shuddered. "Maybe I should wash out Myra Sue's mouth?"

"You shouldn't let her hang around Isabel St. James for the rest of forever," I said in what I considered to be a grown-up tone of voice.

Both women looked at me as if they thought I'd just sprouted from the kitchen chair that minute.

"April Grace," Mama said, "go clean your room."

I looked down at my plate. "But I'm still eating." Given that they'd just been worried about Myra Sue not eating enough, I figured this earned me my place at the table for a few more minutes.

She glanced at my half-full plate of food. "Then sit there and finish, but please don't interrupt, honey. We're talking."

She stopped in mid-chore and poured a cup of coffee. Sitting down across from Grandma, she said, "I've grounded her from that soap opera until Labor Day—watching that thing can't be good for her. And she's going to iron the sheets this morning." She let out a deep breath, then sipped her coffee. "I've always hoped chores will make her more responsible and grown-up, but I just don't know."

"Be patient," Grandma told her. "You've never been the parent of a teenager before. Worst thing you can do is over-react. And Lily, just between you and me and the lamppost, you know having that woman living here isn't . . ."

Grandma's voice trailed into silence as Mama slid a glance at me and shook her head. They dropped the subject, but I knew they weren't through discussing it.

Myra Sue stomped in from outside and plunked down the laundry basket full of clean sheets and pillowcases. She ignored Grandma and slammed a mean glare at Mama. Mama gave her a look that said Myra Sue might very well be on Social Security before she ever watched another episode of *Days*. My sister picked up a pillowcase, put it on the ironing board, and got to work.

Mama and Grandma watched her for a while. Grandma stared at her hair.

"Faye the one who took out that awful black dye?"

"Yes. She wanted to put on a rinse to tone down that orange cast, but I figure this way, Myra Sue will remember how foolish she was. And if she behaves herself for a week or two, I'll have Faye color it so it looks normal."

Myra Sue looked up. "Really? Will you, Mama?"

"If you behave yourself," Mama repeated.

"And eat," Grandma whispered to Mama.

"And eat," Mama said.

My sister stopped ironing. "But look at me. I'm a house!"

Grandma snorted. "If you're a house then I'm a barn. I'm two barns."

Myra Sue rolled her eyes. "You're old, Grandma, so it's

okay to be fat. But I'm too young. And I can't be as graceful as a gazelle if I have the figure of a warthog!"

"You aren't fat!" all three of us said together, as if we'd rehearsed it. Myra Sue rolled her eyes.

Mama sipped her coffee until she drank it all; then she got up and resumed work with the beans.

"Then I hope you like going to school with orange hair, because you will if you keep refusing to eat," she said, looking very calm and determined.

Boy, oh boy, you should have seen ole Myra Sue think about her choices. She didn't say anything, but you could tell her little pea-brain steamed. No one spoke, and it seemed the good stuff was over. I finished my eggs, which had turned cold, and drank my milk, which had turned warm.

Just about the time I got up and started to take my plate to the sink, Grandma said, "S'pose you could show me how to paint my face a little bit, Lily?"

Well, I sat right back down. Myra Sue looked up from the ironing. Mama's lips flew apart.

"You mean use makeup?" she asked, her eyes round.

Grandma nodded.

"Why, you've never . . . have you?"

"I use face powder now and again, and when I was young I used lipstick, but Mike's daddy never liked seeing a woman's face painted, so I quit."

"Why do you want to paint it now, Grandma?" I asked.

She looked at me. "'Cause."

"I'm curious myself, Mama Grace," said Mama. "Why now?"

"Why not now?" Grandma countered with a bright smile. "There's no time like the present!"

All three of us looked at her until she squirmed like a fish worm.

"Well, if you all are gonna hound me this way, I might as well tell you. Jeffrey is taking me to the Veranda Club up in Branson on Saturday night, and then we're going to a music show. I want to look nice. I'm going to Blue Reed tomorrow and buy me a fancy dress. And shoes."

"*And shoes?*" The three of us spoke in unison for the second time. Grandma never wore anything but those ugly librarian/teacher/nurse shoes.

"High heels?" Myra Sue gasped.

"Mercy no. Well, not *high* high heels. I'd break my neck. But something pretty, to go with a fancy dress."

There was a short silence while we all absorbed this development; then Mama spoke up.

"So. The Veranda Club, huh? Pretty classy."

Grandma smiled. "Yes, isn't it? I ain't never been there. Hope I don't spill anything."

I had other things besides table manners on my mind. Grandma driving that sixty-mile trip into Blue Reed tomorrow and me going along, to be specific.

"Is Mr. Rance taking you to Blue Reed tomorrow?" I asked.

Grandma stared into her coffee cup, got up, and poured herself more. "Of course. I'd never drive that far alone." She turned and gave us a tight little smile. "You all would have a fit if I tried. Wouldn't you?"

"Now, Mama Grace, we just want you to be safe on the road." Mama's voice was all soft and nice, like when I'm sick and she's giving me bad-tasting medicine.

Grandma took a sip from her cup. "So, Lily. Will you help me fix up my face?"

"I'm no beauty queen expert," Mama said, "but I guess I know how to put on makeup about as well as anyone."

Now, you'd think my sister woulda had enough sense not to say anything else, wouldn't you? But Myra Sue just had to stop ironing and open her big mouth.

"If you want an expert, Grandma, get Isabel to help you. She's been on the stage. She knows how to look beautiful."

Well, I about choked.

"Your grandmother does not need Isabel St. James helping her with makeup." Mama's voice was strained, as if she wanted to say more but wouldn't. She continued to work without turning around.

"My stars, no!" Grandma declared. "If I wanted to look like a scarecrow, I could do it my own—"

None of us had heard the bedroom door open, but I can tell you every one of us saw Isabel come into the room just as Grandma said this.

Isabel stood in the doorway and looked at us for a minute. Then her lower lip quivered. A second later her eyes filled with tears. Without a word, she turned and ran down the hall, back to the bedroom. The door closed.

Well, I hate to admit it, but for once in my life, I felt some human compassion for Isabel St. James.

"Oh dear," Mama said after a little bit. She grabbed a towel and dried her hands. "Well, I better go see to her."

"Mebbe I oughta—" Grandma started.

Mama held up one hand. "No, Mama Grace. I'll talk to her." She paused at the door and said to me, "While I'm with Isabel, go ahead and stack those breakfast dishes, will you, honey? And Myra Sue, you can just do that pillow slip again. The object of ironing is to get rid of wrinkles, not put them in. I'll check your work when I come back."

For a minute or two after Mama left, Grandma leaned her backside against the edge of the cabinet and stared at the floor.

Pretty soon, without looking up, she said, "Well, now, I feel real bad. I didn't mean to hurt that woman's feelings." She took in a deep breath and let it out real slow.

"Don't worry, Grandma," I said. "We didn't know Isabel St. James had feelings."

She looked up and frowned. "Ever'body has feelings. You know, I'd forgotten for a minute that she was here."

"This Saturday—that's the day after tomorrow, Grandma—they will have been in our house for three entire weeks!" I nearly hollered. "How could you forget that?"

"Oh, I dunno. All wrapped up in excitement, I reckon."

"Excitement over Mr. Rance?" I asked.

She nodded, and I had to force myself real hard to remember our talk about thinking good things about him. If he had Grandma so excited she was starting to forget things. . . . well, I kinda shuddered inside myself.

"Well then, I am just appalled," Myra Sue proclaimed. "Absolutely devastated that—"

"You'd best keep ironing," Grandma told her. "In case you haven't noticed, your mama's nerves is about shot."

Myra Sue blinked a bunch of times. She opened her mouth to reply, then seemed to think the better of it. Instead, her face got as frowny as a bulldog's, and she picked up another pillowcase.

Grandma watched her for a minute; then she looked at me over her coffee cup. She took a good-size drink.

"You been thinking about what we discussed in the café?" she asked me.

Ole Myra Sue's head snapped up again. She eyeballed us both suspiciously.

"We wasn't talking about you," I told her, "so don't get your hopes up."

She stuck out her tongue, and I crossed my eyes. Grandma heaved a sigh.

"Sorry, Grandma. And I been thinking about what you told me," I said before she could lecture us on good behavior. "I'm trying to do my best."

"I hope so," she said, and sighed again.

I looked at my dear ole grandma and realized how much I loved her, and how much I didn't want anyone to hurt her, especially that sneaky old man. But knowing Grandma the way I do, I knew I had to get something factual on him, or she'd never listen to me.

"Grandma?" I said, real casual and offhand.

"Woo?" She looked at me.

"Where'd Mr. Rance live in Texas?"

"On a horse ranch. You know that."

"Yeah, but what town?"

"Town?" She sounded like she'd never heard the word before. "Why, I don't know that he ever said. Maybe he didn't get into town very often. Why are you so interested in that?"

I shrugged, again real casual-like. "Oh, you know. Just trying to get to know him a little better so I can like him."

She gave me this big, bright smile, and suddenly she didn't look so old. I could almost imagine what she might have looked like when she was young and pretty. I felt a little guilty that I had to spoil her dreams of Prince Charming.

"That's my girl!" She hugged me. "You know, now that I think about it, he talks about Beauhide County a lot. You can ask him sometime about the town he grew up in." She paused. "But don't talk about his wife anymore. He don't like talking about Emmaline, and I can't blame him. She ain't been dead a year yet, and it probably hurts him to think of her."

Hmm. Maybe.

Mama popped her head around the doorway between the kitchen and the hall.

"Mama Grace, would you come in here for a minute?"

Grandma set her coffee mug on the counter. She sucked in a deep breath like she was sucking in something to help her deal with ole Isabel. After she left the room, Myra Sue and I looked at each other. My sister developed a snooty little smile, but she didn't speak and neither did I. We concentrated on our chores, and I got busy plotting the next step in my investigation.

NINETEEN

Just Like a Real Detective, Sort Of

❀

Mama came into the kitchen a little later, but Grandma was not with her.

"What's up with Isabel and Grandma?" I asked.

Myra Sue used the excuse of conversation to stop ironing. "Yes, Mother, what's going on in there?"

Mama examined the pillowcases.

"These'll do," she said. "And never you mind about what's going on, either one of you. Myra Sue, when you're finished with your ironing, you may get busy on this other basket of beans. April Grace, you come with me. We need to pick the tomatoes before the sun cooks them on the vine."

I hated picking tomatoes.

"I should probably clean my room," I said.

Mama pulled a billed cap on over her curly red hair, picked up some sunscreen lotion she kept on the shelf next to the back door, and began rubbing it on her face, neck, and arms. She didn't want more freckles.

"I know. You may clean it when we're through picking." She grinned at me like she'd just given me a Mars bar. "Put on some of this sunscreen, then nip out to the garden. Double time."

While we pulled the plump, heavy tomatoes off the vine, I said, "My library books are due tomorrow. Are you going to town?"

She didn't look up. "I need some canning salt and few other things. I can drop you off at the library while I run to the store."

When we went back into the house, ole Myra Sue, Isabel, and Grandma sat at the kitchen table, breaking beans and putting them into big pans on their laps. No one looked mad or even peeved.

Grandma eyed our load of tomatoes. "Well, looks like you girls have been busy!"

"Are you going to town tomorrow?" Myra Sue said. "I need to go to the—"

"You're not going anywhere tomorrow," Mama told her. Myra Sue's lower lip pooched until it nearly reached the floor, but Mama ignored it.

Grandma put aside her pan of beans and got up. She and Mama began sorting the tomatoes.

"Here's a whopper," Grandma said, holding up one as big as a basketball. Well, not that big. But big. "Let's have hamburgers for dinner. I got me some nice, sweet red onions at Ernie's yesterday. April, run over to my place and get a couple of them onions. And bring some potatoes. Might as well have fried taters too."

I sent a glance to Isabel, but she didn't react to the menu. Not even a flicker of a false eyelash. Instead, she seemed real intent on doing the beans, almost as if she enjoyed it, for Pete's sake.

As I braved the blazing sun and crossed the field to Grandma's house, I wondered why Grandma never asked Myra Sue to run these errands for her. In my opinion, ole Myra could do with a trot across the field just to take some of the sass out of her. But it was always, "April, run over to my house and do this," or, "April, trot across the field to my place and bring back that."

Boy, sometimes being a kid stinks.

❀

The next morning, Mama and I left Myra Sue sulking at home while we went into town. It was a treat to be alone with my mama, because usually Myra Sue is always there to whine and complain and take most of Mama's attention. But that day, it was just the two of us. I hoped we'd stop at Ruby's Place for my most favorite treat in the whole entire world.

"Can we stop for a Pepsi slush?" I asked.

"We'll see." Mama navigated around the rocks and ruts, and I figured my best chance at having the treat was to keep quiet. Even when we got out on the highway, I chose to be a perfect little lady and talked only of polite things, like the weather and the dust on Rough Creek Road, and how glad I was that Daisy was our dog. But boy, oh boy, I was itching to know what had transpired between Mama and Grandma and Isabel St. James the day before. I reckon I never will know the details of that meeting.

At one point I said, "Mama, do you like Mr. Rance?"

"Why do you ask that?"

"Well, do you?"

She didn't answer right away, and I could see she was thinking about her reply. Finally she said, "He's good company for your grandma."

"So you don't like him?"

She gave me a Look. I figured I might blow my chance for a Pepsi slush, but I pressed on. "Can you name one thing you like about him?"

"I just said he was good company for your grandma."

"I don't mean that. I mean something about *him*, personal."

She pulled in a deep breath and then took her sweet time exhaling it.

"He has a nice, strong voice," she said at last.

Oh brother. My mama, who'd been able to forgive her great-aunt and nurse the woman until she died, could find nothing good to say about that old man, because believe you me, his big mouth was *not* a positive asset.

"I've been trying to like him but—" I began, and Mama interrupted.

"Good. You just keep on trying to like him, and pretty soon you'll like him for real."

I stared at her with my mouth hanging open. She could not be serious. But she was. And I could tell by her expression she did not want to discuss Mr. Rance further. Boy, oh boy, did I have my work cut out for me.

In the library parking lot, Mama stopped the car and said, "Now, I won't be long. So if you get more books, be quick about it, and wait for me at the entrance."

Hoping I could take care of business in a hurry, I ran into the library, slapped my books down on the return counter, and waited impatiently for Miss Delaine to get off the telephone. Wouldn't you know that would be the day somebody called to ask how to spell *acidophilus* or *ignoramus* or some crazy word like that? The other librarian, Mrs. Heathcliff, was always frowny and grouchy, and she didn't like kids. I hoped I didn't have to deal with her because she'd probably never cooperate.

"Well, Miss April Grace Reilly, one of my favorite library users!" Miss Delaine greeted when she hung up the telephone and closed the dictionary on the desk. "You look all excited." She smiled at me.

"Yes'm. I need some information, and I don't know how to get it."

"You came to the right place. What do you need?"

"I want to find out about someone who died somewhere," I said.

"You mean a historical figure?" Miss Delaine asked.

"No," I said. "I mean a woman who died last year down in Texas."

She gave me a funny look, but she reached for a notepad and took the pen from behind her ear.

"I assume you have a name?"

"Yes'm," I said. "Mrs. Emmaline Rance." I didn't worry too much about her making any connection between Emmaline Rance and Jeffrey Rance. That old man probably didn't read and never used the library.

"And where in Texas?"

"Well, I don't know the town. But the county is Beauhide."

"Beauhide?" She wrote that down too. "I need a date."

"Around Christmastime, last year."

"Hmm." She stared down at the paper.

"Can you find out anything about how she died?" I asked.

That brought her eyes square on my face. "You want her obituary?"

"Will that tell about her and how she died, like if she had been strangled or poisoned or died from a long illness or got kicked in the head by a horse or something?" I asked.

She gave me another funny look, and I don't mean funny ha-ha. "It might. Sometimes all an obituary contains is the bare facts. You know, name, dates of birth and death, names of survivors."

"Hmm," I said.

The expression on her face said she might be fixing to ask me some probing questions, and I preferred not to blurt right out that I thought Mr. Rance might have rubbed out his missus.

I said, "Well, I'd like to know about her life. I'm getting ready to write an essay about Texas women who've died."

She gave me the funniest look yet. "That's an odd topic."

I thought fast. "Well, you know, I'm going into sixth grade, and I hear my teacher expects us to write lots and lots. I want to be prepared. In fact, I'm working on 'What Happened During My Summer Vacation' already."

She kept looking at me as if she thought I had two heads with a horn growing out of the middle of each one. But what she said was, "Well, I'm glad to see that you're getting prepared."

You can tell that Miss Delaine has Real Class.

"Reckon we can locate more information on Mrs. Rance?" I asked.

She hesitated, then nodded. "I think so. I'll get in touch with the library in Beauhide County, see what they have. Will that work for you?"

I was so happy that my grin hurt my face.

"That'll be great!" Then I lowered my voice and added, "But could we keep this just between us? I don't want anyone else writing essays on women who've died in Texas."

"Okay," she whispered. "But I don't think you need to worry."

"Not even my mama." When Miss Delaine frowned, I added real quick, "I want to surprise her and Daddy with all my early writing."

"All right. It'll be our secret." As I turned to go find a book to check out, she said, "April Grace, I hope you'll let me read your composition. It sounds . . . fascinating."

If all went well, my "composition" might get printed right there on the front page of the *Cedar Ridge Teller*, with big black headlines, and right next to it, a photo of Jeffrey Rance being hauled to the Big House for murdering his wife to get insurance money to buy a brand-new, red Dodge Ram and then hiding from the law on Rough Creek Road. If that happened, I wouldn't have to worry anymore about him doing Grandma any mischief.

❀

I guess you could say my backside got sore the rest of the day from sitting on pins and needles waiting to hear from Miss Delaine. I hoped she'd hurry and get me that information about Mr. Rance because the next day was Saturday, and that was the day of the Big Date. But she didn't.

I called the library bright and early on Saturday, hoping for a miracle. Mrs. Heathcliff answered the phone and told me in a real snotty voice that Miss Delaine wasn't working that day.

I asked if she knew anything about the information Miss Delaine was getting for me.

"I do not," she said, all snippy and curt. "If she said she'd call you, then she will. Bothering the other librarians with your questions will not hurry the process." Then she hung up on me. Boy, oh boy.

At lunch, while Mama and Daddy and me and Ian ate beans and cornbread, Isabel said she wasn't hungry. She sat on the front porch and smoked. Myra Sue kept saying she wasn't hungry, either, and needed to go work out, but she wasn't getting away with it. You'd think after three weeks, ole Myra Sue would learn she couldn't get away with everything Isabel did, even though she kept trying. She finally choked down a little yogurt and gagged on a sliced tomato.

Daddy watched her for a while. He sat back in his chair and frowned at her real big. His eyes shone bright blue in a face all brown from the sun.

"I don't have time to sit here and watch you try not to eat, Myra Sue," he said.

"Then don't," Myra Sue said. "I've been eating without your help for years and years."

I stopped chewing so I could hear whatever new punishment would be added to her list.

Daddy looked at Mama. "Honey, I'm sorry to ask this of you, but maybe if you'd fix her a grilled cheese? I seem to remember that being her favorite."

"I can do that, but—"

"Don't bother, Mother. I refuse to eat such a greasy, nasty thing."

Daddy stared at her so hard that even I squirmed.

"Your mother will fix it, and you will eat it while I go back to fixing the fence."

"I won't!" She tried to stare him down, but my daddy is stubborn.

"Wipe that sneer off your face, Myra Sue. You'll sit here until you eat it, or until you're old and gray. Take your choice."

She pooched out her lower lip and folded her arms across her chest. I figured that dumb girl would not see another episode of *Days of Our Lives* until she saw the Pearly Gates.

Right then, the back screen door opened and Grandma came in. I stared at her, and what I saw caused a great big hunk of cornbread to hit my stomach, unchewed.

"Grandma!" I screamed, goggling and choking. "What did you do to your hair?"

Gone was the soft gray bun she'd worn the whole entire time I've known her—which has been my whole entire life. Her hair was now a soft brown with a touch of red, and it was short, short, *short*. I nearly died right there at the dining table. Every one of us stared at her as if she'd lost her mind, which I figured she must have done.

"It's a modified pixie cut. Like it?" She patted that modified pixie and giggled. "I went to Bella Donna's in Blue Reed."

Blue Reed was sixty miles away. Probably Faye at Cedar Ridge, or Jane in Ava, or any other beauty shop person in a fifty-mile radius never in a million years woulda done what had been did to Grandma's hair. I hated it.

She held up a sack from Walmart. "Here's the makeup I bought for the rest of my makeover. Where's Isabel?"

Daddy coughed so hard, I thought he'd collapse all his sinus cavities and both lungs. Ian's eyes grew big, but he didn't say a word.

"We gotta get back to work on that fence on the back pasture before I turn the cows out in it," Daddy said in a strangled voice as he hightailed it out of the kitchen with Ian right behind him. A second later he opened the back door again, stuck his head in, and said, "You eat your food, Myra Sue."

Mama didn't make that grilled cheese right away. She was too busy gawking at Grandma.

TWENTY

Grandma Remade

♫

My sister seemed to forget about gagging on her lunch.

"Grandmother," she said in That Tone, "if you were going to change your hair, why in the world did you choose that silly style?" She must have forgotten her own orange head. "It's much too young for you."

"Myra Sue!" Mama gave her the Look. She finally dragged her eyes away from Grandma long enough to start the grilled cheese sandwich for Myra Sue.

Grandma didn't seem as disappointed by that reaction as you might think. In fact, she looked kinda smug when she replied, "Isabel suggested it. She showed me a picture of an older woman with this same style in one of her dance magazines. Chas at Petite ChouChou Salon knew just who she was talking about. He done a real good job, didn't he?"

My sister blinked a dozen or so times. Boy, she was getting as good at it as Isabel.

"Let me look at it again. Let me see the back," Myra Sue said. "Oh yes! Now I see it. It's darling! Just perfect for you! You look an absolute dear, Grandmother."

Oh brother. I hated it even more, knowing ole Isabel had been the one to think it up.

The hinges of the front screen creaked as the door opened. You could hear the sharp *click, click, click* of high heels on the wood floor, and a second later ole Isabel herself clipped into the kitchen. She brought the stink of her nasty cigarettes right in with her.

"Grace!" she said, beaming. Boy, you wouldn't believe it,

but when Isabel beamed like that, her whole face lit up. I'd never seen such a thing. It actually made her look kind of . . . pretty. "Your hair is darling!"

She put down her cigarettes and empty coffee cup to circle Grandma as if the woman were a mare for sale during the Fox Trotters weekend up in Missouri. "Absolutely darling!"

"That's what I said," said Myra Sue, giving the rest of us a superior smirk.

"She doesn't look like Grandma with that hair," I declared. "And what is this? Everybody Color Your Hair Week? Mama, you'll stay a redhead, won't you?"

"That's enough, April Grace," Mama said. "What's with you two girls, anyway? Where are your manners?" She turned to the woman who clawed into Grandma's Walmart sack like she was digging for gold. "Isabel, would you like another cup of coffee?"

Isabel frowned critically at a bottle of Maybelline foundation she pulled out of the sack. Without looking up, she picked up her cup and held it out.

"Yes," she said.

"Please," I added.

This time Mama didn't say a word to me as she took the cup and filled it. I figured since she'd just brought up the subject of good manners, she didn't want to contradict herself.

"Let's see what else you have," Isabel said to Grandma as she dove into the bag again and emptied it with gusto. "Rose blush, peach blush, blue eye shadow, green eye shadow, pink eye shadow, silver eye shadow, ivory powder, beige powder, light and dark concealer, blue eyeliner, black eyeliner, brown eyebrow pencil. Oh, didn't you get tweezers? Your eyebrows . . . Well, do you really want woolly worms above your eyes? It works for Brooke Shields, but she's a young girl."

"I got tweezers at home," Grandma said.

"Well, we must have them," said Isabel.

"We have tweezers," Myra Sue practically shouted in her enthusiasm to be of assistance. "Shall I get them, Isabel darling?"

"Yes, dearest. Run and fetch them, though I doubt they will be of a quality I need. On second thought, bring me the ones out of my makeup case on the dresser."

I did not approve of this whole business.

"Tweezers is tweezers," I muttered. Isabel looked at me darkly. "Are you gonna paint her face right here in the kitchen?" I asked. "Mama, won't they be in your way?"

"It's okay." She smiled as she sat down. "I want to see Mama Grace transform into a movie star." She looked at the assortment of makeup on the table. "My goodness, Isabel, are you going to put all this on her?"

"I'll use what I need. In the absence of a salon nearby, I believe I can do a reasonable job. I am a professional, after all."

I tried to remember what Grandma had told me, and I thought of Mama's generous attitude toward Isabel. I attempted to find something nice about the woman. I thought hard and came up with this: she's offering to help without being begged.

Well, what did you expect? That's the best I could do with what I had to work with.

Mama eyed the receipt. "Mama Grace, this was quite an expense."

Grandma reached out and snatched the ticket from her.

"It's all right. I want to look nice," Grandma said as she began to remove items from their individual packaging.

"But will you ever use any of this again?" Mama asked.

Grandma stuffed discarded wrappings into the store sack. "If Isabel will teach me how to put it on, yes."

A vision of Bozo the Clown popped into my head, so I had a coughing fit.

Myra Sue trotted into the room with the tweezers. "These are just magnificent," she sighed, handing them to Isabel.

They looked exactly like the ones in our medicine cabinet, and I said so, but no one paid me the least bit of attention.

Only because I did not want to witness the process by which my grandmother was to be transformed, I jumped up from the table and began to clean up the kitchen. No one said a single, solitary word about my industry.

"Eyebrows first," Isabel announced. "Now, Grace, you'll have to relax. And don't draw your face up like that. This won't hurt a bit."

I heard plenty of grunts and yips as eyebrows came out by the roots.

"What are you going to wear tonight, Grandmother?" Myra Sue asked at one point.

"Yes, tell us!" Mama said.

"You did buy something in a boutique, didn't you?" asked Isabel. "You aren't wearing some discount-store bargain, are you?"

"Yowch! Be careful there, sis," Grandma said. "You're gonna draw blood yet. I bought me the prettiest dark-green dress you ever saw at Sally's on the Square. It's got a big, lacy collar and padded shoulders. Y'know, I ain't worn padded shoulders since 1945! Who'da thought that now in the 1980s they'd be in style again? And there's lace on the bodice and a wide belt."

"What did Mr. Rance think of your haircut and new dress?" Mama asked.

Grandma gave her a blank stare. "Woo?" she asked, all innocent like.

"You said he was taking you to Blue Reed," I piped up.

She had the grace to blush. "Well, now, he'd didn't take me."

"Mama Grace! Did you go by yourself?" Mama said. "You shouldn't have—"

"I didn't want to be bothered, Lily! Sometimes I'd like to have some time to myself, do some things without everybody watching me. You people won't even let me go to Cedar Ridge to buy groceries by myself anymore. Gotta send April with me to make sure I don't die on the way there. You act like I'm old!" She sounded plumb disgusted.

"We just want what's best for you, Grandma," I told her, though it was certainly never my idea to ride along with her.

"That's right," Mama said.

"Well, then." Grandma acted like there was no more to be said, so the rest of us shut our mouths. I turned around and went back to my dishwashing. But about a minute later she hollered, "*Oh my!* I just thought of something awful!"

She said this with such panic that I spun around, slinging soapy water across the cabinets, floors, and the makeup artist herself. Isabel sputtered and spewed way more than a few drops of dishwater called for.

"What's wrong, Grandma?" I said, ignoring Isabel's glare. She had plucked away half an eyebrow, and I had to swallow hard to keep from screaming when I saw it.

"My purse!" Grandma nearly shouted. "I don't have a purse."

Now, I figured this meant she had misplaced it again. I dragged my horrified gaze from her brows.

"Well, I can go find it for you," I offered. "Did you look in the crisper of the refrigerator? You left it there just last—"

"No, no. Not that purse," Grandma said. "I mean an evening bag. I need something fancy to go with my new dress and my new shoes."

"And your new hair," added Mama.

"And your fabulous new face," Myra Sue put in.

"Yes, it must be something elegant," Isabel said.

"Something chick," Grandma agreed, nodding.

Isabel and Myra Sue exchanged a look that I did not like.

"If Grandma wants to look chick," I told them hotly, "then that's her perfect right."

"It's not *chick*," my sister said. "It's pronounced 'sheek.'"

"Well, it's spelled *chick*," Grandma said.

"Yeah," I agreed. "*Chick*."

"It's spelled c-h-i-c. It's French," Myra Sue said, all snooty.

"Oo la la," I said. "Who cares?"

"Mama Grace, you are going to look just beautiful whether you have an evening bag or not," Mama said.

"But I want everything to be perfect," said Grandma. "Tonight might be very important."

Mama, Myra Sue, and I all gawked at her. Isabel tilted Grandma's head and began yanking out the little tiny hairs again.

"What do you mean, *important*?" Mama asked.

"Now, you must hold your head still, Grace," Isabel said as Grandma yelped and frowned.

Grandma opened one eye and looked at her. "Well, that blamed thing hurts! Are you plucking out ever' last eyebrow I ever grew?"

"She's—" I began, but Isabel interrupted.

"The price of beauty is pain." She scrunched up her face in concentration and began tweezing again. Grandma scrunched her face in torture and squeezed her eyes shut.

"Well, then, I must be a real find of great beauty," she declared. "And I sure wish I had me a nice purse."

"What do you mean, *important*?" Mama asked again. "You said tonight might be important. Are you expecting Mr. Rance to—"

"I'm expecting a nice evening with lots more nice evenings to follow, that's all. So don't go making up notions where none exist."

"What notions?" I asked. I gave the matter some thought before it hit me. "Boy, oh boy," I said loudly. "I hope you don't plan to make that old man my new grandpa."

Mama gave me a look that caused me to say, "Just kidding, Grandma. I hope you have fun."

Mama held my gaze for a long time before she finally

turned away. But I'll tell you right now, if that bigmouthed old man was to become my new grandpa, I might have to change my name and depart for parts unknown.

I turned back to the dishes while the plucking and yelping went on. When I was almost finished, Grandma whooped so loud, I dropped a glass. It shattered on the floor, but I didn't care. I was ready to jump on Isabel's scrawny back if she hurt Grandma one more time.

"I got one!" Grandma announced, nearly standing up. "I got a purse."

"You do?" we all said together.

"I do. It's a little black beaded thing that I carried to the very first dance me and your grandpa went to."

I stared at her. "You don't dance."

"Not lately. But back in the day, when I was young and skinny and full of vinegar, I could cut the rug pretty good. And I kept that black bag. Oh, it's a pretty thing. Wait 'til you girls see it."

I began to wonder if Grandma was going off her rocker in excitement over her hot date. Just as if she read my mind, she looked at me.

"April Grace, I want you to run over to my house and look in the bottom drawer of that big chester-drawers in my bedroom. That purse is wrapped in tissue paper in a white box. Bring it here so's I can show it to the girls."

Well, I didn't really want to hang around and watch while Isabel continued to mutilate and renovate my grandma for old man Rance.

Quickly I finished the dishes and dried my hands. Just as

I went out the back door, I heard Mama say, "I'm going to make you that grilled cheese sandwich now, Myra Sue."

And ole Isabel squawked, "Oh my word, Lily! Do you really want to make her *fat*?"

TWENTY-ONE

Mr. Rance, the Prowler

☺

The hayfield had been mown and raked the day before, making it look wide and clean while the fresh hay dried in the sun. The tractor chugged on the north end of the field where Mr. Brett ran the baler. It banged and rattled as it scooped up fresh hay, pressed it in a bale, and deposited it back in the field like a chicken laying an egg. By this evening, huge, golden round bales would dot the field.

The sun was bright and hot above me until I reached the edge of Grandma's yard, where the trees threw out plenty of shade. And what do you think I saw? As if he'd tried to hide and not quite made it, Mr. Rance had parked on the far side of her house where we couldn't see his pickup from our kitchen window.

"What's he doing here?" I wondered aloud.

I walked past the house to the pickup. The cab was empty. On the porch, I peered through the front room window, trying to see if he were in the house, but I couldn't see much through Grandma's sheers. I opened the front door quietly. Once inside, I paused a minute to let my eyes adjust from the bright sun.

The odor of Old Spice hung thick in the air, but the old man was not in sight. I didn't see Queenie's spoiled white self, either, and I sure as the world hoped he hadn't let her out, 'cause I did not want to go on another cat chase in the near future. Or the far future either, for that matter.

Mr. Rance was not in the kitchen or the tiny laundry room right next to it. The bathroom door was open, and it was obvious he wasn't in there. Then I heard him in the bed-room, rustling around.

Until I could see what he was up to, I didn't want him to know I was there. I tiptoed to the open door and stood there facing his back. He was looking under the bed. Then he moved over to the highboy—Grandma's tall chest of drawers—in the corner, and felt around on top of it. He went over to the dresser, opened a drawer, and pawed through it. After a bit, he slammed it shut, opened another, and rummaged around in it for a while.

I hollered loud so he'd he hear me good and clear. "If you're looking for Grandma, she ain't in there. She's over at our house."

Guess Mr. Rance had his hearing aids turned on this time, because he jumped like he'd been shot. When he turned, his face was as red as his pickup. For a minute he stared at me, and I could almost see the wheels turning in his brain.

"Well, young'un!" he said at last, grinning real big. "Let's see, now . . . it's Johnny, ain't it?"

I folded my arms and glared at him.

"Why are you messing with Grandma's things?"

"Why am I . . . ? Why, I ain't messin' with nothin', no sir-ree!" He glanced around. "No sirree, I ain't messin' with not one thing." He started toward me, saying, "Let's you and me go get us a little sweet tea in the kitchen."

I didn't move.

"Why were you going through those drawers?" I asked.

He stared down at me, and I wondered if he were decid-ing where to hide my body once he bumped me off. But I wasn't scared, and I wasn't about to be moved.

"You think I was snoopin'?" he asked. "That what you think?"

"Sure looked that way to me."

"Well, I wadn't. Not a bit of it. I wanted to surprise your granny and buy her some flowers to wear on her dress tonight."

I just looked at him.

"You know. Here." He tapped his left chest up by his shoulder. "Some real pretty flowers, but I didn't know what dress she was wearing, or what she'd like. I wanted to find out so's I know what to get her."

"So you were looking through her *drawers*?"

"Well, no. I mean, I *was* looking through her drawers, but I was looking for her hankies."

"Her hankies."

"Shore. Women fold their lacy hankies a certain way and wear their corsages on top of 'em so's their dresses stay clean. Didn't you know that?"

"I never heard such a thing," I declared. But I couldn't swear women didn't do it. I knew zip about corsages. Or lace hankies. "What kind of flowers?"

He cupped an ear. "How's 'at?"

"What kind of flowers in her corsage?"

"What kind?" he asked.

I nodded. The old goofball was stalling, and I knew it.

"Well, sir, I got her some real pretty ones," he said, finally.

"I thought you said you came over here to find out what she was wearing so you'd know what to get," I said.

Sweat was running down that big, red face pretty good.

"That's right, that's right. And now I know, so I better get goin' before the flower shop closes."

Before I could say another single, solitary word, that old man patted me on the head like an old coonhound, and then he left.

Well, you better believe I was going to tell Grandma and Daddy and Mama about all this business. But first, I wanted to see if I could figure out what Mr. Rance was really looking for, because the way he pilfered and muttered, I was pretty sure he hadn't found it.

I looked through the dresser drawers and found nothing but big white cotton panties, big white bras, big white cotton slips, and cotton and flannel nightgowns—some of which were so old you could see through 'em. I found her stockings and two drawers full of material for dresses. In a drawer with scarves and gloves, she kept lots of handkerchiefs. Some were flowered and some were plain. She had white ones and colored ones. But in all that searching, I found nothing that might inspire an old man to come looking for it. I sure didn't think Mr. Rance had taken any handkerchief with him either.

I turned and looked at that highboy. I wagged in a chair from the kitchen and put it in front of the chest; then I climbed up on it so I could see into the top drawer.

The drawers in that big old piece of furniture were as wide and deep as a treasure chest. The top drawer held a ton of old clothes and nothing else. And so did the next three. Why Grandma kept every dress she'd ever worn in the last fifty years is beyond me, unless it was to finally make that memory quilt she talked about so often.

The next two drawers contained more fabric—the kind she made her dresses out of. But there was nothing else in them, or under them. Not a diamond necklace, or a ruby ring, or a million bucks in twenty-dollar bills. Nothing.

When I got to the bottom drawer, I remembered what I'd been sent to fetch: Grandma's fancy evening purse, wrapped in tissue paper, in a white box, supposedly in this drawer. I found a bunch of old purses with missing clasps or torn handles, or falling-apart linings on the inside. Boy, oh boy, I didn't know my grandma was such a pack rat. Finally, there on the bottom was a flat, white box that had turned kinda yellow from age. When I opened it, a musty odor came up. It kinda smelled like old cologne. I pushed aside the tissue paper and finally saw the beaded black evening bag. I lifted it out of the box.

It was beautiful, just like Grandma said. The tiny black beads caught the light and glittered. That purse sure didn't have a missing clasp or broken handle. It looked brand-new. When I opened the tiny clasp, I could see that the silky lining was soft and shiny and not a bit torn. I figured it would look right pretty with Grandma's new dress and shoes. I figured, too, that once I told her about finding Mr. Rance pilfering in her dresser, she'd never want to go to the Veranda Club with him.

But I'd carry that purse to her anyway, because I'd been sent to get it. I had to prove I was trustworthy, so she'd believe me when I told her about that old man.

TWENTY-TWO

A Good Imagination Is a Terrible Thing to Waste

By the time I got back home, I heard female voices coming from the kitchen, and you'd never heard such giggling and talking in your life. Who woulda thought Grandma and Isabel and Myra Sue and my mama would all be laughing and chatting together like they were at a party loud enough to wake the dead?

I crossed the back porch and paused with shock when I heard Grandma go, "Wheee!" like she was dancing on the table or something. I rushed into the kitchen.

Well, she wasn't dancing on the table, but she sure gawked at herself in a full-length mirror that Isabel and Myra Sue held for her. It was the mirror that usually hung in Mama and Daddy's bedroom.

I stared at that woman. If I hadn't recognized her yellow print dress and ugly shoes, I'd never have known she was my grandma. Her eyebrows looked like the arch in St. Louis, or maybe the ones at McDonald's. And she had goop on her eyelids and heavy black eyelashes. Her cheeks were rosy, and her lips were red. In other words, she looked awful. She took her eyes off her own self long enough to glance at me.

"What d'ya think, April?" She patted her modified pixie cut.

Every thought I'd had in my brain that day and probably the day before left me stranded, completely blank. While I stared, everybody laughed, including Isabel—and let me tell you, her laugh is pretty scratchy and shrill. That's probably because she laughs about once a year and her laugh box has rusted.

"I believe," Mama said, "that for once in her life, April Grace Reilly is speechless."

"It's about time," Myra Sue said.

"Did you find my evening purse?" Grandma asked, bending closer to the mirror so she could stare into her own eyes.

I held up the bag.

She straightened, saw it, and, grinning like a monkey, took it from my slack fingers.

"What do you girls think of this?" The "girls" all murmured and giggled and exclaimed over the thing.

"It's beautiful, Grace." That was Isabel.

"Beautiful, Grandmother." That was Myra Sue.

"Really nice!" Mama added.

"Yes!" Grandma said. "Well, I'd better get to the house and finish getting ready. Think I can take a short little nap without messing up my hair or makeup?"

"I wouldn't. Shall I come with you and help you dress?" Isabel asked.

"Yes! Let's gather up this war paint here and scoot on over to my house. Wait 'til you see my shoes!"

"Me, too, Grandmother?" Myra Sue asked.

"You're helping me right here in this kitchen," Mama told my sister.

Myra Sue pooched out her lower lip as Grandma and Isabel went out the back door. Seemed to me if Grandma were going back over there, she didn't need to send me to get that purse. But I have never pretended to understand the grown-up mind. I don't think anyone understands it.

After about another minute, I finally collected my wits.

"Grandma was wearing way, way too much makeup," I said to the world in general.

"Help us with these tomatoes, April Grace," Mama said. "I'm scalding them right now, so you can dunk them in cold water, and Myra can pull off the skins."

"And her hair is ridiculous," I said.

"Don't piddle around," said Mama. "The peels come off easier if the skins are cold and the tomatoes are warm."

"And that old man is a sneak," I added.

Mama was standing by the stove, dunking fat tomatoes in hot water. She gave me a look over her shoulder.

"April Grace, are you jealous of your grandmother and her friend?"

"He's a sneaky old man," I said. "I caught him snooping around in her house."

Myra Sue looked up. So did Mama.

"What do you mean?" Mama asked.

"He was looking through her dresser drawers."

"He what?" Mama asked.

Glad she finally seemed to hear me at last, I said, "He was prowling around in the bedroom, looking through her dresser drawers. When I asked what he was doing, he said he was looking for a hankie. He said women sometimes fold up hankies and fix their corsages on them so their dresses don't get dirty."

Mama's face cleared.

"Oh, that. You're worried over nothing, April. He called over here, said he wanted to surprise her with a corsage that would go with her dress. He asked what she'd like."

"So there really is such a thing as pinning a corsage on a hankie?"

"I've never heard of it, but maybe it's what ladies do in Texas."

I frowned. "Did you tell him to go snooping in her drawers for a hankie?"

"No. But I'm sure if he wanted to have the corsage arranged on one of her pretty lace handkerchiefs, and—"

"Mama!" Myra Sue hollered. "Do you want that water to boil?"

She whirled. "Mercy, no!" She got busy messing with the tomatoes, and when I tried to tell her I didn't trust that old man, she acted like I was a little kid.

"April Grace, your imagination has always functioned in high gear," she said. "Remember last year when you thought you saw a black bear on Rough Creek Road? You called the sheriff! And it was just Mr. Brett's dog."

"So? Taz is a big black Chow. I can't help it if he looks like a bear. And he's not supposed to get out of his own yard. Besides—"

"Come over here and dunk these tomatoes in this ice water, April Grace," Mama said. "And do not say another word about your grandmother, her new look, or her boyfriend."

I figured if I mentioned the old goof reaching for Grandma's purse that time, or pretending to get a map out of the Corolla's glove compartment, or eyeballing everything on the table while he was supposed to be praying, she'd not listen to that either. Sometimes a good imagination can be a real burden.

There are days it does not pay to get out of bed, let alone try to save your own grandmother from disaster.

I decided I'd sneak off over to Grandma's and warn her since Mama wouldn't listen, but you know what? Sometimes it's like mothers can read their children's minds.

She said, "You're not stepping one foot out of this house, April Grace. I won't have you trying to foul up your grandmother's big night just because you don't like sharing her with someone else."

Boy, oh boy.

I hoped that old man didn't steal her wallet out of the beaded black evening bag right there on the dance floor of the Veranda Club.

I thought about calling the sheriff, but I remembered that time with Taz and Mr. Brett, and how the sheriff and three deputies came out, armed to the teeth, ready to shoot in case of a bear attack. . . . Well, I would've felt terrible if they'd shot Taz, who is a real sweet dog, even if he does look like a big black bear. Anyway, I figured the sheriff wouldn't believe me if I told him old man Rance got into my grandma's drawers.

Now, I admit that I have a vivid imagination. And I also confess that sometimes I exaggerate. But I'm telling you, I just couldn't rest easy in my mind thinking about Mr. Rance and Grandma all night.

TWENTY-THREE

Big News.
Big, Bad News.

✳

Mr. Rance proposed.

Yep, that's right. Mr. Rance proposed to my grandma that night in the Veranda Club.

Of course, none of us knew about it until the next afternoon when we were having our big Sunday dinner after church. Mama had made her famous chicken pie, which when you taste it makes you think you've died and gone to heaven. Everyone was at the table in the dining room, including that old man.

I chowed down on a thick, tender, crusty corner of that chicken pie and was smiling at the wonderfulness of the taste and texture when Mr. Rance quit cramming food into his own personal mouth and stood up.

"Here now!" he yelled. "We got us an announcement. Stand up, Miz Grace, darlin'."

Her face as red as sunset, Grandma stood. Mr. Rance grabbed her left hand and held it out so we could all see the humongous sparkler on her ring finger. How had we missed it until then?

"Oh!" Isabel shrieked. "Oh, oh, oh! Grace!" Trust ole Isabel to show life in the presence of a diamond. She nearly broke her neck jumping up from the chair and rushing to goggle that ring.

My own personal self, I thought the thing was way beyond cheesy and gaudy and could hardly believe my very own grandmother would wear such a thing. Of course, I'd never in a million years believed she would doll herself up like a senior citizen teenager, either, but there she sat, with blue and green eyeshadow and blush and red nail polish and everything.

"I ast Miz Grace to be my bride," Mr. Rance announced unnecessarily and at the top of his lungs, "and she said yes."

My stomach clenched.

Daddy and Mama looked a little stunned at first, but soon they smiled and nodded and ogled Grandma's ring. Myra Sue, of course, had leaped up from the table right behind her idol. Ian stayed where he was, but he smiled in a polite kind of way.

You know, after you're around him for a while, ole Ian isn't half bad. Most of the time I think he's too exhausted to be obnoxious.

"When's the lucky day?" Mama said.

"Well, we haven't quite agreed—" Grandma began.

"Two weeks from next Saturday," said the old man.

"Now, Jeffrey, I don't think—"

"I'll do the thinking for both of us, darlin'," he said, and he gave her a big fat smooch you could have heard on the top floor of the TCBY Tower in Little Rock. Everybody else laughed, but I didn't think it was a bit funny, and looking at Grandma, I wondered if her smile were real.

I pushed away my plate.

"April Grace," Mama said, "Don't you want to see Grandma's new ring?"

"I think I'm sick," I said. "May I leave the table?"

"She does look a mite pale, Lily," Grandma said.

Mama felt my forehead, peered in my eyes, and frowned. "Sick, huh?"

I nodded. "Go to your room, then," she said. "Crawl into bed, and I'll check on you later."

I not only crawled into bed—I pulled up the covers and hid my head beneath the pillow. I didn't even have the heart to read.

It must've been midafternoon when I heard my bedroom door open. Figuring it was Myra Sue, I didn't stir and hoped she'd only come in for her hairbrush or something. Whoever it was sat on the edge of the bed, tugged away the covers, and lifted the pillow from my head. I squeezed my eyes shut because I did not want to see anyone from my whole entire family.

"April, honey." It was Grandma.

"I reckon I don't have anything to say," I said. But I did. I had tons to say, but no one would listen to me. No one wanted to hear a word of it.

"Aren't you happy for me, April?"

I opened one eye and looked at her. "Are you kidding?"

For a minute, she just sat there and stroked my head with a real, real gentle touch.

"I know you don't like him, honey, but he's a good man."

I grunted.

"And he'll be a companion for me."

"You got us," I said. "Me and Mama and Daddy and even that dumb Myra Sue. Aren't we good enough?"

"Of course you are! But I—"

"Don't you love us anymore?" I heard my voice crack, but I swallowed hard so I wouldn't bust out bawling like a big, fat baby.

"Now, April Grace, you know I do. But at my age, I need someone around—"

"You said yesterday that you wanted to be left alone! You said you wanted to be able to do things on your own. That old man downstairs wouldn't even let you talk a while ago. He had to answer everything himself!"

She stopped smoothing my hair and clasped her hands in her lap. She sat there and looked at me. Then she said, "You realize I'm a living, breathing person, April Grace? I see you making that face. And I know you aren't going to completely understand what I'm about to say, but I'm going to say it anyway. I've been a widow for twenty years. That's a right long time to be the only person in the house late at night, or when the sun's first peeking into the sky in the morning. Or when your feelings are hurt, or something is so funny you laugh 'til you cry. A real person needs to share her life. Even an old person like me. The good Lord said, 'It is not good for the man to be alone.' Well, I reckon He meant it's not good for woman to be alone either, because I'm mighty tired of it."

"But Grandma. Why Mr. Rance?"

"He's a good man, honey," she said. "And he's tired of being alone too."

I sat up. "His wife's only been dead a few months. He ain't been alone very long. And he's always in town at the Koffee Kup, or else he's hanging around here or your house, so he's hardly ever alone at all." She just sat there, so I went on. "And you know something else? I caught him snooping in your house again yesterday when you weren't home. He said he was looking for hankies for your corsage, but I don't think he was. I think he was looking for something else."

"Like what?" she asked.

"I don't know," I said. "Something valuable."

"I don't have anything valuable."

"But I bet he don't know that," I said. "I bet he thinks you do, and he was trying to find it, and now he's going to marry you so's he can get it."

Then Grandma said, "Did you say he said he was getting me a corsage?"

"Yep. Didn't he?"

She didn't answer that. Instead she asked, real softly, "Don't you think Jeffrey wants me for me?"

I refused to answer that because both of us knew what I thought. We just looked at each other. For a time, she did not move. Then a tiny expression flickered in her eyes, and it grew until she looked really, really sad. I watched as something seemed to go out of her, like air leaking from a balloon.

The two of us had been close my whole entire life. There were a lot of times when I'd rather be with Grandma than anyone else, even Mama or Daddy. Sometimes, when it was just the two of us taking a nature walk, or sharing a glass of sweet tea, or just sitting on her sofa, looking at the old family album while she told me stories about our family, I thought she liked being with me better than anyone too. I thought we were best friends, and now she was going to be best friends with that icky old man. And it wasn't just that I was jealous. I was. But there was something strange about that man, I had no doubts.

But right then, when I saw how Grandma looked all deflated

and empty, I realized how much she wanted me to approve of that old goof. And there was only one way I could ever give him my stamp of approval.

I sat up and scrooched close to the edge of the bed. I leaned close and looked right into her eyes.

"Do you love him, Grandma? Do you love that old man? Does he make you happy?"

She looked away, then she took a deep breath and blew it out real slow. She got up stiffly, as if her bones ached right down to the marrow.

"It doesn't really matter to you, does it, April? Even if I loved him with my whole heart and soul, it wouldn't be enough for you, would it?"

Then she gave me such a look I couldn't speak because my throat ached too much. But she'd answered my question without saying it out loud: she did not love Jeffrey Rance.

Grandma walked from the room and closed the door softly behind her. I lay back down and pulled the covers over my head again.

※

It amazed me that for the next two weeks, all of us went about our regular business with the threat of an upcoming and totally inappropriate marriage in the near future. It's hotter'n blazes in late August, you know, but all us females just kept putting up the garden produce and doing the housework, while Daddy and Ian mended fences or went to town for parts or repaired equipment.

I thought I was going to die with the threat of Grandma's marriage hanging over our heads like a dark, ugly thunderstorm. At least school would be starting soon, and that was the only bright spot in my days.

"Well, is the wedding a week from Saturday or not?" Mama asked Grandma over their coffee the following Thursday.

"Jeffrey says at our age we shouldn't dawdle. And I see his point." She glanced at me. I just ate my Cheerios and tried to keep my big mouth shut. She said nothing else about that old man. Instead, she talked about the visiting preacher who'd held the service at church last Sunday.

"If you don't want to marry old man Rance, then don't," I said, interrupting her. I couldn't stop myself. It just came out.

Mama frowned at me. "April Grace, that was rude. And why would you say such a thing?"

Grandma and I looked at each other.

"I'm sorry if I was rude. I didn't mean to be. But Grandma doesn't want to marry him. Not in her heart where it matters. Right, Grandma?" I asked hopefully.

I waited with my fingers crossed for her to speak up. But she didn't, and I was so hurt and disappointed that I left the kitchen with half my cereal still in the bowl and went to the front door.

Every day for the last five weeks since the St. Jameses moved in, Myra Sue and Isabel had been using the shade of the porch every day to do their dancing stuff before the day got too hot. I very nearly went out on the front porch to exercise with them and work off being mad. Instead, I stood just this side of the screen door and watched for a while. Stretches and bends and crunches and twists weren't very entertaining, especially when being done by those two skinny-bones. I could've watched TV or read, but neither *Card Sharks* nor *Press Your Luck*—not even a book—would have helped right then. I guess I was just too disgusted with everything.

In the new black leotards and a neon pink headband Isabel had given her a couple of days ago, Myra Sue was starting to look as gaunt and spooky as her idol. It was so hot outside, I didn't see how Myra Sue could stand to wear those bright pink-and-black-striped leg warmers, but she did. When she twisted around and I got a good view of her back, I saw the sharp ridge of her spine and could practically count all her ribs. Starving herself seemed to be working, if she were trying to look withered like Isabel.

Watching those two only added to my disgust, so I gathered up my newest book, *The Hobbit*, then went outside and called Daisy. The two of us took off through the woods. I wanted to go off stomping, but we had to go slow because the day was heating up pretty fast, and Daisy is old and her white coat is thick.

We walked through the woods across the road and came out of the trees near the smallest east pasture, where Daddy and Ian were setting fence posts. Mr. Brett was there, too, several feet away, digging holes for the posts. His big arm muscles showed every time he rammed that post-hole digger into the hard ground.

"Miss April Grace!" Mr. Brett called out when he looked up and saw me. His teeth showed through his dark whiskers when he smiled. "How you doin', gal?"

"Hi, Mr. Brett. I'm fine." I wasn't fine, of course, but I

liked him and didn't want to bother him with my problems. Daisy went up to him and accepted all kinds of pats and scratches while she smiled. "How's Taz?"

"Sleeping under that big shade tree in my backyard, so he's happy," Mr. Brett said.

I wasn't in the mood to visit, but Daddy caught sight of Daisy and me and waved us over. I ambled toward him and Ian, and Daisy followed. Behind us, I could hear Mr. Brett breaking the earth with that post-hole digger.

Ian and Daddy had been talking real serious about something, but they quit when I walked up. Usually I'm curious as all get-out when I walk up on a serious conversation and it stops. That means something real interesting has been said. But that day, I was so discouraged that I just didn't care to know about things I wasn't supposed to know about.

"Well, what are you and Daisy up to?" Daddy asked as we got close enough to smell their man-sweat. P-U. Heaving fence posts into the ground and pounding them solid on a blistering day in August isn't the frostiest thing you can do, let me tell you. Ole Ian was getting back to his roots the hard way that day.

"I'll get us some water," he said, and walked toward the red-and-white cooler under a scraggly hickory tree nearby.

Daddy smiled down at me as he drew out an old blue bandana and mopped his face. "Mama give you the day off?"

I made a face. "I can't hardly stand it," I told him.

"What's that?" Daddy asked.

"They're talking about the wedding! Like it's some big deal wonderful thing."

Daddy lost his smile.

"Daddy, I can't stand the thought of Grandma marrying that old man."

"What's that?" His voice was none too friendly, and neither was his expression. I knew he'd heard me. Right then he gave me a chance to smooth over my comment. But I didn't. I just repeated myself.

Ian walked up just then with three Solo cups full of cold water. He handed one to me, which I accepted gratefully and drank down so fast, I belched like a lumberjack.

Mama would have scolded me, but Daddy took a long drink, then said, "Did Mr. Rance say or do something you don't approve of, April Grace?"

"He's loud and bossy and sneaky and snarky, and Grandma is gonna regret getting married."

He and Ian shared a long look in which they silently said something to each other. I gave Ian a sharp study, trying to read his mind, but I couldn't see his thoughts any better than Daddy's.

"Well, I'm sorry you feel that way," Daddy said to me, "but if your grandmother wants to marry him, it's none of your business."

"But Daddy!"

"I agree with your girl, Mike," Ian said, surprising me. "I'd sure hate to see your mother get legally tied to that man."

Daddy took his eyes off me to look at Ian. The two men regarded each other for a minute. Daddy nodded so you could barely see it. Then Ian squatted down and let Daisy lap out the rest of the water in his Solo cup. He patted her head. Guess she'd controlled that vicious, tail-wagging, tongue-lolling, and hours-long napping enough so he could trust her not to rip his arm off.

"Well," Daddy said after a bit. "I will admit he wouldn't be my first choice for her. But she seems to like him. They get along well. She's happy; he's happy. And they're certainly old enough to know their own minds."

"But Daddy—"

"No 'but Daddys.' You have a right to how you feel, daughter, and I won't deny you that right." He pinned a look on me. "But here's the situation as it stands. Your grandma wants to marry Jeffrey Rance, so don't you be trying to cause trouble. That means no pouting and sulking, no smarty remarks, no running off when you're needed. You jump in there and help your mama and grandma get things ready for the wedding if they want you to. No arguments."

"Well, you used to stand up for Mama when she couldn't stand up for herself, and now all I'm trying to do is stand up for Grandma."

"It's not the same thing, April Grace. Not in the least."

"Oh brother!" I yelled. "As if—"

"Don't you raise your voice to me," he said in that quiet tone that made the hair on the back of my neck prickle. He narrowed his eyes, and I knew what that meant. I was on my own in this.

"Okay, then," I said through closed lips. "Since no one will listen to me except ole Ian"—I gave him a friendly look and nearly patted his arm the way he'd petted Daisy—"I reckon I can't do anything. I'm just a dumb kid, ain't I?"

I snapped my fingers to get Daisy's attention and turned

to leave. We took a few steps; then I looked over my shoulder at Daddy.

"Oh yeah. One other thing, even though you might not want to believe me: you can't tell by looking at Myra Sue's face or while she's in her regular clothes, but you and Mama ought to take a close look at her in those leotards of hers. All her bones are sticking out."

TWENTY-FOUR

Getting Under Isabel's Skin

Daisy and I took our own sweet time walking back to the house.

"If Grandma keeps letting Mr. Rance push her around," I told the dog, "that wedding will be in a few days."

I tried to kick a big, loose rock out of my way. Pain shot up from my big toe. Some rocks are made to be kicked, and others aren't.

"Boy, oh boy, I wonder if Miss Delaine has got that obituary from Texas yet. If Mrs. Emmaline Rance died under Mysterious Circumstances, I am calling the Beauhide County sheriff so he'll know where to come to get that old man." Daisy looked up at me with one ear cocked. "Don't worry. I know what I'm doing this time. No dogs will be hurt."

She put both ears back and wagged her tail. I figured that was all the support I was going to get from the Reilly family. At least Ian seemed to be on my side, but since he hardly ever said a word these days, I doubted I could count on him for anything beyond finally getting some sense in his head.

You see, Ian kinda got off on the wrong foot with everybody on Rough Creek Road and in town because he acted like a rude know-it-all. Why someone who'd spent his whole entire life in a big city, thousands of miles away, thought he could tell everyone here how to run their own farms is beyond me. He'd read books, I guess. Big whoop. So had I. But two or three weeks ago, I overheard Daddy tell Mama that Ian had got himself told off pretty good right there in the Farm and Tractor feed store. Apparently more than one fellow told him that he could take his attitude right back to California, or they'd cart him back there personally.

Guess that explains why he lost that attitude of his right quick. Since then, Ian had kept his mouth shut and his eyes open and tried to get along with the "natives." That's his word, not mine. Daddy told him one night at supper that if he'd learn how not to tear up the equipment, he'd be a right good farmer. You shoulda seen Ian's face. He grinned like a monkey all evening.

By the time Daisy and I got home, Isabel and Myra Sue no longer reached and stretched and gyrated on the porch. I went into the house and heard voices in the kitchen. I overheard Grandma say something about the Reverend Hunsaker being available next Saturday night. Isabel asked about orchestra music. That's when I put my hands over my ears and ran upstairs.

Thank goodness Miss Delaine answered the phone at the library. If that snippy, snoopy, bossy Mrs. Heathcliff had answered, I do believe I'd have hollered at her for no good reason or just hung up in aggravation because nothing had gone right all day.

In a quiet and gentle tone of voice, Miss Delaine told me, "I sent a letter to the librarian in Beauhide County with your request, but she hasn't replied yet. Be patient, April Grace. School doesn't start for another few weeks. You've got plenty of time to write that composition."

I started to tell her it was a matter of life and death, but since I couldn't prove anything whatsoever, I figured she'd not understand any better than the people in our house. Even if she is nice and kind and speaks quietly. I hung up the phone and felt downright helpless.

Downstairs, Mr. Rance bellowed for Grandma. In a few minutes they took off in that red truck, going on yet another date. Boy, you'd think Grandma would be sick of the ole goof by now and not want to marry him. Not long after, Daddy and Ian came home for lunch earlier than usual. Mama called me and Myra Sue to come help her get a quick meal on the table. Ian and Isabel joined us, and Daddy ate so fast I don't see how he had time to swallow. Once again, Myra Sue hardly had a bite.

Finally, Daddy shoved back his chair and said, "Lily, I need to talk to you."

They went into the hall. I could hear them speaking in whispers, but even when I leaned back in my chair as far as possible and strained my ears, I couldn't understand a blessed word.

A few minutes later, he came to the door of the kitchen and said to the daughter who hadn't eaten a real meal in a month, "Myra Sue, your mother and I want to see you in your room."

Looking mystified, but not necessarily concerned, she left the table and went upstairs.

In just a little while, the awfullest ruckus came from her bedroom. Myra Sue was yelling and—you might or might not believe this bit—cussing as bad as Isabel. Then Daddy raised his voice above hers, and everything up there got deathly quiet. Ian and Isabel and I all looked at each other, and none of us said one word.

Pretty soon all three of them came downstairs. Mama and

Myra Sue went straight outside, and Daddy came into the kitchen. He looked more than a little agitated.

"Ian, we've got to run into town, so we'll finish that fence tomorrow," Daddy said. "I'll let Brett know on our way out. Why don't you cut the grass at your place since it's been a week or more? And if you want to, when you get back, you can start mowing the lawn here. The riding mower is in the shed."

All three of us in the kitchen were just as quiet as still water for a minute or two. Ian finally fixed himself another ham sandwich and a glass of sweet tea. Isabel watched him. She had gorged herself on half an orange and a tiny container of plain yogurt.

"Well," she said at last, pushing back her chair, "I need to work on my glutes. They are absolutely flabby."

I had no idea what glutes were, but as she walked away, Ian eyeballed her scrawny butt and said, "No, they aren't."

She turned, stared a moment at the mound of potato salad he'd put on his plate, sniffed as though offended, and went down the hall to the bedroom. A moment later she came back, passed the kitchen doorway with her cigarettes and lighter, and went outside. I guess glutes are less flabby after a couple of smokes.

Ian finished eating, took his plate to the sink, and rinsed it off. He was all nice and sun-browned now from so much outdoor work, but he was still pink around the edges in some places, like on the tops of his ears or the growing bald spot on the back of his head.

"Ian," I said, "do you feel you've got back to your roots like you wanted when you first moved here?"

He kinda squinched his eyes a little as he thought about it.

"Yes," he said after a bit. "I think so. Your daddy and Mr. Brett are helping me learn a lot—but I have a long way to go." He grinned, adding, "And now I have to get busy."

"Wait!" I said, as he started to go outside. "Are you glad, Ian? Glad to find your roots even if the work is hard?"

He laughed softly. "Oh yeah. You better believe it. See you later, April Grace."

He gave me a little smile and wave and went out the back door. The place seemed awful quiet after he'd driven away in the old pickup, which used to belong to us.

Well, I'll tell you. I knew I ought to do those dirty lunch dishes, but I sure didn't want to. I was mad as fire at everybody in my family for a number of reasons. Number one: you know about the Grandma and Mr. Rance thing so I won't even go into that. Number two: Daddy and Mama took off for town without asking me to go with them. Number three: they took Myra Sue. Number four: no one told me why.

But I figured if I didn't do the dishes, I'd have to do all the lunch and supper dishes for the next sixty years. My big sigh of martyrdom totally lost its impact since no one was there to hear it. I got up and cleared the table. By putting his plate in the sink, Ian St. James was the only one who had bothered to lift a finger. Good ole Ian.

I'd just filled the sink with hot soapy water when this terrifying, bloodcurdling scream came from the front porch. I was so startled, I dropped the dishrag right smack on the floor and didn't even stop to pick it up. Instead, I tore out of the house to see if killer bees or an ax murderer had attacked Isabel.

She stood near the railing, all hunched over, her right hand clutching the left one against her chest. In between wails of pain she moaned like a pregnant heifer.

"What happened?" I screamed.

"I . . . oh . . ." She had leaned her whole body against the rail by this time. "Oh, oh, *oh*! It hurts! Help me, help me!"

I was thrown back in time to the day she twisted her ankle and acted like she'd shattered every bone in her body. My heartbeat slowed.

"What's wrong?" I asked in a normal tone of voice.

"I impaled my hand on this wretched railing," she managed to choke out.

Maybe Grandma or Mama had left a paring knife out here from when they'd peeled potatoes. Sometimes they sat on the porch and prepared vegetables just to get out of the kitchen for a while. Or maybe Mr. Rance and his nasty old pocketknife had been out here earlier. I looked for a nail or something else sharp, but I saw absolutely nothing on that porch railing. Surely she hadn't gotten a *splinter*. But remember, we're talking about Isabel St. James, the Queen of Imaginary Illness and Pain. It was just like her to carry on over a little ole splinter.

Then I saw the blood. It dripped from the hand she had clenched to her chest and splattered on the gray painted floor of the porch.

"Help me!" she gasped. Her face was chalky.

For a minute I felt frozen by the sight of blood, unable to think or move. But then I remembered all that I'd learned in health class last year.

"Let me see it," I told her.

She moaned and shuddered as I peeled away the bloody fingers of her right hand to look at her left one. A large sliver of wood protruded from the meaty part of her palm, and let me tell you, it was bleeding pretty good. I might have screamed a bit, my own personal self.

"Okay, Isabel St. James, here's what you need to do. First, just take a nice, deep breath. That will help you relax. Here. Like this." I pulled in a deep breath through my nose, then breathed it out through my mouth. "Do that."

I dragged over one of the cane-bottomed porch chairs.

"Now, sit down and just keep breathing that way. I'm going to get the first aid box and take care of you."

"Call 9-1-1," she moaned weakly.

"It's not that bad. Besides, Zachary County don't have 9-1-1. Now, you just sit there and breathe."

I walked calmly into the house because I wanted her to understand she wasn't mortally wounded. Once I was out of her eyesight, I rushed to the hall bathroom and dove into the recesses of the little vanity.

I shoved aside a can of Scrubbing Bubbles, a pair of bright yellow rubber gloves, a can of Lysol spray, a can of rose-scented Glade, two packages of Charmin toilet paper, a package of Handi Wipes, a box of feminine you-know-whats, a bag of cotton balls, and three boxes of Preparation H cream before I could, at long last, get to the first aid box and a bottle of hydrogen peroxide.

Boy, oh boy, when you have an emergency, you shouldn't have to crawl around through a zillion bathroom items to reach what you need. I was gonna reorganize the bottom shelf of that vanity as soon as Isabel's Crisis was over.

I picked up the cotton balls, took a bottle of aspirin from the medicine cabinet, wetted a handful of washrags, grabbed a couple of towels, and got a glass of water from the kitchen. Then, balancing everything, I dashed to the front door where I stopped, took a deep breath, and calmly went outside.

Isabel sat right where I'd left her, eyes shut, breathing the way I'd told her to do. I knelt down next to her chair.

"Okay, Isabel St. James. Here's the thing: this is gonna hurt a little bit." I sounded like the nurse who flashes a needle for my booster shots. "So you have to be brave."

She opened one eye. "Are you positive you can't call 9-1-1?"

"Well, I can call it, but it won't do any good 'cause Zachary County doesn't have 9-1-1 service. I can call the sheriff's office, and they can call an ambulance, but you don't really want me to do that, do you? I mean, for a little ole splinter?" It wasn't such a little splinter, but I didn't want her to think I thought it was anything more. She might pass right out for sure.

She looked at me and made me think of the time Daisy got her leg broke, and she looked at us like she didn't understand why she was hurt. I felt sorry for ole Isabel.

"It'll be okay, Isabel St. James," I said softly. "I promise."

Her mouth quivered. She licked her lips and clamped them together.

Squinching her eyes tight, she said, "Okay. Do what you can for me."

Again, she let me pry loose the fingers of her right hand

and pull her left hand away from her chest. She wasn't bleeding so badly by then.

I took the first aid tweezers from the kit, and as gently as possible got the end of that huge sliver of wood and worked it free of her palm.

"Oh, dear me," she moaned as blood seeped again.

"It's okay," I told her. "I got it all out. Now I just gotta clean the wound." As careful as could be, I sponged the gouge. "Now this might hurt a little, but it'll help kill bacteria." I put aside the cloths and picked up the hydrogen peroxide. Her face was white as a sheet, and she stared in horror at her palm. I tried to distract her.

"Boy, it's a good thing you didn't use this stuff on ole Myra Sue's hair, huh? I hear peroxide does awful things to hair."

"Used by a professional, it works quite well," she gasped. "Of course, I take full responsibility for the way that child's hair turned out. I simply lost track of the time and left it on too long. A few minutes would have turned her into a stunning brunette."

Yeah, right. Stunned brunette was more like it. Anyway, while she was talking and semi-sidetracked, I poured the stuff on her wound. It hissed and bubbled, but at least she didn't scream and faint dead away like I thought she might.

"Did you know our school is going to have performing arts classes this year if they can find a teacher?" I asked.

She broke off mid-groan. "Really?"

"Yeah. You think you might like to teach acting and dancing at our school?"

"Oh, I hardly think—" She paused, looking at me sharply. "Are you sure this is something they're going to do?"

I shrugged. "That's what I heard. Ask Myra Sue. I'm surprised she hasn't already said something to you." I glanced down at her palm, happy that my distraction ploy worked so well. "Okay," I said quietly. "That's over. Now I'll just put on this dressing and bandage it, and you'll be good as new." A little bit later, I gently pressed down the last bit of tape and sat back on my heels. "There you go, Isabel St. James. I think you'll live. Now take these aspirin."

I shook out a couple and handed her the water. I expected resistance, but she was as obedient as a little baby. Boy, if the color of her face was any indication of life, she'd been dead a few weeks already. Once more, she cradled her hand to her chest.

"Thank you, dear," she whispered, then leaned back.

For a long time she sat there with her head against the back of the chair, her eyes firmly closed. Maybe she was thinking about those classes, but she looked kinda sad. Finally, she flickered open her eyelids a slit and looked at me.

"Little girl, tell me something."

"Okay. Pick a subject."

"Why does everyone hate me?"

I blinked in surprise. "Are you kiddin'?"

"No. I want to know, because the only people who treat me with any respect around here are your parents and your grandmother."

Where to begin listing her offenses, transgressions, character flaws, and faults? So many answers popped up that my head buzzed.

TWENTY-FIVE

Isabel's List

☆

"Well, go on." She sat upright with her eyes completely open. "You won't hurt my feelings."

I figured she probably didn't care two shakes one way or the other about my opinions or how I felt, so I sincerely doubted I *could* hurt her feelings. I jumped in with both feet.

"You act like we're inferior to you."

"Oh, now. Really," she said.

"You do!"

She shrugged and made an airy gesture with her un-injured hand.

"Well, after all . . . you do live . . . that is, you are from . . . I mean to say, uh, you are . . ."

"Are you saying that because we aren't from California or New York or Chicago or somewhere like that, we aren't as good as you? Is that what you're trying to say?"

She had this little smile that made me want to bite something. A roofing nail maybe.

"Well, my dear child, after all, being from here, you can't possibly know as much as, well, those of us who are from somewhere else."

I wanted to scream because that was the dumbest thing I'd heard in a long time, and believe me, I'd heard a lot of dumb things lately.

"Do you mean to sit there on your skinny rump and tell me that, after living with us for all these weeks, you still think we're stupid?"

Her mouth wagged and she blinked a dozen times. "I know you aren't stupid, none of you," she said. "And I see you reading a lot, April Grace. But surely you realize Rough Creek Road can hardly be called a mecca of culture. That awful little Cedar Whatever is no thriving megalopolis, and you people are so provincial, it's appalling."

Well, that frosted me good. I squinched my eyes to little slits and stared hard at her.

"So what if Cedar *Ridge* is a little town? There are little towns in every state, even the Fantastic and Golden state of California. And one thing for sure, I know *provincial* means you don't think outside the place you come from. So, okay. Maybe I *am* provincial. But, Isabel St. James, so are you."

She blinked. "I . . . *what?*"

Obviously she had never considered this possibility.

"You don't think anything matters outside the place where you used to live," I said. "You're so provincial, you don't even know the name of the nearest town to where you are right now."

She twitched, an odd expression on her face. "I've . . . I've never thought of it quite that way."

"And you know something else?" I said. "I might not speak good grammar all the time, but I *know* good grammar. And so does Daddy, and so does Grandma, and so does most everyone else around here. We just don't like using it sometimes, so don't even think about using that old saw to insult my family, or any of our friends."

She had her mouth all screwed up and kept twitching in

her chair like she was itching to say something rude. But she had asked me for this information, and I was telling her. After a minute, she allowed her lips to relax a little.

"All right, then. Point taken. Thank you for your honesty." She paused, then asked, "Is that the reason you don't like me?"

I gave her a look, flickering with hope that she was actually listening to me. I kinda hated to say it, but she needed to hear it, so I did.

"That's one reason of about a hundred and ten," I said.

Her eyes opened wide. "Really? Well, you may as well drive the nails in my hands and feet. Pray continue."

I nearly rolled my eyes at her martyrdom. "Well, since you're using Jesus images, it galls my behind that you and Ian won't even bother to go to church with us one time so you can meet the people who are gonna work on your house, free of charge, so you'll have a nice place to live this winter."

Her face got red, and she leaned forward.

"We are not religious fanatics!"

"Neither are we."

"You people pray over every meal."

This time I actually did roll my eyes in a goodly imitation of Myra Sue.

"So? We don't stand on street corners screaming at people about hellfire and brimstone. We thank God for all the good things He has done and all the blessings He has given us."

She sniffed.

"When Ian and I went into town the other day, a foolish little man in a plaid suit had the nerve to invite us to a revival meeting."

"So what? Did he put a gun to your head and force you to attend?"

"Of course not! But just the fact that he approached us—"

"Good grief," I said. "He didn't mean anything. He was just extending an invitation."

Isabel sniffed again and batted her eyes a few times. Then she said, "Your parents have that . . . that hideous prayer framed and hanging in their room."

Mama and Daddy told my sister and me that their bedroom was their private sanctuary, so usually I went in there only with permission. But I'd been in it enough to know what she was talking about.

"You mean the Prayer of Saint Francis? Is that the hideous prayer of which you speak?" I figured if there was ever a good time for proper elocution and correct grammar, this was it. "Have you ever read that prayer, Isabel St. James?"

"No!" she said. "I saw the word *prayer* and didn't read further."

Boy, oh boy.

"That just proves my point," I said. "You are narrow-minded!"

Her mouth flew open. "I'll have you know I'm a registered Democrat."

"Who cares and so what? I strongly recommend you read that prayer sometime instead of making judgments about it. And I'll tell you something else, if my mama and daddy are religious fanatics, then I reckon it's not such a bad thing to be! After all, look at how you and Ian have been treated."

We stared at each other for a long time. Then I said, "You

want me to tell you some more things about yourself, or have you had enough?"

I fully expected her just to reach out and smack me a good one, but instead she took in a deep breath and said, rather slowly, "No. No, I'm willing to hear more. If I'm doomed to live here, then I should at least try to find a way to connect with you."

I was glad to hear it. She was showing a little sense.

"You think you're sick all the time," I said.

She blinked at me a few times. "Well, I have a delicate constitution."

"Yeah. That may be, but nobody likes to hear about it three times a day and six times on Sunday. Hearing about your toe fungus or possible diphtheria makes me tired. Look how you carried on about that splinter. It was all bloody and gross, but it's not a life-threatening emergency. You wanted to call in the paramedics, for crying out loud."

Her back was very stiff, but she said, "I see. What else?"

"You don't do anything around here."

"I beg to differ!" She started ticking things off on the fingers of her good hand. "I have chopped tomatoes, I've broken beans, I've shucked corn—" she shuddered "—and there were *worms*! I peeled peaches, and the fuzz on the skins could have given me a dreadful rash that might have . . ." She trailed off, probably remembering what I'd just said. "I . . . I turned the steaks over on the grill the other day. And . . ." Here she paused to think. "Oh yes. I have never folded so much laundry in my life!"

"So? You could do a lot more. And you have insulted my mother so many times I can't count them all."

Her mouth flew open.

"When? When did I *ever* insult your mother?"

"Oh brother!" I yelled. "Are you kidding? You called her Lucy about a million times until she finally snapped and asked you very politely to call her Lily—which is her name! You refuse to eat her cooking, and she has to drive all the way to Ava, and sometimes Blue Reed, to get food just for you."

She stared at me. "Well, I . . . she does?" This was almost a whisper.

"Yes."

For the first time, she actually looked dismayed. "Well . . . well . . . I never asked her to do that."

"No, but she's nice, and she does things for people."

"But she's so busy all the time. And that's a long way to go for just one person. Why, she's never said a thing to me about it. Are you sure?"

"Positive. She went to Blue Reed one night last week to get mangoes because you set up a fuss for them, and she didn't get home until after ten. She'd been up since five that morning. Then you complained that they just didn't taste like the ones *back home*, so most of them spoiled because they weren't good enough for you."

She pressed the fingers of her injured hand to her mouth. "Oh my."

Well, I was all wound up and couldn't stop. "And here's something else: Our dog Daisy isn't vicious, this house isn't dreadful, we don't have rural diseases, fresh country air doesn't make you sick, and Forest and Temple are nice people, not 'vile creatures.' Furthermore, you've been treated like royalty in this house when the only royal thing you've done is act like a royal pain in the neck!"

Isabel stared at me in a way I've never seen before.

"Oh my," she said again.

Then she looked past me and gazed at nothing for a long time. After a while, she spoke again in a strangled voice, "Does everyone in your family feel this way?"

I took a deep breath and pushed it out. "I don't think so," I said. "I mean, they'd sure never let on even if they did."

"No. No, I suppose they wouldn't, would they? Your parents are wonderful people. They've done more for Ian and me than any of our friends back home ever did."

"And Myra Sue worships the ground you walk on."

A slow, soft smile came to Isabel's lips. "She's a dear girl."

I snorted. "Well, that's debatable. But let's not argue."

I thought about telling her I thought Ian had turned out to be a nice guy after all, and she ought to stop being so crabby and snotty to him, but then I decided maybe the two of them ought to work out their own relationship.

"And I think your grandmother is an absolute hoot," Isabel said.

"You do?"

Finally she met my eyes. "Don't you?"

"Oh yeah," I said. "Grandma is a case. Sometimes I nearly pass out from laughing at the funny things she says and does."

"I used to think she was a dreadful hillbilly, but actually, once you get to know her, she's so clever and wise."

"I know!"

Anyone who loved my grandma couldn't be a complete knotheaded jerk. I began to get a warm, fuzzy feeling for Isabel St. James, so I dismissed that hillbilly remark. After all, since she and Ian lived there now, they qualified as hillbillies, like it or not, deny it or not.

"So you have more to say?" Isabel asked after a minute. "Go ahead. I'm braced for it."

"Just this. Treat my folks with a little more consideration, especially Mama. There was a time when she was treated real bad, and I just . . ." I stopped right there, remembering that Mama likes to keep some things to herself. "Just be nicer to them, okay?"

Isabel sniffed a little and blinked a little and twitched a little more.

Then she said, "Thank you again for your honesty. I shall be more mindful of how I present myself from here on out." She cocked her head slightly to one side. "You know, my dear, you and I are a lot alike."

I gawked at her. "That's one of craziest things you've ever said, Isabel St. James."

"Think about it for a minute."

So I did. I went back over how I had acted and the things I'd said and done since I first met the St. Jameses. I had judged them before I met them, just from the car they drove. And hardly ever tried to see past the things they said and did as a reason to understand them.

I remembered what Grandma had told me that day in the Koffee Kup, how no one was perfect, and I knew then just how right she was. Isabel wasn't perfect . . . and neither was I. That was a hard pill to swallow, I tell you, but once I swallowed it, I had to admit it aloud. I think Jesus would've liked that.

Gulping in a deep breath, I said, "Isabel St. James, you are absolutely—"

The telephone rang in the house. I excused myself very politely to go answer it.

"April Grace?" the voice on the other end of the telephone said. "This is Miss Delaine from the library."

My heart jumped.

"Hi! Do you have some information about Mrs. Rance after all?"

"Yes, I do," she said. "It came in the afternoon mail. But I'm afraid it's not what you were looking for. You might need to choose another subject for your composition, April Grace."

"Why?" I asked. "What do you mean?"

"You want to write about women who've died in Texas, right? Mrs. Emmaline Rance is not dead."

TWENTY-SIX

Joining Forces

☺

What did Miss Delaine just say?

"She's not dead?" I yelped. "Of course she's dead! She died about Christmastime last year."

Miss Delaine cleared her throat in a way that told me I had overreacted and she did not appreciate it.

"I have a letter right here from Eunice Magruder, the head librarian of the Beauhide County Library. Do you want me to read it to you?"

My mind sputtered like the engine of Mr. Brett's old lawn-mower. Words jerked out of my mouth, making no sense.

"Why . . . why . . . if you . . . of course . . . sure."

She cleared her throat again and said, "All right. Mrs. Magruder's letter reads: 'What an unusual request! Please pass on the following information to your patron. Mrs. Emmaline Rance is not dead. She is, and has been, very much an active part of our little community. In fact, Emmaline Ellison Rance is the secretary of our library board. Until last year, she owned one of the largest ranches in Beauhide County. Perhaps your patron heard of Mrs. Rance's troubles and assumed she had succumbed to the devastation brought about by the scheming and reckless man she married just two years ago.'"

I squawked and slid down the wall, flat to the floor on my backside.

"Who'd she marry?" I yelled into the phone. "Does it say who she married? Is his name Jeffrey Rance? What'd he do to that woman?"

"April Grace, honey," Miss Delaine said after a brief

silence. "Why are so you agitated? If you're worried about finding another subject for your composition before school starts, I'll be glad to help you. You don't have to write about deceased people in Texas, do you? There are plenty of interesting women who've lived and died right here in Arkansas. In fact—"

"Does the letter say who Emmaline Rance married?"

"You needn't shout. I'll read you the rest of the letter: 'Mrs. Rance was hospitalized last winter for stress-induced heart failure after she learned J. W. Rance, her husband, had sold a huge part of their estate to a Japanese developer. By the time she recovered, the man had left Beauhide County and, we hope, the state of Texas altogether. She's filed divorce, of course, but doesn't know where J. W. Rance is, so the papers have yet to be served. Please feel free to pass this information along and assure your patron that Mrs. Rance is now fully recovered and busy as ever, although she is now without the ranch and fortune that had been in her family for many generations.'"

I just sat there on the floor, limp as a rag doll and just as speechless.

"Are you still on the line?" Miss Delaine asked. "April Grace, are you there?"

I finally took in air, then swallowed hard.

"I'm here," I said weakly. "Miss Delaine, will you keep that letter for me until I can get to the library and pick it up?"

"Of course. But, honey, I—"

"Thank you." I let the phone drop out of my hand.

For a little while I stayed on the floor, trying to come up with a way to get to Cedar Ridge. Mama and Daddy were gone; Ian was at his place, mowing his weedy yard; today was Mr. Brett's day off, so he'd be at an auction somewhere—his favorite thing to do. Grandma had gone off with That Man. Someone had always driven Isabel anywhere she wanted to go, so she probably could not drive. I felt pretty hopeless right about then.

But just about the time I heard funny noises coming from the uncradled telephone receiver on the floor, I decided that if any air remained in my bicycle tires, I'd pedal my way to town. Rough Creek Road discouraged bike riding unless you hankered after a chiropractic adjustment at the end of your trip. Jouncing over that road's rocks and ruts would rattle my brains loose, probably, and if I got flattened by a milk truck on the way to town, Mama and Daddy would kill me. But I had to get that letter. No one would believe me without it.

I scrambled to my feet, hung up the telephone, and headed outside into the afternoon sunlight.

"Where are you going?" Isabel said as I rushed down the porch steps.

"I gotta get to town." I hurried toward the shed without pausing.

"How?"

"I'm gonna ride my bike."

"What?!" A few seconds later I unfastened the rusty latch on the shed door, and Isabel was right beside me. Boy, I didn't know she could move that fast.

"You can't ride your bicycle all the way to town," she said. "It's dangerous."

"I have to."

I pulled open the shed door, and a field rat rushed out into the daylight. Isabel saw it, screeched, and jumped aside, but she didn't hightail it back to the house like you'd expect her to do. Instead, she eyeballed the thing until it disappeared into the pasture where it belonged.

"I will not let you put yourself in danger, April Grace!"

My bicycle hadn't been out of the shed in two years. To get to it, I moved a small wooden stool, an old bucket with a hole in the bottom, a broken broom, and an empty gas can. I wheeled the old red bike outside and took a look at it. Both tires were flatter than a flitter. Plus, it was covered in dirt.

Isabel looked at it with her nose curled up and her mouth in a wad. "Well, I'm glad to see you cannot use that nasty thing. Now tell me what's so urgent that you suddenly must go to town."

"I'll just have to walk." I took off down the driveway. "But there's no time to waste talking. If you want to walk along, I'll tell you what's up."

Off I went with Isabel teetering along beside me on her high heels. That woman did not own one pair of anything as practical as sneakers. Looking at her long, skinny feet, I wondered if they even made sneakers that would fit. But this was not the time to make snide remarks in my head about Isabel.

"You like my grandma, don't you, Isabel St. James?"

"Yes, yes, I do!" she said.

"Well, that old goof she's fixing to marry is a rotten old goat."

"What? What?" she said. We were stepping along at a pretty good clip. She was panting like Daisy on a hot day and clutched my arm with her good hand for support. "What makes you say that, child?"

So I told her every nasty little detail that I could remember about Mr. Rance, including the parts about apple trees and the little flap on the VCR. By the time I got to the letter from Texas, we had reached the place in the road where Grandma had bailed out of the truck to look for Queenie that time.

Isabel stopped dead. Her clutching fingers were hard as iron and hurt my arm like crazy.

"Let go of me, Isabel St. James! I have to save my grandma."

"Not without me, you aren't!" she declared. "And we aren't walking all the way to Cedar Whatever. I'll drive us to town." She whirled around and marched back the way we'd come. She kept twisting and tripping over rocks and holes in the road.

"Oh, I've had enough of this!" She yanked off those silly high heels and kept on going barefoot. I knew that rough rocky road on the soles of her citified feet must have been painful, but she must've gritted her teeth because she didn't slow down.

"I didn't know you drove!" I hollered, then ran to catch up with her.

"I do in an emergency. And this is an emergency."

"But where are you getting a car?"

"We'll walk to our place and get the pickup."

Well, let me tell you, it was hot as blazes outside—it usually is in August around here. We both worked up a good sweat in a real short time. I didn't even know Isabel *could* sweat.

At one point Isabel asked, "You never liked the old man, did you?"

"Nope. But, of course, no one listened to me when I said he was snoopy and bossy." I gave her a look. "As many times as he's had supper at our house, did you never notice that?"

She blinked a few times. "Actually, I did, but I just assumed he was like everyone else around here."

I bristled. "What's that supposed to mean?"

"You know . . ." She slid a look at me.

"No, I do not know. Not everybody around here is like that, and besides, he's not from *here*. It's snooty remarks like that, Isabel St. James, which make people dislike you. And I'm starting to like you, so don't mess it up."

She drew in her lips and blinked some more. Then, to my utter and complete astonishment, she smiled.

"I'm starting to like you, too, now that I see you are a perceptive, caring child and not always a smart-mouthed little brat. We have totally misunderstood each other, April Grace."

"That's true. But I'm not the brat of the family. And if you'll stop acting all superior and looking down on everyone here . . ."

"That has never been my intention," she said.

Hmm. It sure seemed that way, but maybe I'd been wrong.

She added, "If you'll stop coming up with pointed little barbs to hurt me . . ."

"The truth hurts."

She grimaced, and I continued, "But we're trying to turn

over a new leaf, aren't we? So what the hey. All right, I'll try not to be such a smart-mouth, and you just gotta stop saying things like, 'Back in California, we always had this, or did that.' And, 'You people here are so dumb or ignorant or whatever.' You're not in California anymore, so you might as well learn to love it here 'cause that's where you are."

She got all prickly again.

"Well, April Grace, you really need to stop making snide remarks about anyone not born and raised in these parts. It's very off-putting. Sometimes I think you're making fun of us. And I'll tell you something else for your edification: sarcasm is a very unattractive trait in a child."

I knew she was right. Every thought in my head did not need a Voice. I'd probably hurt people's feelings more often than I realized.

"Well, I reckon I can try to control that."

"I'll make an honest effort to adjust my behavior too."

"And what you said earlier about us being alike?"

"Yes?" She wore a little smile that threatened to become bigger.

"Well, it just about kills me to admit it, but you were absolutely right."

She let out a breath as if she'd been holding it for a long time.

"So let's try to get along as friends, shall we?" she said.

That sounded reasonable to me. I stuck out my right hand. "Deal?"

She reached out, and we shook.

"Deal. But one more thing." She did not let go.

I gave her a look. "What's that?"

"When you speak to me, please call me Isabel or Mrs. St. James instead of my entire name. Will you do that?"

Well, if someone called me April Grace Reilly every time they spoke to me, I'd feel more like a thing instead of a person, so her request was reasonable.

I said, "Okey-dokey. I'll do it, Isabel."

"Good." She released my hand. "Now, let's go save Grandma Grace from the clutches of that wormy old weasel."

I grinned at her. "I like the way you think."

TWENTY-SEVEN

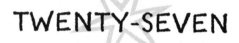

Lily Reaches Her Boiling Point at Last

✳

When we got to their house, Ian was halfway finished mowing the grass. In his spare time, Ian had come over to their place and cut back the seedlings and scrub and burned all the brush. Even though they weren't living there yet, he had kept the yard mowed. Their old place didn't look near the wreck it had a few weeks ago. In fact, it looked right nice and neat.

Isabel beckoned to him. He turned off the mower and walked over to us, wiping the sweat off his face with his forearm. Isabel explained about Mr. Rance and Grandma and the letter from Eunice Magruder that was at the library.

He announced, "I knew that old man was up to no good. I'm going into town with you."

Boy, oh boy, Ian can drive fast when he gets a notion.

After I ran into the library and got the letter from Miss Delaine, we sat in the cab of the pickup, and all of us took turns reading it.

He said, "That explains it."

Isabel and I looked at each other and then at him.

"Explains what?" I asked.

"Yes, darling," Isabel said. "If you know something more, you should tell us."

Ian nodded. "Yesterday, Jeffrey Rance showed up in the lower pasture where I was grubbing out some of those multiflora roses from the fencerow. He asked me for a loan, can you believe that?"

Isabel blinked a bunch of times, but she did not say anything. He continued.

"He said his truck payment was due, and he found himself short of cash. I told him I didn't have a penny to lend him, but he didn't believe me. Kept saying that since I'd sold my Caddie and we were living rent-free with the Reillys, he knew good and well that I had plenty of money. I told him about the deal Mike and I had worked out, how we were using the cash from the sale of our car to buy remodeling for the house. He kept wheedling and trying to strike a bargain, but I stayed firm."

"Oh, darling, it's marvelous that you didn't give in to him!" Isabel said. "I would hate to think you gave money to that awful old man."

"But I'm not finished."

"Oh?" she said prissily. It's such a habit for her, speaking that way. I have a feeling it will be a while, if ever, before she quits doing it. "Then continue telling us, darling."

"Well, old Rance muttered and paced around a bit. Then he said, and I'm quoting, 'I'll pay you back as soon as me and that old woman get hitched. Everything that's hers will be mine, too, and I aim to make good use of it.'"

Isabel and I looked at each other, and she looked as outraged as I felt. I wanted to get out of that truck right then, go find old man Rance, and strangle him with my two little girly hands.

"I was telling your daddy about it when you showed up this morning, April Grace," Ian said. "He was all set to confront Rance, but once you told him about Myra Sue, it was more important that he take care of her as soon as possible."

Just one more reason that we couldn't let that old goof

marry my grandma. Besides, if he succeeded in doing to Grandma what he'd done to Emmaline, he'd take everything she owned and sell it all to Japanese developers.

"Anybody with half a brain," I declared loudly, "would not sell our farm to Japanese developers. Good grief."

"April Grace," Ian said, "that old guy does not have half a brain."

Good ole Ian St. James.

We hadn't been home long when Mama called to say they were going to be late getting back. So, in the spirit of our newfound cooperation and friendship, Isabel and I fixed supper, while Ian helped Mr. Brett with the milking. We took turns peeking out the window above the sink every little bit to see if Mr. Rance's red truck was at Grandma's house yet, but they were still off somewhere.

Isabel forbade me to fry potatoes or make bacon—two of my most favorite foods—but we put together a decent meal of leftover baked chicken, green beans, fresh sliced tomatoes, and cucumbers. I tried my hand at making biscuits, and they didn't turn out half-bad. Over the protests of his little missus, Ian ate six. With butter. And molasses.

But much later, after we'd eaten supper, it was nearly dark outside, and my folks still weren't home. I was worried.

"I wonder where Mama and Daddy are."

"So do I," Isabel said. "I wish they'd call and at least let us know if everything's all right. I wonder where they went."

Ian refused to look at us, and I got suspicious.

"You know where they are?" I asked.

He buttered a biscuit. "I might."

Isabel leaned forward. Her movements made me think of a snake because they were all slinky and smooth.

"Do tell," she said, "and I mean it."

Boy, after the day we'd had and all the progress we'd made, I hoped they refrained from fighting. At least she didn't sound too threatening this time.

Ian sopped up the last of his molasses with the final biscuit; then he looked at his wife.

"Not sure Mike wanted us to know, but since it's taking them all day, I probably should tell you. I think they took the girl to a doctor."

Isabel gasped and sat up straight.

"Dearest Myra? Why? Is she sick? She didn't say a word about feeling ill. Oh, my!"

"I don't know anything," he said. "I just think that might be what Mike decided to do."

Isabel's face was all scrunched up and as frowny as a newborn bull calf. She put down her fork and pushed away her weensy half-eaten meal.

"Well, I've simply lost my appetite to worry."

Now, I'll tell you something. I may have made peace with Isabel St. James, but I had not lost my appetite just because ole Myra Sue had to see a doctor maybe. If she saw a doctor, he'd probably put her on vitamins and tell her to eat something and send her home, and she'd be mad for a week, but that was nothing to worry about.

"How about some ice cream?" I said.

Ian nodded, but Isabel didn't even hear me. I tell you, she did look worried.

While I spooned out ice cream for me and Ian, she said, "That child is not dating, is she? I mean, she would have told me, wouldn't she?"

Ian frowned. "Isabel, what are you thinking?"

"Well, I hear tell that the girls here . . ." She let her voice trail and looked at me kinda guiltily. "I don't mean to say that girls here are the *only* ones who have boyfriends at an early age and indulge . . ."

"Are you kidding!" I hollered, because I'm no dumb kid. "Myra Sue is *not* pregnant. She's never even been kissed, unless you count kissing yourself in the mirror. Good grief, Isabel St.— I mean, Isabel."

She blinked a bunch of times. Right then we heard tires crunching gravel in the driveway.

"There they are!" I yelled.

Leaving my ice cream to melt in its bowl, I ran outside with Ian and Isabel right on my heels.

"Where've you been?" I asked the minute Daddy opened the door.

He looked tired and said nothing. Mama got out, and you could see she'd been crying because her eyes were swollen and red. Myra Sue sat in the backseat, sulled up like a possum. She refused to look at anyone, not even Isabel, who was gawking in the back window at her and tapping on the glass like she thought my sister was a goldfish in a tank.

"Everything all right?" Isabel asked.

Daddy closed his car door and stood there, looking exhausted. He raked his fingers through his hair, and Mama made a strangled sound as she came charging around the car.

"You might ask that," she said. Even in the twilight you could see she looked at Isabel with a peculiar expression on her face. "You might just ask that! Then you might ask yourself what will you do, Isabel St. James, if Myra Sue Reilly has eating problems for the rest of her life just because of you!"

"What?" Isabel's mouth wagged open as she stared at Mama.

"Now, honey—" Daddy said.

"Don't you 'now honey' me, Mike!" Mama snapped at him. I'd never heard her raise her voice to my daddy before. "If it hadn't been for that woman . . ." She rounded and got in Isabel's face. "You and your obsession with weight! You, who do not weigh a hundred pounds, encouraged my beautiful, innocent daughter to lose weight. You sabotaged everything I tried to do to keep her healthy."

"Lily, I didn't—" Isabel began, but Mama didn't let her talk.

"We took you into our home when you were rude strangers. We have sheltered you, fed you, waited on you, helped and encouraged you while you've done nothing but complain about what we don't have and criticize our lifestyle. I want to be charitable, Isabel. I told myself over and over you must have had an unhappy life to make you so callous and bad-mannered. I've done my best to go the extra mile, but this is too much! I tell you, this is too much!"

She opened the back door, unbuckled Myra Sue's seat belt, and more or less dragged her out of the car because my sister refused to get out on her own.

"Come on, honey," she coaxed. "Let's get in the house and get you in bed."

She brushed past Isabel without another word and led Myra Sue into the house. The rest of us just stood there, stunned and silent in the semidarkness.

"Mike," Ian said softly, after a little bit. "Can you tell us what happened?"

Daddy took a deep breath, then let it out slowly, as if he were pondering whether or not to answer Ian's question.

"She has an eating disorder," he said finally. "They call it *anorexia nervosa*. You ever hear of it, Isabel?"

She stood straight as a stick. "Of course. But I never realized . . ."

"If it hadn't been for April Grace telling us this morning how bad her sister looks in those dancing leotards, I guess we wouldn't have noticed until it was too late," Daddy said. "She's always been a little-bitty thing, so her face didn't show how much weight she'd lost."

Isabel pressed her hands to her mouth as tears began to spill from her eyes. "You have to believe, I'd never in a thousand years wish to harm that girl. Why, she's as dear to me as if she were my own child."

Daddy took in another deep breath. "Well, maybe that's what you told yourself, Isabel, but the reality is that now she wants to be a rail-thin dancer, just like you."

"Oh no!" Isabel sagged, and Ian caught her. "I didn't mean for this to happen. Please believe me, I didn't want anything like this . . ."

Daddy just stood there a minute, clenching and unclenching his fists. Then he shook himself like he had a shudder inside that had to get out.

"I can't talk to you now," Daddy said. "I'm too upset and too exhausted. April Grace, come here."

I went to him. He pulled me into his arms and hugged me as if I were the last child on the planet. He kissed my cheek real hard and hugged me some more.

"Your mother needs you," he said. "Go to her."

As I left them, I heard Ian say, "Mike, I know you're mad, and you have every right to be. I sure hate to be the bearer of more bad news, but there is something else you should know."

I wanted to hang around and listen, but if my mama needed me, I had to go to her. I pulled the letter out of the pocket of my shorts and handed it to Ian. I trusted him to tell Daddy all about Mr. Rance.

In our room, Myra Sue was in the bed, all cuddled down, and staring at nothing in the dim light from the small, blue lamp on the dresser. She refused to answer when I spoke to her, so I just stared at her a minute, then went to find Mama.

Mama wasn't in the bedroom, but I could hear the shower running. I knocked on the bathroom door and called to her.

"April Grace, honey, I'll be out in a minute." She sounded weary and weak.

I went back to my room, combed my hair, and put on a clean T-shirt, thinking that, after all they'd been through that day, the least I could do was look as clean and neat as possible.

Myra Sue was lying silently on top of her bed, staring up at the ceiling.

"Are you okay, sister?" I asked finally, looking at her over my shoulder.

For a minute, I thought she was just going to keep ignoring

me, but finally she said, "I guess so." She looked at me. "But I wish you hadn't said anything. Mama and Daddy are all worried, and they'll probably throw Isabel to the wolves."

"They won't either. They care about you, and so does Isabel. And I reckon I do too."

She just looked at me for a bit longer, then closed her eyes. I figured she wanted me to leave, but I didn't. Instead I told her about Mr. Rance.

It was like all of a sudden she'd had a jolt of energy. Her eyes flew open and she sat up. "Really? Why, that old coot!"

"Don't worry," I said. "I have a feeling he's gonna get what's coming to him sooner or later."

"He'd better! Imagine trying to do something like that to our grandma!"

When I heard Mama come out of the bathroom, I went to the other bedroom where she was. She wore her pale yellow summer robe and sky-blue house slippers. Her curly red hair was wet, and she smelled like Dove when she hugged me. For a long time she crushed me into her, and I could hear her heartbeat and feel her chest rise and fall as she breathed.

"Honey," she said, still holding me close, "I want to thank you for telling your daddy about your sister."

"I just told him her bones were sticking out."

"You said more than that." She let go, except for holding my upper arms, and knelt in front of me. "You've been saying more than that for a long time, and we have not listened. You saw Isabel's negative influence and kept pointing it out, but I turned a deaf ear because I thought it was important to see the best in her. I want you to know I'm so sorry."

"But, Mama, Isabel's not as bad as you might think."

She smiled a little bit.

"I'm not saying she's bad, honey. I'm saying she's been a negative influence on your sister, and it must stop."

"Okay, Mama. But Mama, Myra Sue's not going to die, is she?"

She smoothed my hair. "No, of course not. Your sister will need treatment from a good doctor, and we'll have to watch her closely. The doctor told us that sometimes girls with eating disorders eat only to placate those around them, and then they throw up their food later. We have to make sure Myra Sue doesn't do that." She held me at arm's length and looked me up and down. "You don't think you're too fat, do you?"

I gawked at her.

"Good gravy, no! I like food too much. Especially yours and Grandma's food."

TWENTY-EIGHT

Showdown on Rough Creek Road

It was so late when Mr. Rance brought Grandma home from wherever they'd gone that I wasn't allowed to go with Mama and Daddy to her house that night to talk to her. But boy, oh boy, I was there when it all hit the fan the next morning.

Myra Sue and I came downstairs, and there sat all the adults—except Mr. Rance. It was about midmorning, and everyone had eaten their breakfast, but they sat at the kitchen table like they expected another meal. Half of a cinnamon coffee cake sat on the counter and fresh coffee brewed. Myra Sue leaned sullenly against the doorframe until Isabel made Ian move to another seat and patted the chair for Myra to sit beside her. She caught one of Myra Sue's hands in her own and clung to it as if she'd never let her go.

Grandma looked about the same as usual, if you didn't count her modified pixie cut, and new hair color, and the eye shadow and lipstick and blush. What I mean to say is, she didn't look upset or anything.

"Well," she said, looking at me, "there's our own little detective. Come over here, Jessica Fletcher." Everyone laughed. Jessica Fletcher was a sleuth on the show *Murder, She Wrote*, which is Grandma's favorite TV show.

I went to her, and she actually pulled me onto her lap as if I were a little kid and loudly kissed my cheek.

"Here's the girl that saved me from a big fat mistake," she said.

"Are you mad?" I asked her.

"Woo?" she said. "Mad at you?"

"No! Are you mad at that old man?"

"You could say I'm a little ticked off. Am I mad at myself? Oh, my goodness, yes! I've just been telling everyone here that I knew he was a bad egg, but I wouldn't let myself believe it. Reckon he turned my head with his charm."

"Charm? Mr. Rance?" I shuddered. "You're not gonna marry him tomorrow. Right?"

"Mercy me, no!"

"'Cause he does not deserve you," I said.

"Of course he doesn't."

"So have you told him?" I asked.

The adults all looked at each other and said nothing. Myra Sue looked mildly interested.

"What's going on?" my sister asked.

"We're waitin'," Grandma said.

"Waitin' on what?" I asked.

She grinned real big. "Just waitin'."

Well, they didn't have to wait long, because pretty soon, while I ate a bowl of Cheerios with a banana cut up in it, ole Mr. Rance knocked on the front door. Then he came on inside without being invited, just like he thought he was family. Mama and Daddy and Grandma and Ian and Isabel were drinking coffee and eating coffee cake—yes, even Isabel nibbled a small piece of coffee cake—and they all eyeballed him as he walked into the kitchen. Nobody had a smile right then.

"Wal, howdy there!" he boomed.

He made a beeline for Grandma and smooched her real loud. I fought the urge to throw the rest of that coffee cake right at his fat old head. Myra Sue curled up her nose like she smelled dog doo instead of that tiresome Old Spice, which seemed to fill all the extra space in the kitchen. I decided he used so much aftershave 'cause he was trying cover up his own disgusting awfulness.

"You wasn't at home, Miz Grace darling, so I figgered I'd find you here." He spotted me seated beside her and tousled my hair. "Hey there, Oliver! How's the boy? Hee hee."

Boy, oh boy, his worn-out joke was a real knee-slapper. Mr. Rance glanced around.

"This here is a solemn bunch. Who died?" He snorted and laughed and, when no one joined in, he sort of shrugged and said, "How about a cup of coffee for your honey-pie, Miz Grace, on the eve of our special day?"

I nearly choked.

"Coffee's right there," Grandma said, waving her hand carelessly toward it, "and the cups are in the cabinet above the percolator."

He gave her a funny look but went to get his own drink.

"How 'bout a piece o' that cake y'uns are eatin'?"

"Help yourself," Mama told him casually, sipping her coffee.

He raised both eyebrows and looked at Daddy. "Say there, Mike, you need to teach your womenfolks how to treat a feller. It's a blamed shame a man's gotta get his own treat around here, ain't it?"

Again he laughed his loud, obnoxious braying laugh, and again no one joined him.

"Not that I'm complainin'," he yelled as he poured his coffee—and managed to slop it all over the countertop and the floor. Then he cut himself a piece of coffee cake that left only a smidgen in the pan.

"Well, you shouldn't complain, Jeffrey," Grandma said. "You've had things pretty good for a long time."

"How zat?" the old goofball hollered, cupping his ear her way.

"Oh, for goodness' sake, turn on your hearing aids or turn them up!" Grandma said. "I'm about half-convinced you ain't near as deaf as you want everyone to think you are."

"Why, I can't hear a thing, Miz Grace, and you know it! I'm ashamed at you fer sayin' otherwise."

"Baloney!" Grandma replied. "And I said you've had things pretty good for a long time."

He fiddled with his hearing aids for a long time, looking down at them, but I was watching him real close. In fact, we all were, and what I saw was his eyes darting around like he was looking for a good path to take. Finally, he shoved the things back into his hairy holes, looked at everyone, and grinned real big.

"There! That's better. Now I can hear y'uns. What was that you said, Miz Grace, about me having it pretty good? Why, shore I have it good. I got you!" And he smooched her another loud one.

She huffed out a long, irritated breath.

"Don't try charming me, Jeffrey Rance. Your jig is up."

He gave a shifty-eyed glance around the room again and cupped an ear, but before he could say one word, Grandma spoke up again. "Don't you be acting like you didn't hear me."

He sat back and gawked at her.

"Miz Grace, I don't know what's got into you today. Didn't you get enough sleep last night? You look as pretty as a peach, don't she, folks, even if she is a mite tired? And you're in the bosom of your family, and tomorrow you'll be marryin' the man of your dreams. Why, you ain't gettin' cold feet, are you?"

Grandma stayed casually slouched in her chair and didn't move. She twisted her mouth as if she were trying not to bust apart with words. For a little bit, she fiddled with the handle of her white mug, then took a sip of coffee. It was like she drew out the moment we all knew was coming, kinda like when Queenie catches a mouse.

"No, I ain't getting cold feet," she said at last. She sat up straight and looked at the old man. "And I'll tell you something else I ain't getting." She gave him a grim smile. "I ain't getting myself legally tied to a sneak, a leech, or a loudmouthed old freeloader. And I ain't paying any more of your bills, or buying you any more lunches and tires and gasoline. Or new boots, neither. I'm ashamed I've already done all that."

My mouth fell open. I didn't know she'd done any of that.

She took a deep breath. "But here's the thing, J. W. Rance, and I want you to hear it loud and clear, so make sure your ears are clean, those hearing aids are turned on high, and you're listening real close."

She got right in his face, her nose about an inch from his.

"The one thing I ain't never had, never wanted, and the main thing I ain't *never* gonna have in a million years is this: I ain't ever gonna have the husband of another woman."

He looked frozen, staring at her like he was made of rock.

His face was redder than I'd ever seen it. Now, after being caught and embarrassed in front of everyone that way, the old coot ought to have had enough sense to get up and skedaddle out of our house. But you know what he did instead? I'll tell you.

He kinda shook himself all over like a wet dog; then he looked around at everyone with this mud-eating grin on his face. He smirked as if to tell us all that Grandma had done gone off the deep end.

"Why, Miz Grace, I don't know what you're carrying on about, but maybe you ought to go lay down. You've done—"

"Oh, be quiet, you old goofball," I said, because I couldn't hold it in any longer. "We know all about you ruining Emmaline Ellison Rance's family ranch down there in Texas by selling that ranch to *Japanese developers* like a big, fat dope! We know you made her so upset that she had a heart attack, and then you ran away. We also know you're still married to her. But now that they know where you are, you can't hide—"

"What do you mean they know where I am?" Suddenly his voice wasn't all corn-pone and Texas. "Who knows where I am?"

"I mean Mrs. Rance, your wife, and everyone else down there in Beauhide County who might be interested in your whereabouts. They know that you live on Rough Creek Road in Zachary County, Arkansas." I grinned real big. "I had the honor of calling the sheriff my own personal self. You know. Just in case you're also running from the law as well as your wife. . . ."

He stood up, knocking his chair over backward, and cussed like you wouldn't believe.

"How did you find out?" he shouted, but he didn't wait for the answer.

He pointed a thick finger first at Grandma, then at Daddy.

"I thought the two of you were a couple of gullible, dumb hicks from the sticks. Stupid, rednecked hillbillies like everyone else on this fool road in this fool state. So how come you got so smart all of a sudden?"

"You can thank April Grace for that," Grandma said.

I piped up. "And Ian."

Mr. Rance snarled like a rabid dog and started cussing again and calling us names I won't repeat. Daddy stood up and so did Ian; then the rest of us stood.

"Get out of my house," Daddy said through clenched teeth.

"Yes, leave." Mama stared the old man right in the eye.

"Go," said Grandma.

"And don't come back," I added.

Isabel leaned forward and said, "Don't let the door hit you in the . . ."—she looked at the rest of us—". . . backside."

Ian grabbed the old man's arm.

"Let go of me, you pantywaist," Mr. Rance growled, trying to pull away.

I reckon all those weeks of farmwork had toughened up Ian's muscles, because he held on firmly as he steered Mr. Rance toward the back door, which I rushed to hold open. Then good ole Ian escorted that old man across the porch and down the steps.

Everyone clustered on the back porch to make sure Mr. Rance went to that red Dodge pickup of his. He opened the door and put one cowboy-booted foot halfway inside, then turned and looked at us. He gave us a sneer.

"Miss Grace, you don't know what you're missing by turning me down this way."

Grandma rested one hand against my shoulder, and I heard her chuckle quietly.

Out loud, she said, "Oh yes, Jeffrey. I know exactly what I'll miss. Good-bye."

"Yeah!" Myra Sue yelled out. "Good-bye!"

The old man stood there and stared at us. He sneered again and shook his head. He muttered and swore under his breath, but we didn't care. We turned and trooped back into the house, all except for Ian and Isabel. They stayed outside—watching, I guess, until Mr. Rance and his pickup were out of sight.

When they came inside, Mama said, "I'll make us a celebration lunch. Isabel, would you rather have salmon or turkey breast?"

Isabel stared at Mama for a minute; then she ran from the room. We all looked at each other, mystified. A few seconds later, though, she came trotting back down the hallway, high heels clicking against the floor.

"This," she announced as she came into the kitchen, waving the framed prayer that had been hanging in Mama and Daddy's room. "I am not a religious person, as you know. I'm not even sure I believe in God, but this prayer . . ."

She looked at it in her hands a moment, then began to

read. Unlike the shrill bite to which we'd become accustomed, her voice turned quiet, and it was a pleasure to hear.

> *Lord, make me an instrument of your peace.*
> *Where there is hatred, let me sow love.*
> *Where there is injury, pardon.*
> *Where there is doubt, faith.*
> *Where there is despair, hope.*
> *Where there is darkness, light.*
> *Where there is sadness, joy . . .*

She looked up. "I read this last night for the first time." She blinked a bunch of times, but this time she blinked back tears. "Lily, you and Mike exemplify these words every day. I'm sorry I've . . . that I have been . . . well . . ." She cleared her throat a couple of times, then looked Mama in the eye and said, "After what my influence did to dear Myra, you have every right to throw us out of your house and never let us return. What I did is simply inexcusable, but I hope someday you'll forgive me."

"Isabel, of course I forgive you. And I'm sorry I lost my temper—"

Isabel shook her head. "No. I deserved it. And you know something? You cook whatever you want to for the celebration lunch. I'll eat it. I'll even help prepare it."

Mama smiled that warm, sweet smile she held in reserve for everyone. Grandma laughed. Then they all three had a long group hug.

I looked at my sister, and she looked at me. We giggled just like we used to when we were kids. I liked that.

☉

On Labor Day, to celebrate the holiday and the end of summer, and to signal the new school year, the Reillys, the Freebirds, and the St. Jameses all sat at our dining table and ate home-made ice cream—even Temple and Forest, who rarely ate sweets, and Isabel, who was trying to give up smoking. Myra Sue—whose hair looked almost normal since Mama had taken her back to Faye's Beauty Shop and had a color put on it—sat next to Isabel. Both of them had polished off a good meal, just the way they'd done at every meal since the day Myra Sue first went to see that doctor.

You want to know something? Ole Isabel was a lot better looking after she'd gained a few pounds. And she tolerated Temple and Forest because both of them looked and smelled like they'd had a recent bath. Maybe one day she'd like them because they were nice people.

Old man Rance wasn't there, of course, because he sat in jail. It seems he not only had a wife in Texas, but one living in Colorado and another in North Carolina.

"Goodness gracious," Grandma had said when she received that news. "With all them women, what'd he want another one for?"

"Well, since the others all had significant property, I fig-ure he was after this farm," Daddy said.

She snorted at that. "Reckon if I'd told him I had signed it over to you a long time ago, none of this nonsense woulda happened."

"Yeah," I said, "but now he won't be fooling any more nice old ladies."

She had given me a fat kiss. "And for that, we are all eternally grateful."

For myself, I was eternally grateful that the old goofball wasn't at the table having homemade ice cream with us that evening. I sure wouldn't miss that smell of too much Old Spice for the rest of my life.

"April Grace," Isabel said, as I scooped out more ice cream into my bowl.

"Ma'am?"

"I just want to thank you again for your suggestion. For teaching dance at the school. I believe teaching theater and dance is my true calling."

"Well, the younger kids might run you crazy," I said, "but the high schoolers like my sister will enjoy it."

"My lambkins has been a different person, you know," Ian said, smiling at his missus. "She has a new lease on life."

"It just came to me when I remembered the school planned to add those classes to the curriculum," I said. "You have your degree, so it just seems logical that you'd be the one to teach them since you're a dancer and know about acting."

"Way better than Coach Frizell," Myra Sue put in.

"Way, way better," I agreed.

"Just because he's athletic does *not* mean he can dance," my sister said.

"Amen!" I added.

Coach Frizell was as mean as you expect a football coach to be. Could you see him doing a pirouette or a *petit battement*?

Now that it was autumn, work had begun on the St. Jameses' house. Daddy said that by the end of October, the St. Jameses' house ought to be finished, and they'll have something nice to move into. I think I'm gonna miss them some.

But today, I was happy as a pig in mud. I sat down and shoved a spoonful of ice cream in my mouth. Once it had slid its sweet, cold way down my guzzle and settled satisfactorily in my stomach, I grinned, looking around.

Mama and Daddy exchanged tiny bites from each other's spoons. Good grief. Well, but what do you expect from them?

Temple and Ian and Forest were deep in discussion about the rain forests.

Grandma was all dolled up because she had a date. And don't get all excited. She learned her lesson about who to get serious about and who to avoid. She said she refused to dry up on the vine, whatever that means. She and Ernie Beason from Ernie's Grocerteria were going to the movies that night. They planned to see *Karate Kid II*, which wasn't exactly the latest movie, but in Cedar Ridge, if it's been out less than two years, it's new.

I reckon Grandma didn't look so bad with her hair short and colored, and I have to admit I was getting used to her makeup. She took exercise lessons from Isabel too. She looked pretty good, if you ask me, even though she sort of looked like a dolled up version of Angela Lansbury from *Murder, She Wrote*.

Isabel drizzled a little more chocolate sauce on Myra Sue's

ice cream, then added more to hers. She added a dollop of whipped topping on them both and sprinkled a few chopped pecans. Right about then she looked up and met my eyes. She gave me a wink and a smile.

You know what? When Isabel smiles, her whole face lights up.

THE END

Acknowledgments

☆

Growing up in the Ozarks hills, I've had ample opportunity to know people from all walks of life. From the down-home country folks like Grandma in this story to less-than-kind, out-of-town newcomers like Ian and Isabel St. James. I count it a blessing from God that I've had the opportunity to know so many diverse people. They have helped lay the groundwork for building multilayered characters.

Special thanks to my wonderful agent, Jeanie Pantelakis, who saw the potential in April Grace Reilly and cheered me on when discouragement tried to set in. Heartfelt gratitude goes to editor MacKenzie Howard, who "got it" when she read this story. Editor Kristin Ostby exhibited admirable patience and understanding as we polished the final product together. I suspect she's a city girl who was somewhat bumfuzzled by the antics of the country-fried April Grace but loved that little redheaded spitfire anyway. Without people like these hardworking professionals to encourage and guide us, where would we writers be?

Cliques, Hicks, and Ugly Sticks

Don't miss out on book two in the

CONFESSIONS OF

April Grace Series!

ONE

Recovery Isn't As
Easy As It Looks

＊

Isabel St. James is a recovering hypochondriac.

She once thought she had hoof and mouth disease just because she skittered through the barnyard while the cows were there waiting to be milked. Another time she swore up and down and sideways that the air in the Ozarks was full of poison and begged her husband to take her back to the city for the sake of her lungs. She was puffing on a cigarette as hard as a freight-train when she said it, too. Boy, oh boy.

On Tuesday afternoon, the first week of September, right after the first day of school, I walked with my Mama and my older sister Myra Sue along the shiny gray floors of the hospital corridor. I seriously doubted anything in ole Isabel's experience to this point had prepared her for the actual pain of a concussion, a broken nose, a broken arm, four cracked ribs, two black eyes and a purple knot on her forehead the size and color of an Easter egg. This is what her husband Ian reported to Mama this morning, after Isabel's accident. I figured Isabel probably had a good case of the whiplash as well, but I'm no doctor.

Now for a girl of my age (which is eleven) and education (I am in the sixth grade at Cedar Ridge Junior High), I've always been pretty good around blood and scrapes and runny noses. I'm no sissy like Myra Sue who is fourteen and in high school. But that day was my first experience in the hospital. I have to tell you, I felt down-right woozy. Even Mama looked queasy. Maybe it was because of all the busyness and the noise: phones ringing and people talking and nurses scurrying up and down the hallway with clipboards. I guess it made us both want to lose our lunches, but if Mama could buck up and face it down, so could I. We redheads are pretty tough.

Those nurses didn't bother to make eye contact with anyone.

I wondered if they ever looked at the people they took care of, or if all they did was scribble on those clipboards and read what other people wrote.

In one room we passed, the door stood wide open and a blonde-haired lady was barfing right over the edge of her bed and onto the floor. And in the hallway, a gray-faced old man was lying on a hospital bed right out in the open so everyone had to step around him. He kept raising one thin white hand every time a nurse passed. None of them bothered to say to him "good morning" or "excuse me" or, "Are you having a heart attack?"

I smiled at him, hoping to make him feel less invisible, but he just looked at me as if he was on his way out of this world. He'd probably be dead a week and half before anyone from that hospital noticed.

I looked around and saw a chubby nurse with short frizzy brown hair and great big pink-framed glasses. She was just standing there staring at nothing on the wall.

I walked right up to her and said, "That old man over there needs some help. I think he's dying."

She looked at me over the top of those glasses.

"I hardly think you qualify as an expert."

"But—"

"Children have no business on this floor." She moved away from me, and her pale blue-green scrub pants made *shish-shish* noises as she walked toward the desk where two nurses were sipping coffee. "Charlene, I keep telling them that kids don't need to be up here; they're always underfoot. Has the office changed the minimum age?"

Well, as I said, I'm just a little bit under the age of twelve, which is the minimum age to be a visitor on the floor, so I hurried to catch up with Mama and my sister before I could be thrown out for trying to save that old man's life.

I felt downright sorry for ole Isabel if she needed anything because I don't believe anyone in those aqua outfits had time or interest enough to actually take care of the sick and injured.

Right then I promised myself to never, in a million years, go to the hospital in Blue Reed, Arkansas unless I was in a big hurry to be ushered out of this world and in to the next.

"There's Isabel's room," Mama said as quietly as if we were in church. "Room 316."

"I hope she isn't asleep," Myra Sue whispered, her eyes big and scared. She dearly loved and adored Isabel St. James.

Somebody, somewhere, dropped something loud and metallic and it clattered a good ten seconds before it finally collapsed.

"How could she sleep in all this racket?" I asked in a perfectly reasonable volume given all that was going on around us.

"Shh," Mama cautioned. "We're in the hospital."

"Yes, you dork," Myra Sue added. "Speak appropriately."

I hardly saw the point, especially when about ten feet behind us that frizzy-haired nurse yelled for Kelly, who hollered back at her from the far end of the corridor. Apparently Nurse Frizzy had wanted Diet Dr. Pepper, *not* Diet Coke, and in case you're wondering, the vending machine on the third floor of that hospital has never, *ever* sold Fanta Orange, and probably never will. Kelly said so. In fact, she yelled it right down that big shiny hall so all of us could hear.

Mama tapped on the door which, unlike most of the doors we'd passed, was half-closed.

"*Entrez-vous,*" came the unmistakably miserable and somewhat nasally voice of Isabel St. James.

With her shiny blond curls flying, Myra Sue left us in the dust as she rushed into the room.

"Isabel!" she shrieked in the most un-hospital-appropriate and unladylike manner you can imagine.

"Dearest girl!" Isabel did not shriek, but her whimper was not exactly genteel, either.

Isabel looked like she'd been beaten with an ugly stick. She lay black and blue and purple against the white pillow and sheets. Both eyes were black. Her nose was all bandaged and her lips were twice their normal size. Her left arm was in a sling, and I don't think she or any of the busy nurses had bothered to comb her short, dark hair since her car wreck and it stood out all over her head. I have to say, I've seen ole Isabel St. James look much better, and that's saying something, because believe me, even on her very best day, she's no prize in the looks department.

For a minute, you would have thought Myra Sue was going to jump right up on the bed with Isabel, but she stopped herself and tenderly hugged the woman. Isabel attempted to kiss her cheek with those big, ole swole-up lips, then looked past her at Mama and me. She reached out her bruised right hand.

"Lily! April!" she said with a little more spirit than you might have thought. "Oh, it's so good to see you both. I thought I might never see another living soul."

We hugged her as gently as possible. She moaned but she didn't scream, for which I was grateful. Isabel can put on the dog pretty good when it comes to High Drama, and that's the honest truth.

She looked past us. "Didn't Grace come with you?"

"No," Mama said, "She has come down with a cold this morning, and she won't leave her house until she is sure she's no longer contagious. You know Mama Grace."

"She said used up a whole box and a half of Kleenex day before yesterday," I put in.

Isabel shook her head. "And she won't see a doctor."

"You know Grandma," Myra Sue said.

"Stubborn to the very core," said Mama.

"And then some," I added. "I just hope she don't get the pneumonia."

"When I called to tell her about your accident, she said to tell you she's praying for your quick recovery," Mama told Isabel.

Isabel lay back against the pillows and sighed. "That's kind of her. But after everything I've been through in the last eight hours . . ."

Her voice trailed into nothing as Ian came into the room. He looked worse for wear, let me tell you—all wrinkled and droopy, with bags under his pale blue eyes and his shirt half untucked. Ian usually looks well-groomed, even in work clothes. Right then his wispy blond hair was wispier than ever and he had mud on his shoes. He saw us and smiled a little bit. Ian's not so bad once you get used to him.

"Afternoon," he said wearily. I have to say, we three Reilly females greeted him with a lot more enthusiasm than his wife did.

"Is that my coffee?" Isabel said to him without so much as a howdy-do. Have I told you yet that she can be rude? R-u-d-e, rude.

"Yes. I had them brew it fresh for you at Gourmet Coffee, just like you told me." He peeled back the little tab on the lid. Steam came out and the smell of coffee temporarily overcame the icky stink of medicine and sick people.

"There's a coffee vending machine at the end of the hall," I told him. "Right next to the machine that sells potato chips and gum and Oreos."

He gave me a tight smile. "She didn't want that."

"Oh." Enough said.

"And where are my cigarettes?" Isabel took the Styrofoam cup from him.

Ole Isabel says she's going to quit smoking, but your guess is as good as mine as to when that will be.

Ian hesitated. "Your doctor said you must not smoke until he's sure you're all right," he said finally. "You might have injured your lungs in that accident, lambkins."

She glared at him from her black and blue eyes.

"Have a little pity, can't you? I am in deadly pain, I've totally lost the use of one arm, and I haven't had a cigarette since . . . since . . ." Her look of outrage fled as panic replaced it. "Oh! Oh! I can't remember the last time I had a cigarette."

She leaned toward Ian in desperation, "I might have brain damage, darling! Oh! Oh, please don't leave me, darling!"

See what I mean about High Drama? Good grief.

"Oh, *Isabel*!" hollered Myra Sue, as if someone was taking out her own personal appendix without her permission.

"You're recovering from a wreck, Isabel, so it's only natural to have a little memory lapse or two," Mama said soothingly, a complete Voice of Reason.

"Yes, lamb," Ian murmured, all sweet and kind. "The doctor said your concussion was mild."

He tried to smooth her messy hair but she jerked her head away.

"A lot you care. Or know. And I can remember just fine what happened right up until I . . . until I . . ."

It was obvious the way she visibly grasped for memories that she couldn't remember right up until Whatever. I tried to help.

"Why don't you just tell us what you remember, then maybe all the rest of it will come back to you?"

She dragged her pitiful, bruised gaze from her mister and looked at me. When her swollen lips parted in a smile, I saw where her two front teeth were chipped. I wondered if she knew about that. I bet she didn't, because if she did, she would already be screeching for a Beverly Hills plastic surgeon to give her a mouth transplant.

"You always have the *best* ideas, April," she said.